THE LOST TREASURE

A Bobby Holmes Mystery

J.M. KELLY

ISBN: 1484084942
ISBN 13: 9781484084946

Acknowledgements

No successful endeavor is completed in a vacuum. That was certainly true in bringing my manuscript to print. There were many creative hands in the pie, providing editorial expertise, critical appraisal, and downright moral support.

A writer comes to know that a first or even second draft is just that. It is far from the end zone and requires a great deal of tender care to get there. Friends are an early and necessary help. Many thanks to Jeff Cole, teacher and editor. His spot-on comments, suggestions, and corrections were a guide to a better book. My manuscript would not be where it is today without the keen eyes and honest appraisal of teachers from the Lafayette School in Chatham, NJ: Maureen Stryker, Carol Pedoto, Sarah Kimmins, Beth Adams, and Sharon Kiss, as well as teachers from the Richard Butler Middle School, in Butler, New Jersey: Ed Lavorgna and Susan Kempson. The efforts of college professor and reading specialist Mary Saraco to always have my back are always appreciated.

When the going gets tough, it's time to get professional help. I'm thrilled to have worked with two professional freelance editors who, through their encouragement and judicious application of an editorial scalpel, brought this novel to life. Major thanks and heartfelt appreciation to Jude Polotan in Sarasota, Florida. Her knowledge and expertise on several drafts were the backbone of this novel. She also, in fact, taught me how to write, for which I am eternally grateful. Her website is www.judepolotan.com, and check out her blog at www.writetravellove.wordpress.com. My other guardian angel at the professional level was Helga Schier in Los Angeles, California. Helga was a pleasure to work with from the start. Her background and expertise were instantly evident. Her line-by-line and copyediting, as well as her evaluative comments, led to the final draft in a long and fruitful process. She can be found at www.withpenandpaper.com. Any remaining errors of judgment throughout the novel are mine alone.

I also can't say enough about the team from CreateSpace through Amazon.com. They have been extremely supportive, incredibly professional, and through their efforts, brought me across the finish line.

I'd be remiss, in closing, if I didn't recognize my wife Bronwen, my best supporter always, and my children Brianna, herself a teacher, Alex, and Peter. They've always been there for me and are my most important fan base.

Part I

In the Beginning: 1700

PRELUDE

The night was dark as pitch, filled with the acrid smell of the torches carried by the ship's first mate, one Joshua Speed, as well as by the captain. What little light the torches gave was quickly swallowed by the near inky darkness that enveloped the small party of four. Ashore on this ungodly night was Speed, followed by two of the ship's mates—a Mr. Boot and a Mr. Crag, who together carried a heavy chest—and the captain who led the way. Their tattered clothing could not impede the cool breeze coming off the river with increased urgency. It was a damp night and they felt it deep in their bones.

The bare feet of the ship's mates sank in the mud of the riverbank with every difficult step they took under their heavy load. The only noise that penetrated the deathly quiet was a combination of grunts, labored breathing, and the soft sucking sound of the moist ground beneath their feet. Despite the coolness of the evening, the two mates were sweating under the strain. They had a decidedly uncomfortable job, no doubt about it, and as far as they were concerned, the sooner they were done with it the better.

"This is getting heavy," Boot whispered. "I don't know if I can handle it much longer."

"Shut up, you fool," rasped Crag. "If the captain hears you, you'll be worse than dead, eh!"

The captain stopped suddenly, and the rest of the party followed suit. He turned around slowly, took a few steps towards the mate who had spoken first, and looked into his eyes. The captain didn't say a word, but he didn't have to. Mr. Boot swallowed hard and stood still, straining under the load, trying not to return his captain's gaze. Then, abruptly, the captain turned and continued his journey.

Only the captain had a sense of where they were heading, having scouted the area alone for the past few nights. Nobody was to know the final destination; the captain had made sure of that. Back on ship, except for the posted guards, the entire crew had been ordered to remain below decks if they wished to remain alive.

Mr. Speed and the two crewmen who had been chosen to come along on the night's excursion stopped at the captain's command. "Port," he shouted, "and march twenty paces."

They all obeyed and moved inland, away from the river. Despite a slight incline, the land was easier to negotiate as their feet no longer disappeared into the muck that lined the shore, but found more stable ground to move about. The wind whistled eerily as it darted through and around the small scrub that dotted the landscape. The two crewmen peered about fearfully, despite the effort necessary to accomplish their task. They paused at the sound of the captain's voice.

"Starboard," he barked, "and move forty paces this time."

There was no pleading in his voice, no faltering, no hint of a rest coming, and no implied kindness either. His voice was gravelly, its tone deep and booming. It was clear that he expected his commands to be followed instantly and without question. The rapid movement of his dark, bushy beard with every syllable he spoke, and the murky color of his deep-set eyes that never seemed to blink, made any subordinate look away and do as told.

The captain raised his hand. "Port again at fifteen paces, then stop!"

Exactly fifteen paces later, the crewmen's legs locked to remain upright. Their bodies were ramrod straight. Their eyes were fixed forward, as they continued to shoulder their burden. There they remained, not uttering a sound, patiently and painfully awaiting orders as they had so many times in the past.

Just ahead lay a small opening, a cave of sorts, which led into a massive mountain. Seen from the boat, it appeared as the visage of an old man. Wild brush marked and at the same time obscured the opening to the interior of the mountain.

"Enter," the captain grumbled. The crewmen approached the gap, which was just wide enough for them and the heavy chest on their shoulders. Mr. Speed trailed behind.

"Follow me," said the captain as he made his way through a maze of tunnels and caverns, never faltering, towards a destination only he knew. The ground tilted upwards, sending them all up and into the breast of the mountain. With each passing step, it felt like they were entering a deep tomb. On the ground, hard rock alternated with patches of soft earth. Finally, when the two mates thought their wobbly legs could go no further, the captain spoke again.

"Place the chest down and begin to dig at the mark!"

Relieved, the crewmen laid the heavy chest on the ground, then grabbed their shovels and dug into the soft earth. At first, digging was not difficult. The deeper they dug, the more they were beyond the cold effects of the damp cave. It got much warmer in the hole and soon their bodies were covered in sweat.

"Dig it deep, lads!" shouted the captain. "Work hard tonight and yer reward will be great!"

Spurred by the captain's words, the two mates dug and they dug, and then dug some more as the night passed. Finally, when the hole was so deep and dark they could not see, the captain nodded to Mr. Speed, who leaned over the edge and said, "Enough! Throw up yer shovels, lads, and I'll toss ye a rope to scamper out of there."

The shovels shot up, landing quietly in a pile of dirt not two feet away from the hole. Instead of the expected rope, however, a lone torch came flickering down. They leaped aside to avoid it. Blinded by the sudden light, the two mates could not see the first mate lean over the edge with two pistols drawn and cocked. He fired down at them, knowing he couldn't miss.

"Like shooting fish in a barrel," he snorted. With a bark of a laugh, he jammed the two pistols in his belt, thinking that this had been easier than the captain said it would. Before he could turn, though, he felt the cool, deadly tip of a gun barrel placed firmly against the back of his head.

"Sorry, my friend," said the captain, "I'm really gonna' miss you, Joshua. You've been a good lad, but now you know too much, and I just can't have that, now can I?"

Suddenly weak in the knees, the first mate felt queasy. Before he could turn his head and utter what was to be a plea for his life, he heard the click of the trigger. He never heard the delayed thunderclap of the bullet that entered his skull, ending his short, but illustrious career as a pirate. His lifeless body fell, head first, towards the men he had dispatched just moments before.

Slowly and deliberately the captain pushed the treasure chest, which had been resting comfortably on the lip of the new gravesite, into the man-made abyss. Tightly bound with the strongest of rope, it landed with a dull thud on the bodies below. The captain hummed a jaunty little tune that he had made up while the mates were digging:

Along this trail came Boot and Crag
Who carried a load and daren't drag,
Rich we'll be says Mr. Boot
When first we bury the captain's loot.

He burst into hysterical laughter, as he casually pushed the dirt back in. Working alone, it took him quite a while, but he was in no hurry. When the hole was filled, he smoothed it over, covering it with a few stray rocks. Satisfied with his work, he stepped back to take one last look. He grinned, quickly turned, and left.

It was nearly dawn when the captain returned to the ship, still anchored a mile or so down river. As he came aboard, the posted guards wondered about the whereabouts of the first mate and the two crewmen. They wondered but did not dare ask.

As if he had heard their unasked questions, the captain turned to one of them and told him he was now the first mate.

"Make sail!" he grunted as he moved briskly to his cabin. "We return to Long Island."

PART 2

PREMONITION

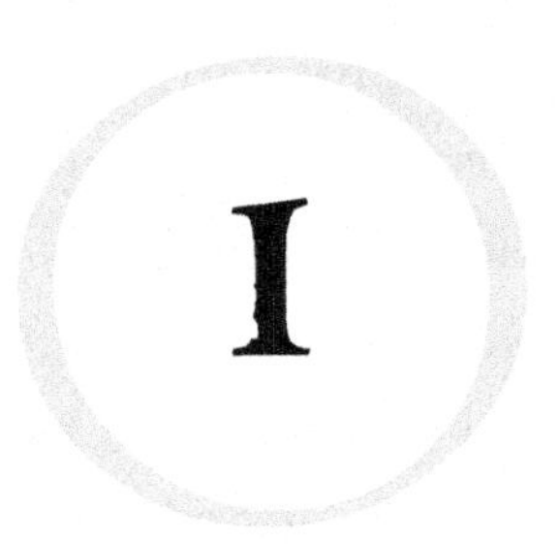

The cabbie took a sharp right through the deserted streets of London like a fox escaping the hounds. He threw his passengers into the side of the cab, shaking Bobby from his deep thoughts. Bobby turned towards his mother, not sure how to begin.

"Mum," he started. "It happened again last night."

"What's that?" Mrs. Holmes replied. "What happened, son?"

"I had another one," Bobby responded.

"Another one? You mean another dream?"

Not for the first time, Bobby worried why he was having these *experiences,* as his mum often called them. She once explained that he had a touch of something called clairvoyance, which helped him see things more clearly than most people. Bobby didn't care what it was called; he didn't like it under any name. He had been plagued by a series of strange visions ever since his mother told him he would be spending a part of his summer holiday with family in America. He turned his icy blue eyes in her direction.

"Yes," Bobby answered. "It was like the last one, and I'm getting quite sick of it!"

Bobby's mum looked down at her son with a smile. She reached over and ruffled his thick blond hair.

"I told you, Bobby, it's rubbish. You're just nervous about going to visit your cousin in America. You and I haven't been away from each other since your father passed away and you're worried about it. Any eleven-year-old would be. I'm sure you'll be fine once you get there and sort it all out. Besides," she added wistfully, "your dad would be proud of you, knowing that you're undertaking this journey alone."

Bobby thought of his dad, and how deeply he missed him. He would much rather be visiting his dad's relatives with both his parents along, but his dad had died two years earlier, making that and a great deal more impossible. And with his mum going to Paris, he was now facing this challenge alone.

"I know you're going to enjoy yourself immensely, once you're there." His mum sounded confident, but Bobby knew better. His dreams were getting more intense and last night's was a whopper. It had made him fearful like never before. He was reluctant to tell his mum too much: about the dark nature of his dreams, about the bad headaches that now accompanied them, and especially about *him. He* appeared in all of Bobby's nightmares recently. There was something dark and sinister about *him.* Bobby couldn't make out all of *his* features yet, but each dream brought them more clearly into focus. The worst thing was that Bobby didn't know who *he* was or what *he* wanted.

"We're almost there, Miss, and I got you there in record time, I did," piped the hackney driver. "Not much traffic this early in the morning, I suspect."

"Thank you," said Mrs. Holmes as she glanced out the window. "Paddington Station does look quite busy, though."

They pulled up to the curb and the cabbie opened their door. He hoisted their bags from the boot, they settled their bill, and Bobby and his mum approached the beehive of human activity inside the station. People were going every which way at once. Bobby and his mum had to serpentine through the crowd, dodging oncoming bodies, as they raced to find their train to Heathrow airport. Bobby pulled away and ran over to the statue of Paddington Bear, the well-known fictional character of his youth. He patted Paddington's bush hat for good luck.

"Good idea," his mum said. "We'll need a bit of that to find platform six."

It was easier than they thought, however, and soon they were on their way. A short ride later, they found themselves hurrying to the boarding call for Bobby's 10:00 a.m. British Airways flight bound for Newark, New Jersey. At the gate, Bobby's mum grabbed his shoulders and turned him towards her.

"Now listen closely," she said. "I love you and will miss you. I'm sorry I can't come with you. I'd love to, you know that, but I have to go to Paris. It's my job."

"Yes, I know that, but why can't I come with you?" Bobby asked, knowing the answer already.

"Well, Scotland Yard won't allow their detectives to take family on assignments. Although they should make an exception with you, given you have such keen senses," she teased him as she gave him a big hug. "Come on, Bobby, look upon this as an adventure. Your dad's first cousin, Auntie Arlene, and your Uncle John are wonderful people, and you're going to adore their daughter, your second cousin Brenda."

"I don't need an adorable cousin," Bobby protested, but his mum would have none of that.

"Well, whether you *need* her or not, you've got her. What *I need* is for you to be on your best behavior. Try not to lecture people when you explain things to them. You have a great command of vocabulary and you know how you can be, especially when you try to explain your dreams and the peculiar *feelings* you get. Most people won't understand your gift and will find it hard to accept."

Bobby rolled his eyes in response. He didn't understand his 'gift' very well himself and couldn't be further away from accepting it. His mum kissed him briefly and promised to call him as often as possible. As he walked down the ramp with the airline agent assigned to children traveling alone, he thought of patting the hat of Paddington Bear and his wish for good luck. He had the uneasy feeling that he was going to need it.

Once on board, Bobby settled in for the long flight and took in his surroundings, playing with the video controls. The crew prepped for takeoff and soon they were in the air. When food service began, Bobby helped himself to all that was available, including the extra dessert a friendly attendant offered. He was watching a movie on the video screen when his eyes began to droop. His head bowed ever so slightly and he drifted into that world between sleep and consciousness where reality mixes with fantasy and he couldn't tell which was which.

All at once, Bobby had visions of darting between mounds of clothing, trying to stuff his most important belongings into a small suitcase. He found himself running through crowds with bits of his clothes fleeing his bag. He stopped suddenly as he heard an ear-piercing whistle and a shout for "All Aboard!" He saw a train pulling out of the station and somehow knew he should be on it. He ran as fast as he could, but desperation set in as he realized his legs were not moving fast enough and the train remained just out of reach.

Exhausted, he stopped, watching the train get smaller in the distance. He looked up when he heard the loud engines of a jet overhead. He looked closely and could see himself in one of the windows. How could that be? The "he" in the plane looked unhappy and was pounding on the window, mouthing a silent scream for help just before the jet was swallowed by a thick, dark cloud.

The cloud descended to the ground and enclosed him. Bobby could not see but five feet in front of him. He was shaking, as it got colder and colder. He had no idea where he was or why this was happening to him. Fear set in.

What was that he heard? He was sure he had heard voices, all of them whispering at once, though he could not understand what they said.

"Hello!" he called out, but the blended noise of the whispers only got louder.

"Hello there!" he tried again. This time, the voices all stopped abruptly. Intense quiet surrounded him.

It was cold in the swirling mist, but he was sweating and breathing much too rapidly. He wasn't sure what he was afraid of the most: the voices he had heard, or the dead silence that followed. He took a few tentative steps towards the echo in his ears, arms extended and hands groping, both hoping and fearing that he would make contact with someone or something.

He walked for what seemed like an eternity before he heard another sound. Yes, he thought desperately, there it is. It was faint at first, a slight tap against something soft, like a mattress. He paused, cocked his head to one side and listened. There it was again! More this time, a cadence in fact, going on for several seconds before stopping. It sounded like a soft leather boot making contact on a hard surface. He closed his eyes tight and leaned forward, as if that could somehow help him hear. At first, nothing. Then, yes, there it was again. Louder this time. Louder, and coming closer.

He opened his eyes wide, looking every which way, not knowing the cause or intent of the noise that continued towards him. The thick, viscous cloud swirled in front of him, and out of the churning darkness emerged the silhouette of a man.

His grin was the first thing to become clear: a long, yellow, toothy grin that stretched from ear to bangled ear and snarled from a thick, oily and matted black beard. The eyes were like pieces of jet-black coal piercing Bobby's very soul. Fear rooted his feet to the ground. Atop the towering figure's bug infested head was a tattered pirate's hat. He donned a dirty, torn cloth coat that seemed much too large for this already large man. The giant leaned into Bobby. When the stranger opened his mouth to speak, the foul stench of death poured over Bobby like shower spray.

"Boy!" the beast bellowed. "Ye best stay away. Yer power draws you to me, I can feel it. I know you do as well, so I warn ye. Stay away. Stay away or I will tear ye to pieces!"

Nearly swooning from the smell of this creature's breath and his own overwhelming fear, Bobby could do nothing. He tried to speak, but no sound would come, no matter how hard he tried.

"You will die if you continue this journey," the stranger continued, "and after I kill ye, I will eat yer rotting flesh. Heed my warning, boy!" He pointed one long, bony finger at Bobby, laughing viciously.

Finally, Bobby could move. He took one step backwards and fell into a vast, dark abyss, with his arms and legs flailing. All he could see above was complete and utter blackness. He panicked as he fell, and let out a desperate, piercing scream. And as he shouted…

...he awoke.

Bobby remained motionless for a moment, except for the pounding in his head. He looked around trying to assess if he was in real danger. His knees were bent upwards and his hands clutched the blanket that a flight attendant must have draped over him while he slept. Not sure where he was, a quick visual survey confirmed he was indeed on a British airways flight to America.

The flight attendant was there in a flash. "My goodness," she said, "you made quite a yelp, there, before you awoke." He noticed that those sitting next to him were staring. "You must have had a nightmare," she continued. "Too much dessert, I suspect." The attendant adjusted Bobby's blanket and asked if there was anything else she could get him.

"Given the circumstances," Bobby stammered, "I think not, thanks."

She smiled and went about taking care of the other passengers.

Bobby's head drummed an uneven beat, as an echoed phrase teasing at the recesses of his mind, came slowly to the surface: "*Along this trail...* "It came in the voice of that man in his dream, but Bobby had no idea what it meant. It sounded like there should be more, but nothing followed, only the fading sound of a few mumbled words. As he pondered these new and terrifying developments in this latest vision, Bobby's head throbbed more steadily. He massaged his temples trying to ease the pain. This was going to be no ordinary vacation; this hallucination, experience, or nightmare—whatever one wanted to call it—had put Bobby on notice to be extra wary and cautious. He sensed that he was on a collision course with something of unknown magnitude and origin.

Something terrible, he knew was going to happen on this trip.

Upon arrival in Newark, Bobby was escorted through customs. Viewing the milling crowd outside of baggage claim, Bobby feared momentarily that no one would claim him and he would be left at the airport all alone.

The feeling was brief, however. Looking up and scanning the crowd, something caught the corner of his eye. Without thinking, he glanced to his right and quickly saw a handful of balloons and a handmade sign that said, "Welcome to America, Bobby Holmes!" Despite his fears, he smiled at the two happy faces that greeted him. A large, stout woman with a kind face that vaguely resembled his father's was waving with great animation. That had to be Auntie Arlene, he thought, and the person with her was sure to be cousin Brenda. Brenda, who was his age, looked about one inch shorter than Bobby's four and a half feet. Her long, brown hair was put in a ponytail and held together by an elastic band. Freckles played tag across her pert nose, fanning out along her high cheeks. Her bright green eyes and carefree smile put Bobby instantly at ease.

Bobby was turned over to his welcoming committee. Almost immediately, Auntie Arlene scooped him off the ground, smothering him in her considerably oversized bosom. After two wet smooches on his cheeks, she released Bobby and practically pushed him into Brenda, who gave him a much briefer but no less heartfelt hug.

With his bag in tow, Bobby obediently followed his aunt and cousin to their parked car for the ride to Mountain Lake, Connecticut.

Bobby noticed that Brenda was staring at him. "It's about a three hour drive," she said, "and we won't be going through New York City." Bobby's jaw dropped.

"How'd you know what I was thinking," he asked.

Brenda smiled. "I'm a good guesser."

But Bobby was getting the tingling feeling on the edge of his brain that told him that something strange was going on. It put him on full alert. He didn't believe his cousin. He thought there was more than guessing going on here.

The ride north was marked by a steady stream of information discharged by Auntie Arlene, who couldn't seem to stop talking. Bobby laughed as Brenda made fun of her mother, who didn't seem to notice. They traveled through rural Connecticut, north of Danbury, when his Auntie Arlene announced that they were close to their destination. Bobby glanced out the window. He noticed that a dark cloud had formed overhead, taking the shape of a man's face in a pirate hat. It grew ever darker, threatening rain, or perhaps something more menacing. His head hurt suddenly, and he drew in a deep breath, experiencing a moment of intense panic. He began to perspire slightly, and he shook from the goosebumps that dotted his arms. He was once again lost in that horrible dream on the plane. What was happening to him? Why was he thinking of these things? What was the source of this fear that gripped him so forcefully?

Then, as quickly as it came, the cloud dispersed from the wind, leaving him feeling cold and wondering if he was letting his imagination get the better of him. He glanced over in Brenda's direction and found her staring at him.

"Are you okay?" she asked.

"Yes, I'm fine, thanks. I must be getting a bit carsick."

The moment he had said it he knew that Brenda wasn't buying it. She looked at him and seemed to know instinctively that something was wrong. Bobby wondered if she could sense his fear, or worse, if she knew what it was that scared him so.

They rounded a corner and all thoughts of his nightmare faded as they came upon a great big sign surrounded by flowers that read, "Welcome to Mountain Lake, Connecticut."

They did a brief car tour of the area and came upon the town's massive lake.

"See that mountain at the head of the lake?" Brenda asked. "That's shaped like the head of an old man, when you look at it from the right angle. There are creases in the face of the mountain where the eyes and mouth should be, and some bushes where the nose should be. They make it look like the old man has a moustache."

They turned around in the south parking lot near the lake's hiking trails and headed for home.

"Brenda will show you the town tomorrow, if you don't mind, Bobby," said Auntie Arlene. "I'll need to get home to start dinner."

"That's fine, Auntie," said Bobby. "I'd love to tour about, but it's been a long trip, and with the time difference I'm probably more tired than I should be."

"You really don't have a choice, you know," whispered Brenda. "When mom wants to start cooking dinner, there's no stopping her. It's like she's prepping to invade a foreign country. She even started cooking dinner this morning, before we left for the airport. She said it needed time in the oven. But you'll see the town soon enough. We'll meet up with my best friend tomorrow—oh, you'll like him—and we'll take you around to all of our favorite places. It really isn't as boring as I sometimes make it out to be. My friend Stevie and I, we have a good time, mostly."

Home was on the south side of town, only another few minutes of driving away. The land was fairly flat, the houses in the neighborhood spread out in a geometrical grid, giving each lot the sense of privacy. They drove to the last house on Doyle Street, a cul-de-sac just off of Arthur Road, pulling up in front of a two-story colonial with a white picket fence. Dark red roses grew up the row of pickets, reaching for the sun, following it as it crossed the sky. There was small, white fencing flanking the circular driveway, supported by bunches of colorfully arrayed annuals that welcomed him with their colors and fragrant scent. Bobby couldn't help but feel relaxed.

"Home again, home again," chanted Auntie Arlene. "We've made it, and all in one piece. I'll get started on dinner, Brenda, so why don't you show Bobby his room and the rest of the house."

"Okay, mom, I'm on it," said Brenda.

"And Bobby, dear, you should call your mother to let her know you arrived safely."

"Yes, I'd like that," Bobby said politely trying to hide the homesickness that swept over him like a tsunami.

Brenda's home was as beautiful on the inside as it was outside. Oriental carpet graced the floors in the living and dining rooms while gleaming hardwood floors radiated throughout the house. Most of the interior was white: white walls, white frames around carefully hung pictures, and white cabinets in the kitchen. It almost felt like walking through a cloud. Although it looked carefully maintained, Bobby immediately could tell that the people who lived here were neither cold nor stuffy, but regular people who enjoyed relaxing at home. Brenda and Bobby went from the kitchen towards the front door and up the staircase in the foyer. At the top of the stairs, they brushed past the master bedroom and made their way to the guest room at the far end of the hall. It was a comfortable room, also light in color, but without the posters and "kid stuff" that decorated his room back home.

Bobby was left alone to use the phone in the room, and he quickly called his mum on the number she gave him.

"I've been waiting for your call," she said after picking up on the first ring. "I miss you terribly."

"Me too," responded Bobby. " My flight was awesome, although I am a bit tired," he continued, trying not to show how much he longed for his mum's embrace.

"Yes, I suspect you must be. After getting through customs and then a three hour car ride, it must be what, about 5:30 p.m. in Connecticut? That would make it…let me see…around 10:30 p.m. here in London. My, you have had a long day!"

"Mum…" he began.

"What's wrong, Bobby. You sound more than a bit fatigued."

"I…oh nothing," he sighed. "I guess I had too much to eat on the plane." Bobby didn't know how to tell his mum that he was lonely, that he missed his home, and that he thought that something was seriously wrong, when he couldn't even identify what it was.

"Are you sure that's all, sweetheart?" she asked.

"Yes," Bobby responded, trying to be the brave soldier he thought his father would expect him to be. "Everything's fine. I'm sure I'll feel better once we have dinner."

"How are Auntie Arlene and Brenda?"

"I love them. Auntie Arlene is cooking dinner right now, and Brenda," he continued, "she's nice, I guess."

"Nice? You two are getting on, aren't you?" His mum's tone of voice betrayed the smile on her face.

"Sure we are, mum! We just need some time to get to know each other. That's all."

They spoke for a bit more, and hung up with a promise to call again soon. After placing the phone in its cradle, he sat quietly for a moment, and then went to look for Brenda.

She was in her room. When Bobby entered, he couldn't help but stare. There were clothes on the bedpost, a variety of hats and necklaces clinging unsteadily to the sides of her mirror, and a desk that appeared invaded by a loose collection of papers, books stacked like a deck of cards, and an army of small supplies: stapler, calculator, paper clips, three hole punch, various notebooks, pens, pencils, and the ever-present laptop. The color pink was everywhere, and the surprised look on Bobby's face said a great deal.

"You got a problem with my room?" challenged Brenda.

"Well, no actually, not really, I mean I didn't..." Bobby stammered.

"Maybe you think girls my age shouldn't like pink?"

Bobby took another look around, studying the posters on the wall. "No, that's not it at all," he said. "I just didn't know you were also a Harry Potter fan."

This time it was her turn to be surprised. She had been prepared to defend her color choice and the lived-in look of the room. After a moment, she realized that he was trying to change the subject and started laughing.

"Okay," she said, "maybe I am a bit too sensitive about the color of my room. My parents call me a tomboy, but it doesn't mean I'm not a girl or I don't like girly stuff. Also, I don't think of things that way. You know, boyish or girly. I either like something or I don't. And I like the color pink. All right?"

"Yeah, super," Bobby shrugged.

An awkward silence ensued for a moment until Bobby noticed something in the corner. "Hey, you've got an X-box and the Harry Potter and the Half-Blood Prince game!" He made a beeline right for the X-box. "Are you up for a challenge?" Bobby asked, despite his growing fatigue.

"You must have read my mind," said Brenda with a sly smile.

They had played for a little while when Bobby finally asked. "Hey Brenda, back when we were at the airport in your car, you seemed to know what I was going to ask before I even asked it – you know, about the ride home and whether we'd go through the city. How did you manage that?" He glanced sideways at her to see if he struck a chord.

Unfazed, she looked directly at him and said, "I've been told I'm perceptive. My mom says I read people pretty well and I get an instant feeling about whether or not I like them. When I was seven, my parents were going to leave me with a sitter for a night. I told my mom I didn't trust her and they stayed home instead. Later, that weirdo was arrested for hitting kids she baby-sat for." She paused, looking at him carefully. "It's happened other times, too," she continued shrugging her shoulders. "I don't understand it really. I just know that I'm usually right. People I tend not to like usually prove to be a bit psycho later. Besides," she smiled brightly, "a team of highly specialized Yale University doctors told me that I have the unique ability to read people's minds."

"Really?" Bobby blurted.

"No, of course not, you British ding-dong. Asking about the car ride home was a logical question for you to ask and I'm good at thinking logically. I anticipated your question, that's all; no mind reading involved." With that she gave a laugh and he joined her like they had been friends for much longer than an afternoon.

A moment later, Brenda stopped playing and swiveled towards Bobby. "But now that we're on the subject, I can tell there is something going on with you, Bobby, and it's more than being far from home."

Bobby slowly put his X-box control down and looked her straight in the eye.

"Brenda," he said, "you wouldn't believe me if I told you."

Their stomachs growled harmoniously as they sat there playing and talking. The smell of a roast in the oven snaked its way up the stairs with cunning and stealth, slipping its way into their noses. Their mouths began to water like broken faucets. All thoughts of explaining his last comment to Brenda were put on the back burner as Bobby focused on what was on the kitchen burner downstairs. They simultaneously bolted for the bedroom door, nearly tripping over each other to get to the source of the wonderful aroma.

As they pushed their way into the kitchen, they were asked to set the table.

"You get the glasses in that cabinet," Brenda ordered and pointed, "and I'll get the rest."

They quickly went to work in the kitchen, while Auntie Arlene was busy stirring this, whipping that, and creating a bit of magic of her own.

All of a sudden, they heard the front door open.

"I'm home!" yelled Uncle John. There was a brief pause, as if everyone waited for something further before reacting. "Does anybody care?"

Brenda rolled her eyes. "He says that every night and has for as long as I can remember. When I was a toddler I used to scream, 'I do, I do', which he hasn't forgotten or let go."

Uncle John entered the room with a big smile. Brenda and Bobby said in fractured unison, "We do, we do," followed by peals of laughter.

"Well, you must be Bobby!" said Uncle John. "My gosh, you look just like your father. It's great to see you, son. I hope your flight was good, and you've managed to settle in here without too much difficulty."

"Yes sir," said Bobby, wondering for a moment how close his dad might have been to Uncle John and Auntie Arlene. Turning to Brenda, Uncle John said, "And you must be Brenda, how nice to meet you."

Slapping her hand to her forehead, Brenda looked at Bobby and shook her head.

"I'm going to wash up," said Uncle John. "Be sure not to eat everything before I get back."

As they waited for him, Bobby and Brenda talked about the next day: where they would go, what they would do, and what they would see. "I'm pretty excited about seeing Mountain Lake," said Bobby.

Before they were able to map out their day, Uncle John returned. They all sat down to eat dinner. Auntie Arlene brought out a pot-roast dinner, complete with whipped sweet potatoes, and fresh steamed green beans.

"It's a new recipe," she said. "I hope you all like it."

Bobby found that not only did he love the food, he also really liked Uncle John. He was over six feet tall and rather thin. He didn't so much enter a room as he glided on air. He had a carefree way about him that put everyone instantly at ease. He was a hard-working man, obviously content with his life, and while he didn't say much (not that anyone could with Auntie Arlene in control of the conversation) he was quick witted, often sliding in fast and funny comments that brought a smile to everyone's lips.

It was a pleasant evening. Everyone was eating, smiling, listening, and throwing in a word or two each time Auntie Arlene allowed herself a mouthful of food. Bobby felt relaxed and quite at home.

After dinner, they all lent a hand cleaning up the dishes and putting things away. When all was done to Auntie Arlene's satisfaction, Uncle John retired to the living room to read the paper. Bobby and Brenda climbed up to Brenda's room to finish their game. They attacked it with enthusiasm and wore themselves out in the process. By 8:00 p.m., Bobby was completely exhausted. After all, it was now 1:00 a.m. London time. They decided to call it a night, and with a quick good night to each other and the adults downstairs, they brushed their teeth, slipped into pajamas, and fell into bed. Within minutes they were both fast asleep. It was a solid, dreamless sleep borne from fatigue, without a doubt the best sleep Bobby had had in several nights.

PART 3

THE LAY OF THE LAND

Bobby awoke early and lay in bed, still tired and jetlagged from his trip. He missed his mum, and truth be known, he missed his dad, too. His dad had been killed in a car crash when Bobby was nine. A barrister, he was rushing to try a case before the town magistrate in the Cotswold's, where they lived at the time. Bobby still felt the pain of that loss, especially now that he was with his dad's family in America. Auntie Arlene, his dad's cousin, had his father's ability to talk non-stop about anything. He remembered that about his father with a smile. He could always ask his dad about any subject whatsoever, and his dad would go on for hours. Once, when he was only seven, he had asked his dad if he would answer his questions even when Bobby was an old man himself. His dad smiled at Bobby, and perhaps for the first time, gave him a brief answer. "Bobby," he said. "I may not always be there for you, but I trust you will always remember do the right thing. No matter how difficult."

Bobby suddenly heard three short knocks on the wall that separated his room from Brenda's. It was a sign that his cousin was up and ready to start the day. He wiped a tear from his eyes and quickly responded with three knocks of his own.

"Beat you up and to the bathroom!" Brenda shouted.

"You mean the loo in the hallway?" Bobby shouted back. He then tripped getting out of bed. When he looked up, Brenda was already at the bathroom door.

"Ha! Beat you?" she said. With a laugh, Brenda slammed the door behind her. She then flung open the door and shouted, "And what the heck is a 'loo'?"

She slammed the door again and finished getting ready in minutes.

When she was done, Bobby took his turn to brush his teeth and throw water on his face. Pulling on his clothes, he hurried downstairs to greet what he knew to be the sweet smell of pancakes on the griddle.

After a quick breakfast and clean up, the two scurried outside to the garage, where several bikes greeted them. A couple of them looked quite old and well worn and belonged to his aunt and uncle. Brenda's bike and the spare one next to it were new and shiny.

"I can't believe it!" Bobby said. "These are Schwinn Classic AL Cruisers!"

"What are you, a bike expert or something?" Brenda asked.

Bobby ignored the question and inspected the bicycles. "Wow!" he said softly. "They both have fully wrapped fenders, whitewall tires, and coaster brakes. My friend Ian back in England has one. He has lots of magazines about bikes, and I've read some of them."

"These don't have the skinny racing tires you see a lot theses days," said Brenda, "but I like them better because they're more comfortable. Mom and Dad say they remind them of when they were kids. And hey, my dad got a great deal on the boy's bike from a friend of his, so you would have one to ride while you were here."

"Where do we go first?" he asked.

"Let's see, I think we'll just go into town and ride around. I'll show you the places I go with my friend, Stevie. We'll meet up with him later."

With that, they pedaled towards town, some two and half miles away. Once out of their neighborhood, they turned up Cobble Avenue, a country road with broad paving and good shoulders for bike lanes. Except for a spotty few, the cobblestones that gave the quiet road its name no longer existed. It was a country road with little traffic, and they had the impression that they were pretty much alone.

"This reminds me of my former home in the Cotswold's," Bobby said.

"What does?"

"The trees and the quiet."

"Get out of the road!" Brenda shouted. Bobby reacted by nearly turning into it as a car suddenly whizzed by.

"I'm not sure what side of the road we're on in America. It's so confusing."

"That's right, I forgot," said Brenda. "You people drive on the wrong side over in England, don't you?" she said with a smile. "Just follow me."

They continued side by side, but pedaled in tandem with Brenda in the lead whenever they heard a car or saw one in the mirror attached to their handlebars.

They were about half way to town when Brenda said, "Hey, let's pull over to Copper Creek just ahead. "

"What are we doing here?" Bobby asked, parking his bike next to hers.

"Sometimes, I like to hunt for crawfish at this spot."

"What are crawfish?"

"They're like little lobsters that grow in the creek. They're fast and slippery, but I love trying to catch them."

"What do you do with them if you catch one?" asked Bobby.

"Just throw them back. I don't eat them or anything. It's just for fun."

With a slight breeze blowing, Bobby and Brenda scanned the creek, scouting for crawfish.

"Hey, I see one!" Bobby yelled.

"Quick," Brenda said, "try and catch it."

"No, the water's too deep here. I'm not getting wet for this little bugger."

"Don't be a baby," Brenda responded. "I almost went face first trying to catch one, the last time I was here."

Brenda walked along the west bank of the creek while Bobby went eastward. He followed the waterbed as it turned north, bending a path through the dense trees surrounding it. Sunlight streaked through the entangled branches, painting splotches of bright light on the moss covered canvas below, creating an artistic masterpiece that changed continuously with the wind. As he trudged along the riverbank, the wind picked up and a slight keening whistled through the trees. The trees got thicker, and less and less light came through; in some places it was almost completely dark.

There was no other sound but the wind. It was soft at first, and then picked up in strength before going soft yet again. Bobby was nervous. It was the kind of anxiety that sneaks up from the subconscious. Fear, similar to the fear he had experienced on the plane, bubbled to the surface.

"What was that?" Bobby whispered and jerked his head. A fleeting shadow moved in the corner his eye. He glanced left. All he saw were moving branches. All he heard was the eerie sound of the growing and waning wind. He stood there just listening and staring, hoping his eyes were merely playing tricks on him.

But there it was again. Movement to his right! A dull ache pushed at his temples, as if someone were trying to get in.

Something was amiss, but he couldn't determine what. It was as if the air had been sucked from the space around him. The hair on his neck stood up, and goosebumps appeared on his arms and legs. He turned to the right, yet he saw nothing but clawing branches and whispering leaves. Bobby's head began to pound and he felt faint. Then he heard a voice. It was deep, and low, with a mocking tone. "Along this trail…" it whispered. Bobby's body weaved, things became blurry, and he thought he would fall as heard..."came Boot and Crag." Suddenly, a hand fell on his shoulder.

Bobby screamed.

"What is it?" asked Brenda. "You look like you've seen a ghost."

"I don't know," he said, regaining his composure while his eyes were darting everywhere at once. "For a moment, I thought I had seen something. I…I don't know," he concluded. "I just got spooked by the wind. Let's leave this place," he whispered and headed for his bike.

As the two rode off, Bobby took one last look into the darkened part of the forest and thought he saw the moving shadow of a large person. He paused for a second rubbing his eyes and then fled the area as quickly as he could.

They soon reached the southern edge of town. Brenda stopped her bike, put both feet on the ground and turned to Bobby.

"You haven't said much since we last stopped. Still creeped out by the woods?"

"A little," said Bobby.

He felt Brenda's stare upon him. It was uncomfortable, and he was hoping she wouldn't pry any further. He wanted to tell her, and promised himself that he would, but not just yet. He wasn't ready.

"I'll take you on a tour of the town," she said. "It's pretty big. You have Cobble, which we're on, on one side and Turner on the other. Connecting to both of them are Broad, Main and Baker Streets. In the middle of all three is a large park that runs from Broad all the way down to Baker. We'll meet Stevie in the park later."

"Brilliant!" said Bobby, relieved to put his fear behind him. "Let's be off, then."

They made their way up to Broad Street, which was aptly named. The street was indeed broad with angled parking on both sides of the street and plenty of room in between. There were crosswalks for pedestrians and a bike path between the parking stalls and the sidewalk, with room enough for two bikes to travel side by side. Small maple trees lined the sidewalks. In between, the town's gardening club had placed old-fashioned barrels cut in half and filled with red and white geraniums.

"This is quite nice," said Bobby, losing himself in the beauty of the town.

"Is it that much different in England?" Brenda asked.

"In England the roads are tighter and the cars are smaller."

"And the people talk funny," laughed Brenda. "What else is different?" she asked.

"I'm not quite sure, since I've only just arrived, but I'll let you know what's different in a few days." Truth be told, Bobby didn't want to compare America and England. He didn't want to think about home because he missed it so much, so he changed the subject. " I would like to stop into that comics store you mentioned last night, if that's alright."

"Hey, good idea," said Brenda, "it's just down on Main Street. I go there once in a while. The owner is a funny guy."

"What makes him funny?" Bobby asked.

"He likes to tease people. My mom doesn't like him because of that, but I think he's pretty funny. Mom said she thinks he graduated from Yale Law School, but decided to run a comics book store rather than be a lawyer. Come on, I'll lead us over there."

They continued down Broad and took in the sights. At the east end of town, they made a right on Turner and continued down to Main. They parked their bikes outside of *Conan's Comics Shop* and stepped up the curb onto the sidewalk. They opened the shop's wooden screen door, and as they did, a bell attached to the upper end of the door tinkled, signaling their arrival.

Conan was behind the counter, skinny arms folded and holding up his slight frame as he leaned forward on the glass display case. His long, brown, curly hair was flecked with gray and pulled back into a ponytail. His clothes were a cornucopia of bright colors. Bobby read the words on his T-shirt: "*Bad Spellers of the World Untie.*" Led Zeppelin music leaked quietly from the back room, which was partitioned off with a gray cloth curtain that hung to the floor. The store consisted of several rows of glass-enclosed counters surrounded by open shelves filled with the latest in comic book production. The glass cases held the more valuable, and therefore expensive, collectibles.

"To what do I owe this enormous pleasure, Ms. Watson?" Conan gently enquired. "I haven't seen you for donkey's years, young lady. Where have you been keeping yourself?"

"Oh, I've been around, Conan. I just haven't been uptown lately. This is my cousin from England, Bobby Holmes."

"Hello, Bobby," he said and extended what appeared to be a massive paw attached to a stick. "I'm pleased to make your acquaintance."

Bobby lost his hand to the big palms of the proprietor.

Turning his attention back to Brenda, Conan said with a smile, "And what can I sell, uh, do for you today?"

Conan reverted to his stationary position leaning on the counter, moving nothing but his jaw, looking at the two of them through lizard-like eyes that never blinked. Bobby wandered through the store examining the treasure trove that lay about the room, as Brenda spoke with Conan.

"I got some money for my birthday, and I was thinking of adding to my collection. My dad told me about *The Shadow,* and I was thinking that might be just the right thing. As long as they're not too expensive, that is," she added with a side-glance.

"As I've said to your ilk ad nauseum, princess, if you have to ask you can't afford them. What about purchasing a *Watchmen* book for such an occasion? You would be increasing your appallingly limited literary taste to something on a scale akin to novels such as *The Hobbit,* or maybe even *The Shining,* a true classic. I also have a limited selection of some of these favorite novels for my elite patrons, such as yourself."

"Gag me, Conan, I don't have the time to be reading comics in general, let alone a huge cartoon book like *Watchmen.*"

Without visibly showing any emotion, Conan feigned shock.

"You cannot be serious! *Watchmen* is the most critically acclaimed illustrated novel of all time, probably better written than anything you have read to date, I'm sure. How dare you refer to such a treatise as a *cartoon* book!" he added with obvious disdain. "I couldn't sell it to you now even if you begged me for it. Good day to you."

"Okay," sighed Brenda, "sorry if I insulted your precious little picture book, but if you want us gone, we'll go. I was, however, going to buy these two *Shadow* comics, but I guess you don't want me to now."

"Wait!" shouted Conan holding up a beefy mitt. "Let us not be hasty. Those are, of course, relics of another age, and as such they are extremely valuable commodities. Although it pains me to do so, I would be willing to part with them for no less than $5.00 apiece."

"I looked them up on the Internet before I came in today, Conan, and they go for $3.00 each, provided they are in mint condition."

"I sell product that is better than mint condition, young skeptic, but six dollars for the pair it is then. You drive a hard bargain, young lady, but I assure you I shall not be so accommodating in subsequent negotiations with you."

Conan clutched the two comics and stuffed them into a brown paper bag while Brenda handed over her six bucks. After receiving her purchase, she collected Bobby and they hurried out the screen door as Conan called out, "Farewell fair maiden and her knight from England. See you again soon."

"That was the coolest shop!" Bobby exclaimed. "He has quite a collection in there. We're going to have to do some research online and then come back. I saw some things I may want to get. But after hearing your conversation, I thought I should wait and get some prices first."

They hopped down the curb to retrieve their bikes.

"Conan is quite...ah...different," said Bobby.

"Yup, that's for sure," replied Brenda as she stuffed her purchases in her backpack. "We go on like that sometimes for half an hour. I think he likes talking to me because I get him and laugh at his jokes. Some people get offended by what he says, though, and walk out of there angry. Mom says he has family money so he doesn't care what people think."

They cruised to the park, just a block from Conan's, where they'd meet Brenda's friend Stevie. They found an empty bench and just sat there for a while relaxing in the warm summer breeze. Shoppers hustled by dragging their kids and carrying bags, looking like mules on a wagon train. Workers carried boxes on handcarts to the backs of buildings, making their deliveries. All seemed to be in a hurry, but everyone bore the same happy grin that only a beautiful summer day can bring. Looking up brought a big smile across Brenda's face as she announced, "There's Stevie!"

Stevie, with his hat on backwards and an unbuttoned, untucked shirt over his tee flapping behind him, was hurtling down the path towards Brenda and Bobby. Even from a distance, Stevie gave the impression of someone always ready to take a dare. His long, brown hair flowed around his baseball cap, giving a fuller look to his slight frame. He glided in on his bike as if on wings. He pulled his right leg over the bar and stood upright on the moving bike with his left foot firmly planted on the pedal. Then, without hitting the brakes, he stepped off his bike and ran it to a full stop right in front of them.

"Hi, Stevie," Brenda called out.

"Hi, Brenda!" They high-fived. "You must be Bobby."

"Yes, hello," replied Bobby. "Nice bike, but doesn't it have brakes?"

"Yeah, it does, but I like to glide it to a stop. More fun that way."

"Yeah," said Brenda, "Stevie likes to take risks."

"Like you don't," said Stevie, not knowing if her comment was a compliment or a criticism.

"Oh, not like you, pal. Remember two years ago, Stevie?" She turned to Bobby. "The river was swollen because we had a tough winter, and what did genius here do? He decided to walk across the bridge handrails like he was on a tightrope. Halfway across he slipped and fell into the river. And guess what? He can't swim!"

"And I guess," said Bobby, "you jumped in right after to rescue him."

Stevie stared at Bobby. "How did you know that?"

Bobby didn't pause for even a second. "It's elementary logic, really. Brenda told the story like she was there. I know she is quite athletic, because I saw a swimming trophy on the dresser in her bedroom. I assumed she wouldn't have just stood around and wave as you went under. She speaks about you as her best friend and you seem to respond the same way. Didn't take much to figure it out."

Brenda stared at her cousin, obviously impressed. Stevie blushed, embarrassed that it was so easy to identify how he felt about Brenda.

Eager to change the subject, Stevie said, "So what have you guys been doing?"

"We just came out of *Conan's,*" said Brenda as they crossed to the section of the park that continued on the other side of Main Street.

"I can't stand that guy," said Stevie.

"Why not?" asked Bobby.

"Conan threw him out last summer," responded Brenda.

"I didn't do anything!" protested Stevie. "He had it in for me. I was looking over some new stuff that he still had in a box on his counter, when he came out of his back room. He then pitched a fit, yelling at me for touching his precious comics, and threw me out of there. Called me a vagrant, or something like that. He removed the box so fast, I swear he was hiding something in there. I tell you, Brenda, I don't trust that guy."

All three glanced in the direction of the store and saw Conan staring back at them from the smudged window of his shop.

"Hey," said Stevie, "why don't we ride over to the school and play box ball?" Turning to Bobby, he asked, "You know that game?"

"I don't think so. But I wouldn't mind trying," Bobby responded.

"Great. The rules are easy. We use chalk to draw a box on one of the walls of the school. You pitch a ball, and the batter tries to hit it with his fist or a bat. I always carry a rubber ball in this pack on my bike, but since we don't have a bat we'll use our fists."

"Let's go," said Brenda. "You learn best by playing."

Emerging from the park, they turned left onto Baker Street and out to Turner Avenue. From Turner, it was a straight run to the school. The road sloped downward at about 35-degrees before leveling off again. Stevie, of course, was the first to stand straight up on his pedals, arms outstretched, with the wind hitting him in the face as they coasted downhill. Brenda and Bobby weren't quite as fearless. They flung out their arms but did not dare to stand.

At the bottom of the hill, they hit School Drive, appropriately named, as the school was the only building on the road. It was a long, narrow road going on for about a quarter of a mile before the school came into view. Although not a modern school, it looked new. The grounds were well kept, and the building was clean and free of graffiti.

"We'll go this way around to the back of the building," said Brenda. "That's where the gym is. We'll have a big area of brick wall to draw the box."

They sped around the front of the building looking through the front doors as they passed. It was dark inside and not at all welcoming. A far contrast to when school was in session and crawling with kids. The classrooms they passed were now stripped of all artwork, colors, and children's window dressing. The entire building exuded a cold emptiness, like the surface of a distant planet: no people, no warmth, and no discernable emotion. Rounding the side of the school, they crossed the playground with stilled swings, empty monkey bars, and other lifeless forms, like the skeletal remains of some great hulks of the dinosaur age frozen in time. No one was here today and an eerie gloom lay over the area.

They circled the school and proceeded to the gymnasium, which was perfect for their game. There was a vast expanse of blacktop that hugged the rear of the gym. The windowless brick wall rose about 60 feet high.

They stepped off their bikes and dropped them on the ground near the back entrance to the school. Stevie went to work drawing the box, making sure the strike zone covered each of their heights. Brenda raced into the outfield as Stevie took the hastily drawn pitchers mound on the blacktop. Bobby was the first at bat.

"I know you're new at this," said Stevie as if he were talking to a three-year-old. "Just relax and try to do your best."

Stevie smiled a smarmy smile and pitched one at moderate speed, which curved to the left but stayed in the batter's box, clipping it in the lower left hand corner. Bobby watched it go by without swinging his arm.

"Strike one!" Stevie yelled. "I know I'm a pretty good pitcher," he continued, "but I practically lobbed that one to you. You're going to have to keep your eye on the ball and try to hit it." Stevie turned to Brenda and gave a big grin. Brenda smiled back as Stevie wound up his next pitch like Mariano Rivera in a World Series game. He paused before firing the next one right down the middle into the center of the chalk box. It went by with a whoosh and Bobby merely glanced at it.

"Steeeeeeeerike, two!!" Stevie yelled, and now Brenda's grin was even bigger.

"You know, it's okay to hit the ball Bobby," taunted Stevie. "I know this is an American sport, but you've got to try harder. Maybe Brenda should take my place and pitch it to you underhand." Brenda and Stevie got a loud laugh out of that one, but Stevie had no intention of giving Bobby an easy pitch. He was enjoying this bit of showing off. He did his exaggerated wind-up, squinted at the box as if figuring just exactly where he was going to place the ball, and let fly his patented sinker, designed to fool the batter into swinging just as the ball drops into the lower end of the box.

But as the ball sailed towards the plate, Bobby did a roundhouse, like a one arm pinwheel with his right arm. Just as the ball came over the swing area, his arm came up hard like an uppercut punch from a professional boxer. His fist met the ball perfectly and sent it soaring over the monkey bars. Brenda's mouth immediately dropped as her eyes followed the ball up and then behind her. She had moved towards the infield with each strike, assuming that if Bobby hit the ball at all, it probably would not even get past Stevie.

When Brenda finally retrieved the ball, she and Stevie gathered at the wall with Bobby. With a stunned look on his face, Stevie blurted, "Please tell me that was beginner's luck. How did you do that?" Brenda still had her mouth open.

"Years of playing Cricket in school," Bobby replied. "When batting in Cricket, the batter hits the ball with an uppercut swing and not with the straight on swing of American baseball. Took a while for you to finally throw me a decent pitch," he added. Bobby's comments brought a smile to Brenda and Stevie was speechless, but the spell was soon broken as the rear doors of the school burst open and hit the walls with a loud boom.

"What do you kids think you're doing here?" shouted the disheveled looking man who burst through the open doors. "I don't want none of you brats around here messing up the place when school is out! Do you hear me?"

Brenda, Bobby, and Stevie were stunned by the verbal assault and unable to move. All they could do was stare at the unkempt figure charging in their direction. He was tall, nearly 6'2" and, although thin, he looked quite strong. He had dark, deep-set eyes as black as old oil and looked as if he never smiled. His rotten teeth showed when he snarled, and his black hair was greasy.

"Uh oh," whispered Brenda, "that's Carl, the cranky janitor at our school. He always looks like someone at the end of a hard day's work, no matter what time of day it is," Brenda quipped. "Nobody likes him and everyone tries to avoid him at all cost. He's just plain nasty."

"Smells, too," Stevie added.

They searched for an escape route but quickly realized that their bikes were near the now open doors of the school. They were effectively blocked from getting them. As he came closer, Carl's hands bunched up in a threatening manner. Fearful, all three of them backed up a step.

A short, rotund, middle-aged man with round glasses stuck his bald head out the door and yelled. "Is there a problem out here, Carl?"

Carl never took his eyes off the kids as he replied, "Uh, no sir, Mr. Batelli, just some kids causing a ruckus is all. I asked them if they could play elsewhere since we have too much work going on here right now."

"Right. Okay, kids, you move on now like Carl asked you to. Carl, come on in, I need to show you which desks need to be moved."

Carl cast a final sneer in their direction, leaned over and towards them, and whispered, "Too bad our conversation was interrupted. It would have been nice to confiscate your bikes for a while. Maybe next time. And how about detention in the custodial office? Maybe you could do some work for me over the summer." He turned as he responded to the principal, "Coming right in, Mr. Batelli," and then he disappeared back inside.

As soon as they heard the school doors click shut, the three ballplayers broke free from their rigid spots, picked up their bikes, and mounted them in one smooth movement. They pedaled as fast as they could and didn't stop until they reached the end of the School Road. Only then did they dare to disembark.

They all felt as if they had narrowly escaped serious trouble. Realizing they were now safe, they laughed hysterically and collapsed onto the grass next to the road.

"Did you see Carl?" said Stevie. "I should have hit him with the ball right between the eyes."

"Yeah, sure, hot shot, so why didn't you?" challenged Brenda.

Bobby smiled at his cousin.

"Next time I will!" said Stevie.

"Forget it," said Brenda, "you'd really get into some trouble if you did that." She turned to Bobby. "Stevie does have a good eye. By that I mean, nine times out of ten he could hit a bird on the fly with a small rock."

"Who was the other man?" Bobby asked, distracted by what happened.

"That was Mr. Batelli, our principal," said Brenda. "He's just a fat toad, and nobody likes him either. Whenever kids complain about anything, he just tells their parents, 'well, you know how kids make up stories.' Carl doesn't want to get on his bad side, though, so he tries to suck up to him by keeping the bathrooms clean." Bobby looked at her quizzically. "Whenever he lectures us, Mr. Batelli is always going on about keeping the bathrooms clean. I swear it's the only thing he cares about. If he's not checking on the bathrooms, he's hiding in his office."

"He is one scary guy, that Carl," admitted Stevie. "Kids avoid him whenever he's around. There were rumors that he tossed kids who misbehaved into the school furnace at his last job."

"Don't be stupid," mumbled Brenda.

"Funny, though, I've never seen him that nasty before. I wonder what's gotten into him?"

"Your presence brings out the best in people, Stevie," quipped Brenda.

"He did seem a bit over the top," Bobby mused, concerned far more deeply than he cared to admit

Stevie glanced at Bobby as if wondering why he would make a statement like that about a person he had never met before.

"I mean, why would anybody get so upset about a bunch of kids playing on the school yard?" Bobby added quickly, hoping that his comment was casual enough to diffuse the questions he was sure were burning in Stevie's mind. But his own worry about the janitor's demeanor was far too real to be brushed away with his hands that now massaged throbbing temples.

7

The trio headed towards town, biking fast through Stevie's neighborhood, which was full of colonial style homes on neatly trimmed lawns, framed by summer blooms. The leaves of the poplars, which lined both sides of the streets, hummed with the warm breeze that still cooled their faces as they rode. They meandered northward through the neighborhood, eventually making a right turn onto a narrow alley. The alley was not open to cars and other vehicles, but served as a main connection for pedestrians and bikers to enter town. It was lined with cobblestones the way Cobble Avenue used to be. At the end of the alley, they paused to catch their breath.

"Did you hear that?" whispered Stevie.

"What?" inquired Brenda.

"Yes!" he said with mischievous glee. "It's Tony!"

"Who is Tony?" Bobby asked.

"He's the Italian Ice man who comes around in summer!" said Stevie. "I can hear his tune."

Stevie peered around the corner of Betty's Beauty Salon to confirm that Tony's small handcart was parked just down the street. Tony had his back to them as he served Italian Ice to a handful of enthusiastic children lined up near the entrance to the park. Italian Ice was a favorite in summer, drawing large crowds of kids and adults alike.

"Oh, this is great," said Stevie excitedly.

"No, Stevie!" shouted Brenda. "Leave him alone."

"This is too good to pass up!" responded Stevie. "He's within earshot and we're hidden by the building. He can hear us, but he can't see us." Stevie was arguing his point, but not debating it. He had already decided his next move.

Bobby was a bit bewildered. "What are you two talking about?"

"Stevie likes to torment Tony," said Brenda. "He calls out his name and then hides. Tony keeps looking around to see who is calling him. When he finally figures out someone is messing with him, he gets really mad." She threw a stern look at Stevie. "It's childish."

"Look, Stevie," said Bobby. "Perhaps you shouldn't do this. I've had a bad feeling about a few things, lately. I don't think this is a good idea." But Stevie had already moved to the edge of the building and, after drawing in a deep breath, began to shout.

"Hey, Tony!" he hollered before quickly ducking behind the building.

Bobby and Brenda had no choice but to follow Stevie's lead. Hearts pounding, the three of them pressed themselves out of sight against the brick siding of the building.

"How do you know he won't just come charging down here like a bull in a tea shop?" challenged Bobby.

"I think the phrase is 'china shop,' genius," said Stevie.

"He doesn't want to leave his cart unattended," whispered Brenda. "But if he finds out who is doing this, he will pack up his stuff and chase us down."

"He won't find out," murmured Stevie as he peered around the corner. "He just gets crazy mad. It's fun to watch him trying to serve his customers while looking for whoever is yelling at him. When he gets going, he hops around like a madman."

Tony's head was whipping in all directions as he scooped out the lemon and cherry ices. He kept turning his head this way and that, the red kerchief he wore around his neck flapping like a flag on a windy day. His shoulders seemed more tense and hunched. He dropped a half-filled cup and his free hand flexed as he scanned the buildings to pinpoint where the shouting came from.

"Hey, Tony!" shouted Stevie once more, his voice echoing off the store windows.

Now the muttering began. Not only was there a decided change in Tony's demeanor, they could also hear his random, angry comments in broken English as his temper rose. The ices he handed out got larger as Tony scooped deeper to work off his rage. Kids were getting a double scoop when they had only ordered a single. Tony simply couldn't help himself. He took out his growing anxiety on the buckets of flavored ice in front of him.

Stevie fell on the ground laughing hysterically. Bobby and Brenda joined in. They couldn't help it, either; Tony's reaction was funny. They would be ashamed to admit it, or tell their parents about it, but that made it even funnier.

Now on the ground, they leaned over in unison and snuck another peek around the corner. Tony was mumbling incoherently, digging in his freezer in a frenzy. His young customers looked a bit on edge. Some parents began drifting over to the cart, gently corralling their kids and moving them away from this Italian volcano that seemed ready to erupt.

"Hey, Tony boy!" Stevie shouted once more. As they carefully gazed around the building, almost stretching their eyes from their sockets, trying not to make any sudden movements that would attract attention, they realized they had probably crossed the line. Tony was now in full-blown hysteria. He threw his scooper down on the ground sending customers running for cover. When he slammed down the lid of his freezer, it sounded like the cannon the town shot off on Memorial Day and the Fourth of July. Tony whipped around, head swiveling like a top, his eyes darting every which way, framed by a thick, down-turned unibrow.

Then the shouting started.

"You filthy little animals! I catch you, I gonna break you neck! You bother me, I gonna bother you. I break you neck and gonna stuff it down you stomach! I gonna...

"I think we should go," Bobby cautioned quietly.

Brenda and Stevie were already running to their bikes. They rode back down the alley as fast as they could. It was a slight downward slope, and as they picked up speed they could hear a variety of colorful curse words in broken English, convincing them that Tony wouldn't be selling any more Italian ices at the park that afternoon.

They took a right turn at the end of the alley and continued with great speed, laughing all the while. They put as much distance between themselves and the furious Italian as possible. When they could no longer hear Tony, their laughter subsided and was replaced by fatigue. They stepped off their bikes and walked. The park was quite a distance away, so they weren't afraid that Tony was looking for them. He hadn't seen them anyway, and they were sure that he had packed up and moved on to another location.

As they rounded Cobble and turned onto Baker, they passed the Baker Street Café.

"Let's stop in for a soda," said Brenda. "My treat!"

They were about to cross the street, when Stevie held his hand out to stop them. "Hey look!" he said, "There goes the town retard."

Brenda rolled her eyes and elbowed Stevie in the ribs.

Walking away from them was a boy who was holding hands with his mother. He was at least a foot taller than them, with a crew cut hairstyle.

"Why did you call him that?" asked Bobby.

"For one thing, look at him, he's a dork," said Stevie. "Secondly, he's weird. He moved here from another state sometime in May. He walks around with his mother all the time. She home-schools him and I don't think she ever lets him go out to play. He doesn't smile at anyone and just stares if he catches anyone looking at him. Freaks me out. Sometimes I sneak up to his house with a friend of mine, since I live in his neighborhood. I try to peek inside to see if they're doing anything strange. I'm telling you, he's downright creepy."

"He's not weird, Stevie, he's different, that's all," said Brenda. "You shouldn't pick on him or make fun of him."

"I'm not making fun of him. I don't like the way he looks at people and I don't trust him."

"You don't trust anyone!" Brenda challenged.

"You hardly ever see him walking around in broad daylight," countered Stevie. "He only comes out at night with his mom. At first I thought he was a vampire. Seeing him in the daytime gives me the willies."

"Don't be stupid!" shouted Brenda. "He probably had a doctor's appointment or something." Although she did wonder about this boy, too, she was pretty sure Bobby would never behave that way, and so Stevie's open dislike of a boy he didn't even know embarrassed her.

At that moment, the strange boy turned and gawked as if looking right through them. Then he got into his mother's car. As the car drove by, its peculiar passenger kept locking eyes with them.

"See!" said Stevie, "I told you. He's weird *and* scary."

The Baker Street Café was a blast from the past, a true small town icon. As Bobby entered, the first thing he noticed was the long soda fountain counter. It curved at the two edges and went on for nearly twenty feet in length. Cushioned stools stood at attention in front and around the two sides of the Formica-topped counter. A large, vintage Coca-Cola sign hung on the wall behind the counter, flanked by two milk shake machines. A soda machine was to the left and a multi-pot coffee machine to the right. There were only a few small booths near the entrance. Beyond them, glass-enclosed counters, similar to the ones at *Conan's Comics Shop*, housed a variety of candies for sale. A narrow aisle separated the two areas and led to a section in the rear with large, comfortable booths on either side. There were eight in total, but at the moment, only one was occupied.

The screen door slammed shut behind them, setting off the bell attached to the frame. The waitress behind the counter was busy brewing a fresh pot of coffee, and barely looked up.

"Hi Sharon," Stevie greeted her with a short wave.

"Hi kids, be right with you," she responded mangling the gum in her mouth. Gum was a permanent fixture between her teeth. The snapping that came from her face always gave away her location, like sonar pinging off a hidden submarine. Sharon was tall with size ten feet boxed into white shoes, the kind old ladies wear when they decide to lose the high heels and go for comfort. Sharon loved them even though she was only forty years old. She donned a pink dress covered with a white apron, and wore her uniform as proudly as a flight attendant. She also had a well-sharpened #2 pencil stuck at a dangerous angle in her oddly bound up hairdo. It was hard to imagine how she could penetrate the varnished helmet created by the use of so much hairspray with the pencil she rarely used. The smell of her hair lingered on in an area long after she left, mixed with her inexpensive perfume. While she carried a fresh pot of coffee to the rear of the café, she told the kids to saddle up to the counter.

They each took a stool, threw one leg over it to sit down, and got comfortable. Looking around the place, Bobby marveled at the fact that the shop managed to look new and old at the same time. Brenda leaned over to whisper, "It's the Baker Street Regulars back there."

"Who?" asked Bobby.

"The Regulars, for short," chimed in Stevie. "It's what we call that group sitting in the back. They're always here. The one in the uniform is Sheriff Musgrave. We don't know the real names of the other two, just their nicknames—Moss and Jinx."

Sharon refilled the cups of the Regulars. "You know, boys," she said in between snaps of gum, "you are definitely taking advantage of the bottomless cup policy. It doesn't mean you can live here, you know."

"Now, Sharon, you know that's not fair," said the sheriff. "Me and the boys here are deep in discussion about the state of affairs in this country. Besides, we're waiting for the *mayor.*" He pronounced the word 'mayor' as if the President himself was on his way.

"Well, don't hurt your brains in the process," she said and gave them a wink.

The sheriff smiled, winked back, and returned to the serious business at the table. He was a big man in a tight uniform, wearing a belt with a gravity-defying buckle that seemed permanently stapled to the underside of his vast and growing belly. He was overly paternal to the kids in town, treating them as though they were perpetually five years old. He was a small town sheriff and liked the lack of challenge the job provided. He often held court here at the café, and his court jesters were always Moss and Jinx.

People didn't know if Moss was a name or nickname, but suspected it had something to do with the rumor that he sat in the café for so long that moss grew on the seat of his pants. That might have been an unfair characterization, but his rear end did indeed fit perfectly into the depression in the seat of 'his' booth. Moss owned the gas station on the edge of town, and always wore a Gulf Station shirt to prove it. He was also a big man who seemed to prefer clothes from a younger, slimmer time in his life. His pants were bunched up from being pinched in the rear and were short enough to be called "capris" by the kids. His shirt was a size too small, providing a real challenge for the buttons. As it was, they were greatly strained, with tufts of stomach and chest hair protruding through the gaps between them. He didn't even bother buttoning the top two, which would have been a pointless gesture anyway.

Jinx made no secret of the fact that his was a nickname. It seemed that no matter what he tried to do in life, it never worked out to his advantage, as if he were permanently jinxed. The funny thing was, he seemed to take pride in this, almost bragging about his constant failure to anyone who would—or wouldn't—listen. He worked for Moss at the station and was usually by his side, providing a willing audience for his boss.

Jinx also wore a Gulf shirt, though his hung loosely on his scarecrow frame. His hands always appeared dirty, but he never seemed to work long enough for them to get that way. He never buttoned the sleeves on his shirt, which had the name "Jinx" stenciled on the left chest pocket in red. He always had a toothpick dangling from the top of his lower lip, as if it were glued on permanently. No one had ever seen him throw a toothpick away, and it was rumored that he had used the same one for years. Sometimes he took it out and slipped it behind his ear for later use.

"What can I get you kids?" asked Sharon, back at the counter.

"We'll each have a cherry coke," replied Brenda.

As she was preparing their drinks, the screen door opened and Mayor Block waddled in.

"Hello, Sharon. How is my favorite waitress? And how might you three future voters be today?" he asked.

Sharon smiled, but Brenda said, "We're fine, Mr. Mayor, thank you for asking."

"You are indeed welcome, young lady, and I hope you are all enjoying your summer." Grinning from ear to ear, he patted them all on the back and hurried to the back to meet with his cronies.

"Now the group is complete," said Stevie. He turned to Bobby, who sat between him and Brenda. "His name is Mayor Block, which we think is really funny because his rear end is as big as a city block. In fact, we all call him 'city', which he likes because he thinks it refers to his being mayor and the king of the city, when we're really making fun of the size of his butt."

The mayor plopped down next to the Sheriff, who jumped a bit in his seat as a result. Moss and Jinx stumbled over themselves greeting him and trying to fill him in on their deep discussion. "And we were wondering what your position might be, Mayor?" Jinx managed to ask the pertinent question.

Only too anxious to provide an opinion on any topic at any time, the mayor began to pontificate. Only too anxious to listen intently and agree with everything he said—mostly because it meant they didn't have to go back to work—the men nodded eagerly and provided encouragement. Their accord always earned them a fresh pot of coffee purchased by the mayor, of course.

While he never paid for it, at least he put it on his tab.

Part 4

Dire Warnings

Their cherry cokes finished, the threesome decided it was time to drift homeward. After Brenda dropped a small tip for Sharon on the counter, and as the coins rattled to a stop, they hoisted themselves off the stools and headed for the door.

"Thank you, sweetie," Sharon called after them. "Don't you kids forget to check out the poster in the window about the carnival coming to town. It promises to be a good one this year."

They gave one another a quick look. A split second later, they were pushing their way out the door to view the poster. There, in the lower left corner of the front window, lay a multi-colored 15"x20" sign with a large face of a clown dominating the left side. Smaller in scale, as if behind the clown face, was a menagerie of carnival creatures—elephants, lions, and dog acts, all prancing around the center ring under the direction of a man with a tall hat and a whip. The colorful title that curved along the top of the poster was framed with fireworks and said it all: **"The Carnival is Coming to Town."**

The lower right-hand corner of the poster listed the specifics.

Come One, Come All!

Kroft Brothers Carnival

At the Mountain Lake Fairgrounds

August 11-13

Thurs./Fri: 5pm-11pm

Sat: 1pm-11pm.

"Oh boy!" exclaimed Stevie. "It's only one week away. I forgot all about it. It's always such a blast!"

"It sure is," Brenda agreed. "We are so going, Bobby. There are games, and rides, and tons of attractions. I love the food too. Mom lets me eat all kinds of junk she would never let me eat any other time of the year."

"Super!" Bobby chimed in. "I can't wait. We don't have anything quite like this in England. Our carnivals are more like a street fair, or cultural celebration. Do they really have elephants there?"

"Yeah," Stevie responded and rolled his eyes again. "England must be boring as heck. Usually, this town is pretty dull, too, but during the carnival, we've got elephants, tigers, lions, you name it. Nothing more exciting than that all year."

They knocked the kickstands up and hopped on their bikes. Stevie sped ahead, took the first left turn, and with a last wave headed home.

Brenda thought about making a stop at her father's shop, just across the street, when suddenly, a truck pulled out of the parking space right in front. It backed all the way across the street with its tires screeching, then sped forward and ran through the stop sign, fishtailing down the road. Watching the truck disappear, Brenda changed her mind and decided they should go home instead.

"It's late and Mom will be wondering where we are. Dad will be home for dinner soon anyway," she said starting to pedal off. "We'll stop in another time."

Bobby continued to stare at the truck as it vanished in the distance. His head was throbbing.

"You coming?" Brenda called over her shoulder. "It's just a stupid truck."

"I know," he said, more to convince himself than answer Brenda. He took a deep breath and followed her south on Cobble.

They entered the house through the mudroom, slamming the door behind them.

Brenda's mother was busily preparing the salad. "And how do you like our fair community Bobby?"

"I love it, Auntie Arlene, it's brilliant."

"Oh, I wouldn't say brilliant, but there are some smart people about."

Bobby laughed. "No, Auntie, by brilliant, I mean smashing... you know, fantastic."

"But of course you do, dear," she said more interested in dealing with the food in front of her than with Bobby's language lesson. "Brenda, will you begin to set the table, dear? Then the two of you can go play while I finish dinner. Meatloaf tonight!" she exclaimed with a bit of pep in her voice. "It's one of our favorites around here, Bobby, so I hope you'll like it, too."

"Yes, Auntie, I'm sure I'll love it."

Bobby helped Brenda set the table before they went up the stairs to play Brenda's X-box.

At five p.m. the front door opened and closed, followed by a loud but lonely "I'm home!" Just inside the door Uncle John paused, his usual does-anybody-care-teaser stuck in his throat. He heard shouts of glee coming from upstairs, where Bobby and Brenda were engaged in a fierce video game struggle, oblivious to his return home. He never understood the attraction of such things, preferring the simple machines he worked with, but knew it had pleased his daughter immensely when she got one for her last birthday. He trudged into the kitchen and kissed his wife on the cheek, without his usual good cheer.

"Is everything alright, dear?" Auntie Arlene didn't seem to appreciate his distracted embrace.

"Yes, everything is fine," Uncle John sighed. "Just a busy day at work, I guess."

"I see."

They stood looking at each other for just a moment. "I'm going upstairs to wash up for dinner." With another quick kiss followed by a weak smile, he made his way upstairs to the bathroom. Auntie Arlene thought it best not to press further.

Only minutes later, her loud and cheery call for "Dinner!" bounced through the house. Bobby threw his control aside and raced for the bathroom. Brenda refused to give up. "No fair quitting!" she hollered.

"Sorry!" said Bobby while washing his hands. "Can't keep your mum waiting!"

"Yes, we can, since I'm just about ready to crush you."

Bobby stuck his head out of the bathroom. "Sorry, cousin. I respect your mum too much and wouldn't want to disappoint her," he said with a smirk. He then raced down the stairs and heard

Brenda washing up before he hit the last step. He turned into the kitchen and took a moment to breathe in the wonderful aroma. Unsure if he should sit in the same spot at the table as the night before, he waited for Brenda.

"You don't play fair," she huffed as she bounced into the kitchen.

Bobby was taken aback. He wasn't sure if Brenda was serious or not.

"It's a good thing we're having meatloaf tonight, or I would have finished you off before coming down," Brenda stated with a smirk, putting him more at ease. "Sit where you were before, Bobby. It'll be your seat from now on."

At that moment, Uncle John joined them at the table. He took his seat, folded his hands on the table, and looked at Brenda with a faint air of fatigue. "So," he inquired, "how was your day?"

"We just tooled around town," she said absently.

"Since *tools* are my business," he said, stretching the word 'tools' as he spoke, "I would love to hear all about it."

Brenda groaned at her father's attempt at humor. Bobby smiled, but looked at his uncle with concern. He was going to say something, but then paused. Finally, he could no longer contain himself.

"Uncle John, what happened with Mr. McCormack today that got you so upset?" Bobby asked.

No one moved or spoke. His uncle, poised to take a sip of water, held the glass inches from his mouth. His mouth was pursed to sip, but instead he sat there frozen in position. Auntie Arlene was in mid-step, just a foot or two from the table. She grasped the meat-loaf dish with oven-gloved hands and stood there staring at her husband with concern. Brenda, clearly taken aback by the question, looked at Bobby with narrowed eyes.

"What?" his Aunt screeched, breaking the silence as she addressed her husband. "John, what happened with Mr. McCormack today? You know he can be violent! Remember when he would get into fights at that bar out on Route 7 all the time? Did he do something to you? What happened at work today? Why didn't you tell me about it?!"

Her husband sat, almost in shock.

"John!" she demanded. "Why don't you answer me?!"

"Largely because you haven't given me the chance to respond, Arlene," he said quietly. "Nothing serious happened," he finished, turning his attention back to Bobby. "But just how, young man, did you happen to know about Mr. McCormack?"

Bobby hesitated at first, not sure that he'd done the right thing asking the question in the first place. He remembered his mother's admonition against being too direct. So far, he had kept personal things to himself: his deductive and logical reasoning abilities, his usual outspokenness, and most definitely his dreams and premonitions. But the truck had rattled him, and so he had just blurted out the question without thinking it through. Nothing to do, he decided, but plow ahead.

"Well, I, uh..." he stuttered. "I'm sorry, Uncle John, but when you announced that you were home this evening, even from upstairs I noticed that you failed to ask if anyone cared. Since Brenda indicated that you ask that very question each night, and have done so for as long as she can remember, I thought that rather odd. When I came downstairs, I looked for confirmation and noticed that you do appear tired and not quite yourself. Also, a truck pulled out of your parking lot today around closing time.

I had a bad feeling about it, especially when he ran a stop sign and continued to speed down Cobble Avenue, giving the impression that he was very angry and in a hurry to leave your shop. The truck had the name *McCormack Farm* painted on the side. I merely assumed that the man in question was Mr. McCormack, that he was agitated, and that perhaps, you were, too." Well, there it was, and he hoped he hadn't offended anyone.

By now, everyone was looking at Bobby and his uncle managed a faint but surprised smile. He wondered how he had been able to keep his own family in the dark about what happened today, but not his visiting nephew.

"Dear," he said addressing his wife, "you can put the meatloaf down now." When she did, he told her to take her seat and promised he would tell his story. Once they had all filled their plates and started to eat, he began his tale.

"There isn't much to tell, really. Arlene, you know Tom McCormack is nothing but an old loudmouth. He came in to see me this afternoon. Before I could even say hello, he threw a couple of tools on the counter and told me he wanted replacements at no cost. He said I'd sold him faulty merchandise that broke on him. I offered him a discount on some fresh tools. When I looked his old ones over, I noticed that they were clearly abused, likely in jobs for which they were not intended, but he got nasty when I suggested as much. He used language I will not repeat at this table. But when he called me a liar and a cheat, I lost my temper and threw him out. I can take a lot from someone, but not that. I pride myself on taking care of my customers and treating people fairly. So, yes, I was a bit out of sorts when I came home. That's all there is to it."

There was absolute silence at the table. When Uncle John picked up his fork, his wife placed her hand on top of his and looked straight into his eyes.

"Thank you," she said. "I appreciate you sharing this with us. You should know how much we love you and don't want to see you upset. You are a good man and that dirty old…"

"Arlene," he said and nodded towards Bobby and Brenda.

"It just makes me mad that he would even *think…*" She let her final thought go unsaid, leaned over and kissed her husband on the cheek.

"Now," she finally said with gusto, "who's hungry?"

The next few days went by agonizingly slow as the trio got to know each other better. Bobby and Stevie established more of a friendship, each more accepting of the differences in the other. Bobby's nightly phone conversations with his mother took on a lighter tone, as he gained more confidence in his new surroundings. He was still very homesick, but Brenda kept them all focused on the excitement of the carnival that lay just out reach.

The local newspaper, *The Daily Mirror,* was filled with stories about the upcoming event. There were stories of carnivals past, highlighting heart stopping rides and attractions that captured everyone's imagination and attention. Rides such as *Chuckie's Up-Chuck Coaster,* where Joey Smythe had lost his lunch on a curve over the midway (too much cotton candy, the article said). There were stories of unanticipated happenings, such as the one two years ago when someone left the gate open at the petting zoo and an odd assortment of goats, sheep, rabbits, and pigs ran around the *Fairgrounds,* chased by the many children in attendance that day. And there were stories of the upcoming event itself, mentioning the enormous growth in size this year, the abundance of new rides and attractions, and exciting "not to be missed" events like the trained elephant show.

Bobby and Brenda poured over the details as if studying for final exams.

"This is going to be the best carnival ever! There are so many new rides and things to see and do, I can't wait. And it's only two days away!" exclaimed Brenda.

"I'm anxious to see it as well," said Bobby. "I told my mum about it the other night on the phone. She said it reminded her of a country fair in England. She sounded almost as excited about it as I am." He suddenly fell quiet, as if mentioning his mother had reminded him that he was far away from home.

Brenda and Stevie couldn't help but notice. "Why is your mom not here with you?" Stevie asked.

"Oh, she's in Paris, working. She's with the Scotland Yard."

"Paris!" Brenda exclaimed.

"Scotland Yard!" Stevie repeated.

"Yes, I wanted to go with her, and see Paris, but the Scotland Yard has this silly rule—no family at work, ever. "

"Wow, I bet you miss her," said Stevie.

"Yes, I really do. I didn't think I would, or maybe I was just mad at her for going without me and sending me here instead. But I missed her as soon as I boarded the plane."

"I can't imagine leaving my parents to go on such a faraway trip alone to visit with people I never met," said Brenda. "That was pretty brave, Bobby."

"Oh heck," added Stevie, "I could go anywhere without my parents. Nothing much scares me."

Bobby looked at his mates and smiled. "I feel as if I've known you both forever," he said. "And I'm glad we're going to the carnival together."

The night before the carnival finally arrived and sleep was not easy to come by. The thrill of the next day's events filled them with adrenaline pumping excitement, making sleep an elusive goal. It was quite some time before visions of rides, food, clowns, and animals eventually guided them to slumber.

The caravan of cars and trucks rode into town late the next morning. The carnies spent the better part of the day setting up tents, rides, and stands. Ropes of different sizes were crisscrossing each other, resembling a giant cat's cradle, while somehow, magically, holding up the various oversized tents. The animals—llamas, elephants, and horses—were all herded into their tents, corrals, and holding pens. The acrobats, clowns, trapeze artists and other performers walked about juggling, throwing knives, and practicing their jumps, dives, and back flips. Like bees in a beehive, people were milling about every which way. But what seemed like chaos to the outside observer, was in fact part of an established routine. Like a well-oiled machine, the carnies accomplished their tasks quickly and efficiently, moving about with precision-like effectiveness.

Bobby, Brenda, and Stevie spent the day on edge. Each moment lasted an eternity. Trying to kill time, they rode into town on their bikes, and stopped outside *Conan's*. The familiar tinkling of the bell sounded as they opened the screen door to the comics shop. Conan was at his usual post at the counter, arms folded and leaning forward.

"Bless my soul, if it isn't the princess and her English knight, and you brought the court jester along with you."

"Hello to you, too," responded Stevie, sarcasm dripping from his lips.

"To what do I owe this enormous pleasure so soon after your last visit, Ms. Watson?"

"We're trying to pass the time before we go to the carnival tonight."

"Ah, yes, the annual youth-driven Bacchanalia."

"The what?" they all chorused.

"Oh, look it up, I don't have time for a vocabulary lesson," he said with feigned exasperation. "My day is filled with conducting important financial business dealings, which will make me much too tired to attend tonight's frivolous festivities."

Suddenly someone plopped a half dozen comics on the counter with a loud slap. They all turned to find themselves fact to face with Carl, the school custodian, disheveled as ever. No one had noticed him when they came in.

"Hello, children, come to do some summer study?" Carl laughed but it was clearly without mirth. It was, in fact, not even a laugh, but rather more of a growl.

They all stared, but said nothing as Conan rang him up and collected his cash. Carl tipped his dirty hat and lumbered outside to his truck.

"I don't like that man," Brenda said. "He's mean and angry."

"Young lady," Conan replied, "he is a paying customer and as such is deserving of my considerable respect…at least until I have his money. I do, however, share your astute assessment of his innate personality."

"He's probably reading preschool picture books," quipped Stevie.

"Actually, young man, he favors a local writer from Danbury who has translated some of his historical work into pulp fiction format—a comic book to you. I do doubt, however, if the man has ever owned a library card. I, on the other hand, am quite a scholar on local history and frequent the library often."

"Interesting," murmured Bobby. "Conan," he said, "is there a particular time in history that interests the custodian?"

"Now why would you ask a question such as that?" murmured Conan.

"Just curious is all. Would he be researching a time when pirates visited this area?" he asked.

Conan's eyes narrowed ever so slightly. "There were no pirates here ever, young man, and to suggest otherwise is ludicrous. The very idea of it, which seems to be proposed in the comics our school employee just purchased, offends my scholarly instincts." His face brightened slightly as he continued. "Now then, let's see what you owe."

They gathered up their comics, paid, and said their goodbyes.

"A pleasure to meet with you again, Conan," said Bobby and reached out his hand for a shake.

"My word, a true gentleman. The pleasure is mine, Sir Knight, and I bid you a fair adieu."

They made their way to the park in thought.

"Did you notice that Conan said that those comics Carl purchased hinted at pirates coming to the area?" asked Bobby.

"He did? I swear, I can't understand half of what that guy says," muttered Stevie.

"Yes," said Brenda, ignoring Stevie, "but so what?"

Bobby shook his head and changed the subject. "We'll be going to the carnival with your parents, Brenda, right?"

"Yes, they insist on taking us since it is a little out of town, but I think the real reason is they want to make it a family thing. I've never even gone off on my own before. Tonight will be the first time they will let me run loose on the fairgrounds with you guys. I think it just makes them feel better to take us and pick us up."

"I don't know what they're worried about," crowed Stevie. "What could happen if I'm around?"

Bobby and Brenda both stared at Stevie as if he had two heads.

After a while, they divvied up their comics. For the next few hours, they sat, read, and drew, comparing sketches as they did.

"Why is this day taking so darn long?" Stevie remarked to no one in particular.

"I must confess," said Bobby, "I'm anxious myself."

To Brenda it seemed as if some unknown force was holding back the minute hand, deliberately slowing things down. At some point, when they were all engaged with their drawings, her Casio wristwatch alarm went off, shocking them all out of their stupor. They looked at each other for a brief moment. Then they scooped up their belongings, grabbed their bikes, and headed for home. It was time for the big event.

Before long they veered into Brenda's driveway and jumped off before coming to a full stop, their bikes crashing on the front lawn. Without stopping, they ran into the house through the mudroom and into the kitchen.

"Mom!" Brenda screamed. There was no indication that her mother was even home. A panic set in as Brenda thought, for the briefest of moments, that something had happened to prevent them from going to the carnival this evening. Just as she was about to scream again, she heard her mother's footsteps coming down the stairs.

"What are you screeching about, Brenda Jean? I'm here, not to worry. Oh, hello Stevie, how are you? And how is your family, dear?"

"I'm good, and everyone's fine, Mrs. Watson, thanks for asking. Can we go now?"

"Well, I, uh, I suppose," she stuttered. "Yes, let's go. Out to the car..." Before she had a chance to even finish her sentence, the door slammed and the kids were getting comfortably lodged in the back seat of the family van. By the time Brenda's mom found her keys and decided which bag she was going to sling over her shoulder, the three young passengers had grown impatient. Their legs were bouncing up and down as they sat, unable to control the excitement that coursed through them; their hands were rapidly tapping out some indecipherable tune on their knees. Brenda's mother seemed to take forever to haul herself into the driver's seat, shut the door, and turn the ignition.

"Oh my goodness, Mom, where's Dad? Isn't he coming?"

"Unfortunately not, dear. He's at work. He has several repairs that are due tomorrow and he can't break away. He will be coming with us tomorrow night, however."

"That's too bad. So, if Dad isn't coming, what will you do?" Brenda asked tentatively.

"Oh, I was thinking I'd hang out with the three of you," she responded, confirming Brenda's worst fears. Her comment provoked a breathless silence in the car, and Brenda's mom was listening for that proverbial pin drop. "Gotcha!" she burst out suddenly. "No worries," she continued between laughter. "I don't intend to spoil your evening. Mrs. Johnson is joining me. The two of us will stroll around together and maybe try our luck on some of the games. You don't have to contend with me."

The sense of relief in the car was palpable. And when after a short car ride, they finally caught their first glimpse of the tent tops peeking up over the hill, everyone was chatting excitedly, pointing out this and that, discussing what they'd do first. Minutes later an attendant directed them towards the parking area, which was nothing more than a huge section of uneven field to the right of the main entrance. Once they were parked, they got out of the car and walked over the ruts in the dirty, worn patch of grass between the car park and the entrance. The kids wanted to run, but Brenda's mom had made it very clear that they were to stay close by until they had reached the entrance and ground rules had been established. A bright, arc-shaped neon sign with a clown face greeted them from afar. The clown's right eye blinked with each on-again, off-again flash of the lights. His mouth went alternately from a round "O" to a broad smile, with the eye winking as the smile shone. He seemed to stare at everyone as they entered.

Brenda's mom paid the entrance fee, and they received lime green, snap-on bracelets that covered most of the rides.

"Now listen and focus, my dears," Brenda's mom told them. She waited a moment until they were all looking directly at her. "I'm trusting the three of you tonight a great deal. If you lose that trust, it will take some time to get it back. Am I clear?" she asked to check if they were listening.

"Yes, we get it," Brenda responded for the group, as the others just nodded.

"Good. It is now 5:20 p.m. Brenda, check your watch. "

"Yup, it's 5:20."

"Good. We will meet at the end of the midway near that huge cotton candy machine sign at 8:00. Brenda, set your alarm. That will give you time to spread out a bit and check things out. But stay together. And you are not to leave the park under any circumstances. If you need me for any reason, just go over there." She made a slow, deliberate turn and pointed to the sign that read *Lost and Found.* "They will page me. Otherwise, I want you to think and act smart."

The kids had one foot facing Auntie Arlene and one foot towards the midway, but they knew they needed her permission before they could turn their other foot and get their bodies in motion. They paused, looking at her and leaning towards the inviting depth of the carnival at the same time. She returned their gaze and finally, with a slight hitch in her voice, whispered the magic words: "Go on. And be sure to have a good time."

In all this excitement Bobby failed to notice that his body tingled and his head was beginning to throb.

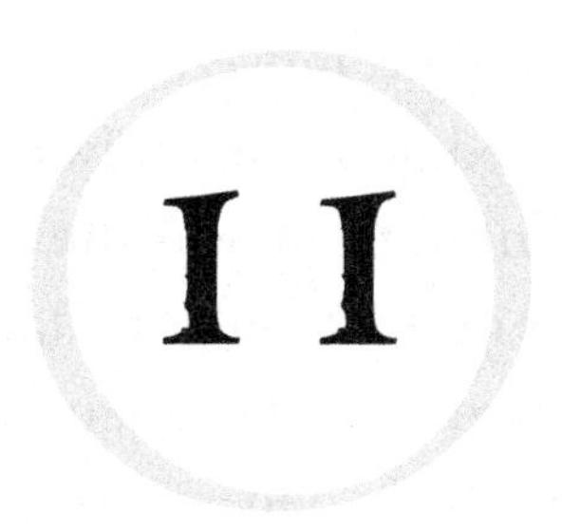

11

Brenda, Stevie, and Bobby took their first leap and walked briskly up the midway. The soft sawdust crunched underfoot, giving off the sweet smell of freshly cut wood. Game barkers shouted for customers on either side. "Hurry, Hurry, Hurry!" they squawked. "A winner every time!" There were squeals of delight from the few winners in front of each game and groans of defeat from the many losers. The cotton candy machine at the end of the midway sent its cloying syrupy scent wafting down the aisle like water from a burst dam. It mixed with the sweetness of candy apples and the savory sizzle of sausage and peppers frying on the grill, causing their stomachs to growl.

They stopped in front of the nickel toss and dug into their pockets for loose change and the chance to win a stuffed St. Bernard. It was a prize they all desperately wanted, although they knew they could not possibly carry it out to the car.

Brenda was the first to go. She lost three nickels in quick order as they hit the plates and bounced out. Bobby went next with much the same results. Stevie smirked at them both, convinced he would have to pick up his winnings on their way out. Even though he employed every skill he possessed, Stevie could not land a nickel on the top of any plate. Frustrated, he kicked up sawdust, pronounced the game fixed, and moved on.

As they rounded the edge of the midway, they turned right and stopped. Directly in front of them was the *Horrific House of Horrors.* There was an enormous animatronics fat lady at the entrance. Her arms pointed at the crowds while she laughed hysterically, triceps wiggling as she did. Her curly hair was bright red and she had on way too much poorly applied make-up. She wore what looked to be a dress from the 1920s and a feathered band around her sizeable head. Every few minutes she would stop laughing and her face would contort into a frightening grin. She would lean forward and say, "Enter if you dare!" in a sultry voice, and then resume her hysterical laughter.

They took their place in the growing line. When they reached the front, they settled into the first of a group of red cars. Brenda refused to sit in the middle and made Stevie do it, proving she had more courage than he. Even though he protested that only girls sit in the middle, he was happy to do so. Bobby took the other side and they all scrunched together.

The restraining bar lowered and the car set off with a loud BANG as it glided through the doors that led inside. They were immediately plunged into a sea of black.

The car moved rapidly up inclines and around bends, whipping around the corners, and careening through the darkness. The speed sent them rocking from side to side. As they slowed in certain spots, a light would flash and some nightmarish character would reach out to them with a growl. Bobby's body began to tingle and, worse, his head throbbed so much he winced. He tried to ignore it and was reluctant to tell the others, hoping it would soon pass. After they passed a huge spider encased in a web, they moved on through the murk, feeling what they thought were silk web strands being dragged over their heads and necks. Despite Stevie's false bravado, all three sported nice sets of goosebumps.

All of a sudden the ride stopped. They could hear each other's hearts beating, but could not see their hands before their eyes, it was so dark.

"Aren't lights supposed to come on in an emergency?" asked Stevie. "Shouldn't someone be here to help us? I'm getting hot in here, are you guys getting hot?"

Brenda and Bobby remained quiet, straining their eyes to see in the silent gloom.

Bobby grabbed the sides of his head as a pain shot through him. He could hear faint whispering and tilted his head in response. He couldn't make out the words. It was just low-level noise but he knew it was there. "What?" he muttered.

"You say something?" Stevie whispered.

"Along this trail…," the voice whispered. "Along this trial came Boot and Crag…"

"Hey, Bobby!" Stevie called and jabbed Bobby in the side. Just then, the ride jerked forward and they were once again hurtled forward through the darkness.

After a few more jump-in-your-face characters and unsuspected steep hills, they finally approached the end of the ride. A large, life-sized skeleton in tattered pirate clothes waved to them as they approached the exit door. A creepy voice congratulated them on their survival and bid them pleasant dreams before braking out in a caustic laugh. Bobby thought the pirate seemed to stare right at him and instinctively reached for his head. Before he could react, there was a loud BANG, as they burst through the exit doors and slowed to a stop in the waning light of early evening.

"I loved it," shouted Brenda.

"It was Okay, I guess," said Stevie, "but not as scary as I thought it would be."

"Yeah, sure," Brenda teased, "is that why you had a death grip on my arm?"

Bobby, on the other hand, was silent. The dark, evil feel of the ride and his thrumming head frightened him. The voice he thought he had heard and the pirate figure that had stared at him had brought back his nightmare.

Before Stevie had a chance to defend his honor, Brenda grabbed the arms of both boys and scooted off down the walkway towards the unmistakable smell of elephant. They soon came upon a large outdoor ring surrounded by spectators and jostled their way through the crowd to a front spot. Inside the waist high ring was a baby elephant balanced on a pedestal with one rounded, flat front foot. Its other front foot and its trunk were lifted towards the sky as the trainer tossed peanuts into its mouth.

"Ladies and gentlemen," the trainer bellowed. "Welcome to the highlight of your evening. I am known as The Major and this is my partner, Suzie the Elephant."

"Boy, they smell a lot worse than I imagined," whispered Stevie. "And the elephant doesn't smell so good either," he added with a laugh. Brenda looked at him and shook her head.

The elephant trainer didn't explain why he was called The Major, but he took obvious pride in the military-style uniform he wore. He had on oversized pantaloons that puffed out at the pockets as if he needed to hide gigantic hands from time to time. They were tucked into high, brown boots that reached up to his knobby knees. He donned a tight red jacket that looked at least a size too small, covering a ruffled white shirt pulled together at the top by a black, clip-on bowtie. Gold braided epaulets hung on his shoulders, wriggling like a bucket of snakes with each dramatic movement. Completing the ensemble, atop his comb-over hairdo lay a slightly askew, black top hat that looked like it was retrieved from a luxury wedding gone bad. He delighted in tipping it to the crowd each time the elephant did a trick, as if he had done it himself. Stevie swore that he saw The Major pop a peanut into his own mouth once or twice, causing his face to turn as red as the candy apples being hawked by vendors everywhere.

After watching a few more tricks, the three moved on to the tent with a sign that read, *"Human Diversity Show – Enter at Your Own Risk."* They hesitated for a moment, not quite sure if they wanted to go in, but intensely curious at the same time. They were dismayed at an additional five dollar fee to enter, but it was billed as an 'extra special' event by Danny, the Diversity Show barker.

"Gather around my friends and listen to my tale," Danny shouted from the small stage at the entrance. When he first appeared on stage there was an audible gasp from the small audience, because Danny could easily have been confused with being in the human diversity show himself. His bulbous nose hung so low it nearly rested on his chin, which itself protruded far enough that it looked as if it wanted to escape his face. His ears were almost as large as The Major's pockets, with a yellow viscous substance clogging the entrance to each, like a mustard colored glacier slowly making its way downhill. Simply put, Danny was good advertising for his own show, and the crowd rapidly grew.

"I have traveled the seven continents in search of the most interesting people in the world," he continued. "I have been to the darkest corners of Africa and to the lofty heights of the Himalayas. I have crossed the mighty mountains of Europe and traversed the deserts of Asia and brought back to the show inside an unbelievable collection of human diversity. For the small charge of five dollars, you can bear witness to what I risked my life to bring to you."

He stepped aside and shouted, "Behold!"

Three figures crossed the stage as he announced each one in turn. First came Lizard Man, whose loose skin was dry and patched like an alligator's. Tattoo Man, who was covered from head to toe with ink designs, followed him. He had so many tattoos that they appeared as one, and he looked more like a bad bruise. Lastly, *The Man With Two Heads* waddled out. This character sported a bulbous fatty growth on his shoulder, with dark make-up outlining two eyes, a nose, and a mouth.

"This is just a small sample of what you will find inside," he continued. "Please step up. The next show is in three minutes." As the crowd began to disperse, Danny panicked. Realizing he was losing his audience, he hurriedly announced, "For one night only, my friends, the cost of this incredible exhibition is just two dollars! Hurry now, before the tent fills up!"

That seemed to do the trick as many in the group decided it was worth the two bucks to see what else he had. Some were tentative as they paid, and marched into the tent as if summoned to their own funeral, frightened by what they might see. Brenda made a face and Bobby concurred that they would rather keep moving. As they drifted away, Stevie was the first to announce what they were all thinking.

"I'm hungry," he said.

They followed their noses to the nearest concession stand. "Bobby, I'm going to treat you to one of the most magical things in food history," said Brenda. "It's a true American classic and you can't possibly leave the carnival without getting it."

Brenda plopped down her cash and ordered three corn dogs. They sat at a small picnic bench and devoured the popular carnival delicacy. Bobby loved it and convinced his mates to have another. Still taking the lead, Brenda, suggested they coat their stomachs with an ice cream.

Done eating, they walked on through the attractions area, taking mental notes on what they wanted to come back to on other nights. They were anxious to get to the rides before they had to meet with Brenda's mom later. Picking their way through the crowd, they couldn't help but notice a small tent set up outside the perimeter of the main activity. A small, wooden sign announced a hand-painted message: "Madame Tarot is in! Stop now and have your fortune told." A little old lady sat in a chair near the entrance. She was smiling in their direction.

Brenda and Stevie started to drift away. But Bobby's body tingled so much he thought he was getting a chill. He grabbed his companions and walked towards the self-proclaimed psychic. Surprised at his interest, they went along at a brisk pace.

"Hello, young man," the woman cackled. She had deep set, dark brown eyes and a smile that commanded attention with several missing teeth. Pulling her earlobes down on either side of her small head were two large, round hoop earrings that glistened under the lights of the fairway. Her skull was wrapped in a multi-colored silk turban, and her billowy blouse gave way to small, delicate hands adorned with gold and silver rings. Her voluminous, colorful skirt was patterned with large flowers. It hung down to the ground and hid the chair upon which she sat.

"Won't you come in? I seem to have some time right now," she said so quietly they barely heard her.

"What's it going to cost?" challenged Stevie, ever the skeptic.

"For you three, nothing," she said slyly.

Stevie heard "free" and was all in. Brenda was wary, but followed the other two into the confined tent. The tent was empty except for a small card table set in the middle with four chairs around it. On the table sat a small, round crystal ball. Madame Tarot sat down and wrapped her hands around the sphere. She closed her eyes and mumbled incoherently. Bobby sat directly across from her while his friends sat on either side. Everyone looked nervous except Bobby. He somehow knew he needed to be here. The sounds of the carnival outside suddenly became muffled.

Madame Tarot reached across the table, and as Bobby placed his hands into hers, she stiffened. Her eyes popped open revealing a stark whiteness. She had rolled them way back into her skull. Bobby's body became rigid and began to shake, as if charged with electric current. His eyes closed and drool fell from his lips. He had fallen into a deep trance.

"Bobby, are you all right?" breathed Brenda, quite concerned. But Bobby didn't answer. He couldn't.

Madame Tarot moaned slightly. Her mouth opened wide and she tried to speak, but no sound escaped. Brenda and Stevie shuddered at the sight of her white eyeballs and cavernous mouth.

Madame Tarot had an iron grip on Bobby who was still shaking in his chair. Then, without warning, Madame Tarot spoke. Her voice was deep and distorted as if it came from under water.

"Boy! I warned ye to stay away, didn't I? It is my time and he is willing. I will collect that which is mine and anyone in my way will die! Pay heed, boy, and stay away or suffer a painful death! I warn ye no more." And then, in almost a lilting whisper, the voice continued:

Along this trail came Boot and Crag
Who carried a load and daren't drag,
Rich we'll be says Mr. Boot
When first we bury the Captain's loot.

This was followed by loud, high-pitched laughter that caused Stevie and Brenda to cover their ears. Madame Tarot eased her grip on Bobby's hands and dropped her head on the table. Bobby immediately fell from his chair onto the sawdust below. Brenda and Stevie, who had been staring at the scary scene, jumped from their seats, each grabbing one of Bobby's arms, and pulled him from the stifling tent. Once outside, Bobby seemed to revive, although he was still wobbly and was sweating profusely. They turned to Madame Tarot, who looked pale and sickly as she tumbled into the chair outside her tent.

"You better not have hurt him," barked Stevie. "My dad's a lawyer," he added, which was his answer to any problem he couldn't handle or explain.

"Shut up, Stevie!" said Brenda. "Can't you see she's as spooked as Bobby?" Brenda walked over and bent down on one knee. She placed an arm around Madame Tarot. "Are you okay, ma'am?"

"Yes...no...I mean, I don't know," she stammered. "What happened? Is the boy all right?"

"He's okay, now that he's outside. What happened in there? Why did you say those things to him?"

Madame Tarot looked her straight in the eye and Brenda could see her fear. It was the kind of fear that made every goosebump stand at attention. The kind of fear that made someone's ears prick when a strange noise was heard. The kind of fear one had when lost in a dark and unfamiliar place.

"*I* didn't say anything," she said with finality as she stared at Brenda. "It was *him.* And *he* is coming." She raced back into her tent and zipped it behind her.

The trio made their way back to the table near the corn dog stand and sat down. Brenda went to the counter and got some ice wrapped in a paper towel. She brought it back to Bobby and placed it on the back of his neck while he sat forward with his head in his hands.

"Are you okay?" Brenda asked. "That scene freaked me out. I thought she would break out the cards and give you a lame, 'Gee, you are going to have a long life,' kind of fortune. What happened in there? What was she talking about?"

Bobby, who hadn't yet said a word, reached up to remove the ice.

"My head keeps pounding and I'm feeling wobbly."

That's when Brenda's watch alarm went off.

"Almost 8:00," she said. "We'll need to head back to the meeting point. Can you make it?"

"I'm very tired. That bloke seemed to be speaking right inside my head. And there was something else, but I'm not sure what."

"Hey, that fortune teller is just a ventriloquist, making herself sound like some old pirate," said Stevie, not sure if he believed what he was saying. "And she's a really bad one if you ask me," he added with growing bravado. "It's just a trick!"'

"I don't think so." Bobby finally looked at his companions. "I think this is all real."

Brenda and Stevie stared, waiting for an explanation.

"I'm sorry mates, I can't think straight with my head pounding, but I know this is real."

In the moment of silence that followed, Brenda decided to trust her cousin and go with it for the time being. "Stevie, help me with Bobby. Let's each put an arm around our shoulders."

They retraced their steps until they saw the *Cotton Candy* sign where they were supposed to meet Brenda's mom.

Bobby and Brenda collapsed on a bench. Stevie stood next to them and gazed over to the side of the midway they hadn't yet explored.

"Are you sure you can't talk about it?" she asked.

"I…I don't know. *He* was threatening me…warning me about finding something of *his.*"

"Who threatened you, Bobby?" Brenda's voice had a slightly higher pitch than usual.

Bobby gazed, as if in a trance. "I…I'm not sure. I'm sorry, my head is pounding…I can't…"

But Stevie, still convinced Madame Tarot was a fraud, continued to stare across from where they sat, where a balloon-shot game beckoned. At a dollar for four darts, the objective was to burst balloons that were tacked to a wall. A small smile spread across Stevie's face. Without speaking to his friends, he slowly walked towards the game.

"Where do you think you're going?" Brenda yelled. "My mom will be here any minute!"

Stevie paused without turning and spoke in a monotone. "I'll be right over there. This will be much easier than the nickel toss."

Focused, Stevie stood behind a few players waiting his turn, observing the game. Stevie noticed there was just enough air in the balloons to make them look penetrable, but not enough to make them burst easily. The darts would often push into the balloon and bounce off after contact. He guessed the darts had been dulled. With the last player before him was done, he stepped up to the counter and laid down a five-dollar bill. "I'll take twenty darts, please."

The nametag on the vendor's shirt read *Vince.* He wore a perpetual sneer and seemed to take special joy in seeing the darts fall when contestants threw them. His sweat-stained T-shirt and tight, dirty jeans reminded Stevie a little of Carl, the custodian. Despite the snug fit of his trousers, he sported rainbow-colored suspenders. He had a toothpick perched on his lip, always ready to fall off but never able to make the jump.

Vince smirked when he picked up Stevie's five-dollar bill, examining it with a light bulb behind it, as if he knew how to check for a counterfeit. Then he plopped the darts on the counter.

Stevie gave him the briefest smile before picking up four of the darts. He kept three in his left hand and shifted the fourth one to his right. He confirmed the dull point and knew the balloons would pop only with some force behind the throw. Stevie spotted a small fan, almost hidden from view that gently blew air on the balloons, causing them to move around slightly, which made them an even harder target. Stevie acted as if he had never done this before and asked how the game was played. With an even bigger sneer, Vince shifted his toothpick by moving his lips, uncrossed his arms and picked up a dart.

"Like this!" he said. Vince jammed a dart into the nearest balloon without taking his eyes off Stevie. Stevie smiled, nodded, and threw his first dart as hard as he could. He popped the balloon right next to Vince's hand. With a start, Vince jerked his hand away.

"Hey, watch it, kid!" he snorted. When he noticed that Stevie popped a balloon on his first toss, Vince mumbled something about beginner's luck and took a prudent step to the right, just out of range. The sneer had disappeared.

Stevie took another dart in his right hand and did a wind-up worthy of a pro baseball pitcher. He let the dart fly and POP; there went another one just to the right of the one he had already hit. "How many do I have to hit to win the grand prize, that iPod over there?" Stevie asked quietly.

Vince looked at the iPod. He knew that no one ever won the grand prize, not in any town they've ever been. He also knew that the advertised number of popped balloons to win it was six in a row, an impossible feat, given how the game was fixed. Vince inched over to the iPod and blocked Stevie's view of the small sign next to it. He picked it up and dropped it face down on the ground. Turning back to Stevie he said, "Ten in a row, kid. But don't worry, people do it all the time." The sneer was back.

Stevie smiled himself. "Just checking," he said.

By now, Brenda and Bobby were right behind him, urging him to finish the game. "Mom isn't here yet, and it's 8:05," Brenda whispered. "I can see if she shows up from over here, but if she doesn't, we're going to have to leave and have her paged."

"Not to worry," said Stevie calmly, "I'm almost done here."

A siren blew in the distance, too muted to cause them concern, yet Brenda looked up nervously.

Stevie threw the other two darts in his hand and popped two more balloons. He picked up four more darts and threw them in rapid succession, all hitting their targets with a loud POP accompanying each one.

A crowd started to form. Adults and kids alike began to push their way closer to see who was popping all the balloons. It was if the mob could smell a winner and they all wanted to be a part of it.

By now Vince was getting nervous. He'd paid for that iPod himself and didn't want anyone winning it.

"Gee," said Stevie, "I've got eight in a row and only two to go. Ohhhh," he said with a mock shudder, "I wonder if I can do it."

"Stevie," said Bobby with his hand on Stevie's shoulder. "We have to go. Something is wrong."

Stevie shrugged off Bobby's hand. "In a minute," he said, not taking his eyes off the balloon board. With slow and deliberate fanfare, he picked up four more darts and made a great show of examining the weight of them as well as the feathers lining their shafts. The crowd was poised on their toes, silently waiting for the finale. He then let them fly at the board, hitting and popping the next four balloons. A cheer went up from the large audience.

Before Vince could even react to the realization that he'd lost his precious iPod, Stevie kept going. He was rapidly picking up darts, winding up, and hitting every target in his sights until all twenty darts were exhausted. The crowd cheered anew with each hit. Twenty darts now replaced balloons that were nothing but shredded latex remnants. They drooped like the hangdog look on Vince's face.

"Wow," said Stevie, "I just got twenty in a row. I guess that means I get *two* iPods."

Vince looked at Stevie with daggers in his eyes. He leaned in to Stevie as close as he could to prevent others from hearing him. "I bet you think you're a smart guy. Well, smart guy, what if I don't give you the iPod? What if I say you cheated by leaning over the counter?"

"You could do that," whispered Stevie, "but my dad's a lawyer, and I don't think you would want that publicity on the first night of the carnival. Besides, this crowd expects you to give me my prize," Stevie added, jerking his thumb over his shoulder.

Bobby turned Stevie around. "We've really got to go! It's 8:20 and Brenda said Auntie Arlene would never be this late."

Just then, a voice boomed over the loudspeaker:

"*WILL BRENDA WATSON AND COMPANY PLEASE REPORT TO THE LOST AND FOUND CENTER NEAR THE ENTRANCE*!"

Brenda gasped and her stomach fluttered. She feared her mother was hurt, or worse.

Stevie looked straight at Vince, held out his hand, and said loud enough for the surrounding crowd to hear, "I'll take one and let you off the hook for the other one."

Vince looked at the expectant crowd and licked his lips. He reached over and removed the iPod from its perch in the center of the game prizes. He cast one last longing glance at it and then handed it to Stevie. The three hurried away to the applause of the crowd.

"A grand prize winner here! A winner every time! Hurry! Hurry! Hurry!" Vince said loudly as the crowd dispersed.

Under his breath, he added, "Somehow I'll get even with you, you little creep! You just wait and see!"

Part 5

The Plot Thickens

As they approached, Brenda noticed her mom standing right outside the *Lost and Found,* talking animatedly with her friend Mrs. Johnson and Tim Carver, the town deputy. The police car sat just outside the entrance gate, still running with roof lights flashing. Something was definitely wrong.

"Mom, what's going on?" Brenda asked out of breath.

"Oh dear, oh dear, Brenda. It's your father. He's in the hospital," she blurted. Brenda, Bobby, and even Stevie turned pale at the news.

"He's all right, please don't worry. He has a nasty bump on the head, but he's coming home tonight. They wanted to keep him overnight for observation, but you know your father," Auntie Arlene added as if that explained everything. "I'm so sorry I couldn't meet you all on time. Officer Carver arrived with the news just as I was ready to go find you."

"But Mom, what happened?" persisted Brenda.

"Oh my, someone broke into your father's store while he was working late in the repair shop. They hit him over the head, knocked him out, and then stole some tools," she explained, sobbing through it all. "How could anyone do that to such a nice man? And for what? *Tools*? I just can't believe it! Nothing like this ever happens here."

Bobby leaned over to Brenda and whispered, "This may sound weird, but I know this is related to my experience with Madame Tarot. My body is tingling like crazy. I think we're all in danger."

"Mrs. Watson," said Officer Carver, "do you need anything else? Would you like a ride to the hospital? Would you like me to take the kids home?"

"Yeah," shouted Stevie, "and we can let the sirens wail!" Brenda shot him a disapproving look.

"No, thank you, Officer. I'll drive everybody home.

Officer Carver tipped his hat and left.

Exhausted, Brenda's mom sighed and waved everyone along towards the exit. She hugged her friend and followed the kids to the car.

"Do you want me to drive, Mrs. Watson?" asked Stevie solemnly.

"No, Stevie, I think I can handle it," she said with a rueful smile.

Brenda shot him another disapproving look as they all piled into the van as fast as they could. No one spoke on the ride home. No doubt everyone was trying to process the news. Madame Tarot, her frightening message to Bobby, and then this news about Brenda's father…

They dropped off Stevie and headed home. Pulling into the driveway, Bobby felt both a sense of comfort and of dread: comfort at the warmth and safety of being home, dread of the danger he suspected lay ahead.

They were all in the kitchen sharing a cup of tea before bed when the front door opened and closed quietly. A couple of steps on the hardwood floor and then a shout, "Hello, I'm home! Does anybody care?"

A split second passed before they all raced into the living room nearly knocking Uncle John down. It was the best reception he had ever received.

"Why don't we all go back into the kitchen?" he said.

They took their places around the kitchen table, holding their cups as if holding on to them would ground them all and provide some safety. Auntie Arlene poured her husband a cup of coffee, which he preferred over tea, and set it on the table before him. The steam rose off the cup. He let the aroma of the strong brew reach his nose. He smiled with his eyes closed and sighed. Other than the periodic tinkling of a teaspoon in a cup, the only other sound in the room was the ticking of the clock over the window just above the kitchen sink. Uncle John gradually opened his eyes, took a sip, and looked at each of them in turn.

"I suppose you are all waiting to hear what happened. I'll tell you what I told the police, but right off the bat I need to tell you that I don't know who did this. I didn't see who it was and I only heard..."

"Are you okay, Dad?" Brenda interrupted.

"Yes, sweetheart, I am." He reached over to her and stroked her cheek until a tentative smile appeared on her tired face.

"What happened?" Bobby asked, curious and fearful as to what he would hear.

"It was just after six o'clock. I was still working on Joe Johnson's ride mower at the time. I knew that his wife Jane was with you at the carnival tonight." He nodded in his wife's direction. "I wanted to tackle this job tonight since it was a big one, and I knew I wouldn't be able to get to it again until next Monday. I had the radio on, listening to the Beach Boys belt out *Good Vibrations.* Anyway, I was moving right along pretty well, thinking I could finish it up by about 8:00, and after cleaning up, I'd be home no later than 9:00." He paused briefly and his voice dropped almost to a whisper. "I didn't even hear him come in. I had locked all the doors and double-checked them before starting the repairs so he definitely picked the lock. He must have worn soft shoes because I never heard a step. I was kneeling on the floor, bent over the mower when it happened. One moment I was absolutely fine, tinkering with the starter, and the next moment I felt a sudden pain in my head. Then, nothing but blackness. I was hit so hard, I passed out. When I woke up, I realized I had been unconscious for about thirty minutes. My head was spinning and I was still in some shock, I think. I had the presence of mind to call the police, however. It didn't take much to figure out I had been attacked and probably robbed."

"But they didn't steal money," murmured Bobby. Brenda cast him a questioning glance.

"No. The money was still in the cash register and the only things I noticed missing were a few brand new shovels I had just laid out this afternoon and a handful of oil lit torches. Odd choices, I thought, for such a determined thief." He paused, scratching his head near the spot where he had been hit.

"The sheriff looked the place over while we talked and he sent his deputy to find you all. I didn't want to go, but they insisted on taking me to the hospital to be checked out. When they wanted to keep me overnight, though, I put my foot down. They weren't happy about it, but I signed myself out and the sheriff drove me home."

He shrugged his shoulders as if to confirm that everything was just fine, but then added "I am tired, though, and just want to go to sleep."

"I think sleep is a good idea for us all, dear," responded Brenda's mom. "Brenda, would you and Bobby go get ready and settle down for the night?"

Hesitantly they obeyed. As they climbed the stairs, far more slowly than usual, they overheard parts of the adults' conversation. "I don't think I will sleep well tonight," Brenda's mom said, oblivious that the kids were listening. "I plan to check on you throughout the night. Head injuries are nothing to take lightly."

"I'm fine, dear," Uncle John said as he got up, walked around the table and embraced his wife.

Bobby went straight to his room, and Brenda snuck in before he could close the door. "How did you know that they didn't steal any money? Did the Tarot lady tell you about the robbery at my father's store?" Brenda approached him so fast, Bobby had to take a few steps back so she wouldn't collide with him.

"Brenda, I know you have some questions," he said quickly, holding up his hands as if to defend himself against an invisible attacker. "I just don't have many answers."

"I don't need *many* answers," Brenda countered. "All I need to know is what's been going on! Things are out of whack since you got here!"

"Out of what?" Bobby was confused, but she didn't answer. "Look, Brenda, I've tried to ignore it, but something's been happening to me since I left London. It's confusing and frightening and I don't know what it is or what to do. But I do know that if I," he paused, "if *we* are to make sense of this, we need to have a good night's sleep. Nobody thinks straight when they are tired."

Brenda looked at her cousin. "Okay," she said. "But it has to be tomorrow. I need to know tomorrow what has you so afraid and what that has to do with my father."

The next morning Bobby awoke energized. Brenda heard him moving about and burst into his room fully dressed. She ran over and jumped onto the foot of his bed, nearly bouncing him from his perch.

"I've been waiting for you to get up! You, Stevie, and I are getting together to talk this through. He'll be waiting for us at the park in an hour."

"Can we meet him at the Baker Street Café instead?"

"The café? What can we find out there other than what Moss and Jinx had for breakfast by looking at the crumbs in their lap?"

"I'm not sure... I know that... actually, I don't know why, but I just have a strong feeling that the café is the place we need to be."

Brenda stared at him.

"Can you just trust me?" Bobby pleaded.

Brenda nodded and raced off to call Stevie while Bobby hurried out of bed and into the bathroom. He washed up and brushed his teeth before dashing down the stairs, ready to bounce out the door.

"Sit down the both of you," Brenda's mom said, stopping them cold. "I have some scrambled eggs and fresh baked banana muffins ready for you. They're your dad's favorite."

"How is Uncle John this morning, Auntie?" realizing that it would be best to slow down and do as his aunt requested, or else she'd be asking too many questions he couldn't answer.

"I'm doing wonderfully, Bobby, thanks for asking," said his uncle as he strode into the room and over to the table. "You can't get food like this in a hospital," he exclaimed. "Or care from such a special nurse," he added as he cast a glance towards the stove, much to the delight of his wife.

"We were going to meet Stevie in just a few minutes," Brenda mentioned casually with a glance at Bobby.

"You can spare a minute or two to have just a bit of breakfast," her mom looked at her with furrowed brow. "What do you say, Bobby?"

Bobby's eyes were glued to the basket of muffins being brought over to the table. "I guess we wouldn't want to insult your mother by denying her the pleasure of serving us breakfast. So, just to be polite I think we should eat something."

They all sat to enjoy what was to be the best part of their day.

After breakfast, Bobby and Brenda participated in a fast cleanup.

"May we go now, mom?"

"And where would the two of you be off to?" her mother asked as her father sat reading the morning paper.

"We thought we would ride into town, meet Stevie, hang out in the park, and then maybe go for a bike ride."

"Okay, dears, go on out and enjoy the day, but be safe and stay out of trouble," cautioned her mother, still a bit rattled from the previous evening. "And be home for dinner if you decide to eat lunch in town!" she called after them, as they ran out the front door towards the garage.

The door slammed behind them while they hustled to their bikes. They raced into town as fast as they could, arriving in front of the café just minutes before Stevie. This was a town where everyone knew everyone else, explained Brenda, so they mustn't look like they were up to something. The boys murmured their agreement and entered the café. As usual, the bell signaled their arrival as the screen door closed after them.

"Hi, Sharon."

Sharon nodded in their direction. She did not have a shellacked piece of hair out of place. "Be right with you, kids," she shouted, as she headed towards the back of the restaurant with the familiar pot of steaming, black coffee glued to her right hand.

There were a number of booths filled with diners, all out enjoying a late breakfast or brunch. Some were shoppers out for an early start. Some were out-of-town visitors about to go to the carnival. And, judging by the loud guffaws coming from the booth in the back, the Regulars were in session, too.

They slipped into one of the small booths opposite the counter and huddled up like referees debating a call.

"What'll it be, kids?" asked Sharon, breathless after racing back up to the front.

Brenda spoke for the group. "Chocolate milks all around, please. We just ate breakfast and aren't too hungry yet."

As soon as Sharon went to retrieve their chocolate milks, they leaned back into their conversation. "Okay, so what happened last night?" asked Brenda, getting right to the point.

Bobby paused for a second or two, unsure how to begin. "There is more to this than last night," he started. "Something so bizarre you may not even believe me. It started before I arrived here. I tried to believe I was just dreaming or imagining things. But the headaches I've gotten lately are getting worse. Also, I get a tingling feeling whenever this is happening. When I heard about your father's attack, that feeling came on very strong, and I felt that it was somehow related to the message given to me by Madame Tarot."

"Look, you British buzz kill, you put a damper on last night by making us go see that fake fortune teller, and you promised to tell us all about it today, but this rambling of yours makes no sense. Headaches, tingling…what the heck are you talking about?" blurted Stevie.

At that moment the door opened and they all turned when they heard the bell. Michael came in, alone, and walked over to the counter not too far from their small booth.

"Uh oh, the town retard," whispered Stevie loudly enough for Michael to hear. "And he's alone in broad daylight. I guess he's not a vampire."

Michael gave Stevie a dirty look and twirled on the stool, while Brenda jabbed her elbow into Stevie's ribs. Bobby quickly inserted a quarter into the jukebox on the wall beside their booth and picked out three songs at random, hoping the low music would provide enough background noise to camouflage their conversation.

"You're right, Stevie, I need to tell you everything," he said when the music began.

"My mum says I have a gift and I've had it since I was born."

"What, you mean like a new baseball or something?" asked Stevie.

"Stop interrupting," said Brenda. "Let him tell it."

Stevie frowned and shrugged. Bobby was about to continue, but waited for Sharon to drop off their order and hurry back to her customers in the rear.

"I noticed it when I was very young. I could always tell when my parents were upset about something. At first, mum called it intuition. But as I grew older, I began to show other talents. Often, I knew where things were that people had lost. Sometimes, my mum would talk to me about a case she was working on, and I was able help her solve it, usually by noticing things she might have missed."

"Like what?" Brenda asked.

"Oh, you get to interrupt him?" Stevie threw in, a slight edge in his voice.

"Just little details," Bobby continued. "Like one time I noticed that someone had said he was home watching a soccer game on TV at a certain time, when that particular game had been delayed for half and hour because it was raining too hard. So that ruined his alibi and…"

"What had he done?" Stevie interrupted again.

"He was the getaway driver in a robbery," Bobby said, uncomfortable with what seemed like growing distrust from Brenda and Stevie. "It wasn't a big deal, really. It was just fun at first, like a puzzle or a guessing game. Sometimes I would show off to my schoolmates. I'd mention things about them they thought nobody knew. But, they began to laugh at me and think I was strange, so I stopped."

"Well, they were right there, it is a little…"

"Stop it, Stevie. Can we get to the point? Today some time?" Brenda was impatient.

"I'm getting there. Lately things got worse somehow. I've been having dreams." Bobby took a deep breath before he finally admitted what spooked him so much. "Bad dreams. I should say *a* dream, because it's versions of the same dream over and over again. Each time I wake up my head hurts. Sometimes my head feels like it's going to burst. Meeting with Madame Tarot was the worst yet. That felt like someone else was actually inside my head, and it left me drained and exhausted."

"What kind of dream is it?" asked Brenda.

"It's about a person," Bobby said, and paused.

"Who?" encouraged Stevie, still skeptical, but showing some interest.

Bobby looked at them both and wondered if he should continue. He steeled himself before telling them. "He's the spirit of a dead pirate. And I believe he's seeking a buried treasure."

Stevie snorted a laugh and Brenda elbowed him again. "Sorry."

"Sure, go on then, I don't blame you for laughing!" Bobby said louder than he had intended. "It's true, though. On the plane over here, I fell asleep and the spirit of a vicious, dead pirate appeared. He threatened to kill me if I didn't turn back."

"I knew there was something bothering you when you arrived," whispered Brenda.

"He warned me to stay away. He said he knew my growing powers drew me to him and he didn't like that. He feared me, knowing I was coming here, and I believe it's because he thinks I can stop him somehow." Bobby looked straight at Brenda, avoiding Stevie's gaze for fear that he would laugh at him again. "I'm sure his spirit tried to make contact when we went craw fishing. I felt his presence among those trees." He stopped for a sip of chocolate milk, and then began again.

"At the carnival, I felt his presence in the horror ride. Then there was the incident with Madame Tarot. It was definitely *him* speaking through her. I could feel *his* hatred. *He* said something about another man, saying 'he is willing' and that *he* wanted to collect 'that which is mine.' I believe *he* wants to collect *his* treasure and *he's* trying to get someone to help *him.* When *he* was in my head I could see another figure speaking with *him.* I couldn't make out who it was, but I saw that figure hit someone with a shovel."

He turned to Brenda, not sure whether he should say what he thought needed to be said. "And I believe the person *he* hit was your father."

"Why do you say that?" asked Brenda.

"Because it can't be a coincidence that at the moment I had this vision, someone was actually hitting your father!"

"Who's the other guy?" asked Stevie.

"I just told you, I don't know," said Bobby with a sigh. "I couldn't make out his features. But I'll tell you this, we're going to have to find out who that person is if we hope to find out who attacked Uncle John and prevent anyone else from getting hurt. And I think this person—whoever he is—is going to lead us to our pirate."

Brenda and Stevie stared at him. "*Our* pirate?"

"Well, yes. I mean… That is, if we're in this together."

Bobby waited for a response of some kind, but Brenda and Stevie seemed incapable of giving him any indication of their thoughts. Perhaps it was too much to process at once; perhaps they thought he was crazy like most people did when he told them about his gift. But no matter, Bobby felt better having told them everything. He knew he couldn't have just told them half the story. By being honest and telling them everything, he felt he had at least established some credibility. He thought so, that is, until he sat there looking into their blank faces as Elvis sang *Viva Las Vegas* in the background.

"There's one more thing to help convince you," he continued. "The poem *he* recited at Madame Tarots."

"What poem?" asked Brenda. Bobby was dumbfounded she couldn't remember. "I didn't hear any poem," Brenda added. Bobby looked at Stevie. Stevie shook his head to indicate he hadn't heard it either.

"I don't understand," said Bobby. "I heard it clearly."

Brenda and Stevie looked at each other, then back at Bobby. "I'm sorry, Bobby," Brenda said, "we didn't hear anything. That must have been in your head, because it didn't come out of Madame Tarot."

Bobby was dismayed, but there was no turning back now. "So… forget the poem. What do you think? Are you in?" Bobby probed. As soon as he asked the question, Bobby realized he was not ready for a negative reaction. Stevie and Brenda were his new best mates. They had forged a bond in his short stay here and he valued their opinion as well as their friendship. He knew it would devastate him to know they didn't believe what he was telling them.

"Bobby," Brenda began, "I knew there was something different about you the moment I met you at the airport. I also knew there was something deeply troubling you. You know how this sounds, though, don't you?" she asked him.

"It sounds nuts," offered Stevie, blunt as ever.

"For once, I agree with Stevie," she continued. "It does sound nuts. But," she continued and paused briefly, "I know that you aren't,

Bobby. I've gotten to know you a little since you arrived, and I don't think you are making any of this up. Especially when it involves my dad. I just don't think you would do something like that, and I believe you, Bobby. I don't understand it all, but I do believe you."

Bobby relaxed visibly. Both he and Brenda turned to Stevie, who was now slurping the rest of his drink through his straw. Wiping his chin with his sleeve when he was done, he cleared his throat.

"I don't get it either, but if Brenda's in, I'm in. And if it is a spook, I'll nail him between the eyes with a rock and send him back to spook world."

"Good," said Brenda, who smiled and reached over to put her hand on Stevie's shoulder. "So, what now?" she asked as Stevie blushed the color of a juicy red apple.

"We formulate a plan," said Bobby.

"Maybe we should get help from the mayor or the sheriff," posed Brenda.

"I don't think that's a good idea," said Bobby. "They'll think we're stark raving mad."

"The sheriff already knows I'm crazy," muttered Stevie, still sipping bubbles from the bottom of his glass.

"Look," said Brenda, "we need to know more about the town's history. There must be a reason why this is happening here. Why did this pirate come to Mountain Lake? Just because you came here?" Brenda paused, thinking. "There must be more to this. Maybe someone in authority knows something that happened in the past that could help explain this mystery."

"And maybe somebody else is in danger," offered Stevie. "Maybe somebody's already been attacked and we just don't know it. We should ask if they know anything about that."

"I agree with you both that we don't know enough, as yet. But if we involve the authorities we could be asking for trouble. I'm sure they won't believe us. Look how much difficulty I had persuading the two of you."

Brenda reached across the table and grabbed Bobby's arm. "Bobby, I know you're right about that. But I can't help feeling that we should at least try."

Bobby nodded. He didn't feel good about the prospect of speaking to town authorities, but knew he should do so for Brenda's sake. If she put her faith in him, he would need to put his faith in her. "Okay," he said. "Perhaps they'll find out who attacked your dad and why they stole the tools. If they do, it might lead us to this pirate. And if we find him, maybe we can stop him. But we need to do it soon. I'm getting a very strong feeling that something very bad is about to happen."

"Something bad?" asked Stevie. "What exactly do you mean by bad?"

Bobby didn't answer right away. Finally, he looked Stevie in the eye and said softly.

"Someone is going to die."

Despite the obvious risks, they all agreed to talk to the authorities. Not talking to them seemed to have even greater risks. Bobby was chosen to do the talking, as he was the one to express their questions and concerns most clearly. Backed by his friends, Bobby approached the booth with Mayor Block, Moss, and Jinx, who were deeply involved in a serious conversation concerning the merits of decaf vs. regular. All three seemed to be in agreement—no surprise there, since the mayor was buying—that decaf was something terrorists had dreamed up. Jinx then looked around for Sharon as he loudly proclaimed 'Baker Street Joe to be the best there is in the whole state' hoping that would get him a free donut to go along with the mid-morning jolt.

Moss tended to sit there and nurse his coffee as if it were nitroglycerin, wrapping both hands around the cup as he brought it up to his sizeable lips for a careful sip. Sharon tried to ignore them in her frequent sweeps of the area especially since they sat forever, ate little, unless someone else was buying, and left a meager tip. Occasionally, she was summoned for a refill. It was bad enough that they continually asked for the refill, but they did so by holding up their empty cups, wiggling them, and shouting Sharon's name. If it weren't for the mayor, she would tell them off and send them on their way. An argument could have been made that bottomless cup didn't actually mean that, but she had long ago concluded that arguing with this group just wasn't worth the airtime.

The Regulars were so heavily engaged in their intellectual pursuits, they didn't even notice Bobby approach; he seemed to pop up at their side like a sudden apparition. Moss was the first to notice him as he raised his cup with both hands, lower lip extended to receive a slurp. He did a double take, shaking his hand as he did so, spilling some liquid from his newly topped-off mug. This was an unthinkable breach of coffee etiquette that would have garnered the reproach of both the mayor and Jinx, especially in light of their conversation, but both were also turned towards Bobby in surprise.

Bobby took advantage of the gap in their chat.

"Hello, Mr. Mayor. My name is Bobby Holmes. I'm a cousin of Brenda Watson, and Stevie Nichols, here, is our good friend." He pointed at his mates who hung back a few feet.

The mayor, never one to miss an opportunity to connect with a voter, or perhaps the child of one, reached across Jinx with his catcher's-glove-sized hand to greet this young intruder.

"Well, hello there young man," said the mayor, after an enthusiastic and elbow-bending handshake. "And what can I do for you young folks today?" he asked loudly enough to impress any would-be voters in the restaurant.

Now that he had their attention, Bobby cleared his throat. "Mr. Mayor, I've enjoyed my brief visit here in Mountain Lake, but I'm here to warn you. Something strange has been happening here in town. I would even use the word sinister."

At first, the mayor wore the smile of a true politician. His grin was ear to ear as he pretended to care about what Bobby said. But with each syllable uttered, even though the smile remained, the mayor began to look like someone with serious indigestion.

"Son," he bellowed. "What are you jabbering about?" now forgetting his concern about the electorate.

Bobby realized that his idea to withhold some of the information was not going to work. He was going to have tell it all, to make any sense. "I'll cut to the chase, as my mom says all the time. My friends and I believe," he said, nodding to Brenda and Stevie, "that there are evil forces at work here in town. The spirit of a long-dead pirate is working with someone here in this community to recover his treasure. We also believe that Brenda's dad has been attacked by that person. To prevent any further injury or even death, we need to know some things. First of all, are there any strangers or suspicious characters in town? Secondly, have there been any pirates in the town's history? And finally, has anyone been murdered or gone missing recently?"

Jinx simply couldn't help it. At the mention of the word murder, he choked on an intake of the café's finest and spewed it across the table with a direct hit on the dull, thick space between Moss' eyes. Even Sharon, who was cleaning up the next booth, stopped in her tracks, her jaw falling like a brakeless elevator. Brenda whispered, "way to be discreet," while the mayor smiled on, as if, like Batman's Joker, the affliction was permanent.

At first, not a sound could be heard. Even the clock seemed to have stopped ticking. Then, all at once, the mayor let out a howl of laughter that echoed off the walls of the buildings clear across the street. The mayor clapped Jinx on the back, encouraging him to join in the laugh fest. All he succeeded in doing, however, was to have the poor man jettison more coffee into Moss' face. Moss was not amused. The laughter began to subside with the wobbling of the mayor's considerable triple chin. He shook his head back and forth and dragged one hand from his forehead to the back of his neck with a waning giggle. Sharon went back to her cleanup and life seemed to resume as normal.

The mayor leaned towards Bobby with furrowed brows, which stood at attention like two elongated caterpillars.

"Son, let me try and explain this to you so you'll understand," he said, in what he would have called his *teaching* voice. "Number one, there are no strangers in town, at least not any we would call suspicious. Everybody knows everybody else, and that's just the way we like it. Number two, there are no pirates around here, nor were there any ever, because, in case you haven't noticed, we live quite a ways from the ocean. And number three, the very last person to have died in town was ninety-five. She lived a very long and fruitful life and since her husband of seventy-five years died two years earlier, she was happy to go."

The mayor was more than pleased with his long-winded and, as far as he was concerned, thorough answer. Bobby started to object, but the mayor waved him off. "Run along now, sonny, we adults have important business to discuss." He then called for Sharon with his cup raised, shaking it a bit.

Dejected, Bobby and his friends returned to their booth at the front of the cafe to lick their wounds. They had received no answers to any of their questions and they'd failed in their attempt to warn someone in authority of the danger Bobby believed was coming.

"Now what?" posed an exasperated Stevie.

"I'm sorry," said Bobby. "I gave it my best shot. But at least we have some firm assumptions to guide us."

"You're kidding, right?" asked Stevie.

"Let's examine what we believe so far." Bobby said. "To begin with, we can assume there's a historic connection with the town of Mountain Lake and our dangerous pirate, even if the authorities don't think so. Secondly, I've received several warnings from that pirate who believes I can interfere with his plans in some way. Simply put, the spirit we are dealing with thinks I'm a threat. And each time I feel his presence, he's gotten bolder and stronger. Thirdly, based on my encounter with Madame Tarot, I now believe that he's seeking help from someone; someone here in town, although I don't know who that someone is. I do believe that if we find out who is helping him, we'll know who attacked Uncle John. Then, hopefully we can stop this fiend before he hurts someone else."

"How are we going to do all of that?" asked Stevie. "We don't even know where to begin looking."

"I think you're wrong, Stevie," said Bobby. "If we believe the pirate is an angry and dangerous killer, we can assume he's trying to work with someone who also exhibits such characteristics."

"Which would make him stick out in our town," answered Brenda.

"Correct!" said Bobby. "And we've had a number of encounters with some strange people, giving us some first class suspects. Moss and Jinx for example. They're very odd characters, wouldn't you say? Maybe they don't look like criminals, but they certainly are a bit strange. Then there is Conan. He's friendly to us, but many people in town do not like him, including you, Stevie. Can we truly trust him? Perhaps he poses as someone who tolerates us, but secretly he's in league with this spirit. He says he frequents the town library, so perhaps he has a handle of the town's history and knows about the treasure. Tony, the Italian Ice man, has quite a temper; we witnessed that first hand. He could go off on people with little or no provocation, just like the *Hulk* in the comics. Our pirate could certainly exploit Tony's anger for *his* own designs."

"And don't forget about Carl," added Brenda.

"Yes," said Bobby. "Talk about bad temper! And he seems to have an interest in local history, given he bought those comics. And let's not forget about Mr. McCormack, either. He actually threatened Uncle John and, according to Brenda's mum, he also has a mean temper. And," he said with emphasis, "he left your father's shop in such anger just before your dad was assaulted."

"My money's on Conan!" said Stevie, now getting into it by slapping an open hand on the table. "Ever look him straight in the eyes? That guy is shifty. I didn't like the way he stared at us when we left his store the other day."

"Stevie, we can't just accuse people without proof," said Brenda, "but some of these people do seem suspect."

"I'm not retarded," Michael interrupted loudly. Brenda, Bobby and Stevie whirled around, staring at Michael, who had jumped off his stool and walked over to their booth while they had been lost in their discussion. Now Michael stood about three feet away as he continued. "And that's a bad word anyway," he said gazing at Stevie. Turning towards Bobby, he added, "and the mayor doesn't know what he's talking about. I know a lot about pirates, and there were definitely some around here at one time. I could help you, if you want."

With that, Michael abruptly left the café, the bell attached to the doorframe tinkling after him.

16

It was nearly noon. The sun was high and the bright light nearly blinded them as they fell out of the doorway looking up and down Baker Street for Michael. He seemed to have disappeared into thin air when Brenda finally noticed that Michael had jaywalked across the street and was approaching the park already. They took their bikes and raced after him, shouting his name, which earned them odd looks from passersby, but no response from Michael. When they finally caught up to him they were out of breath, but Michael seemed unaffected by the distance they had covered.

"I walk all the time," he said, intuiting their unspoken question. "Mostly at night with my mother when there aren't so many people around. It's nicer then, and we get pretty far each time. She says I go faster than she does and a lot farther before resting."

Michael plopped down on a park bench. Bobby dropped his bike on the ground and sat next to him. Brenda and Stevie looked at each other, shrugged their shoulders, and squeezed in next to Bobby.

Michael told them that he had something called Asperger's, which he pronounced loudly and carefully.

"I heard of that," mumbled Stevie. "Isn't that a Butt Burger with cheese?" he asked, laughing, which drew an elbow to his now sore ribs from Brenda.

"It was something I was born with," Michael started to say, but it came out as "IssomethinIwsbornwif."

"Can you speak more slowly, please?" Bobby asked, because he had trouble discerning what he said. "I am from England, and the American accent is hard for me at times," he added, wanting to make sure he didn't offend Michael with his request.

"Okay, okay," Michael said, holding up his right index finger. "My mom is working with me on that. She is encouraging me to speak slower. I hold up my finger to remind me to do that."

Michael repeated his previous statement and went on to tell them his story, correcting himself if he mispronounced something.

"Me and my mom moved here not too long ago. My mom didn't like my old school because the kids there were mean and made fun of me."

Brenda stared at Stevie until he squirmed a bit.

"We like living here. It's a pretty town with lots of stores and things to do. We go for lots of walks at night when it's not too dark. We go up and down the streets and through the park. Sometimes my mom takes me on walks to teach me things, but most of the time we just come out to have some fun."

"Why didn't you enroll in our school when you first moved here?" prodded Brenda.

"My mom wanted to wait until September. She kept me home to teach me things until school ended for the summer."

"Where do you live?" she asked.

"I live by him," he said and pointed at Stevie. "I've often wondered why he always walks past my house but never stops to say hello."

Stevie turned beet red.

"Why are you alone today?" asked Bobby.

Michael's loud giggle interrupted the heavy silence. "I snuck out!" he exclaimed. "My mom thinks I'm playing in my room."

"Is that the first time you've done that?" asked Stevie. "Cause I've done that at least a dozen times."

Brenda looked at Stevie as if a dozen is an estimate that might be ten times two many. "I have, too," she said, "but only once, and my parents knew I was going over to my girlfriends house. I didn't know it at the time, but they followed me there to make sure I arrived safely."

After a pause in the conversation, Bobby asked the burning question.

"You said you could help, Michael. How?"

Michael looked at Bobby for a full minute, as if making up his mind whether or not he really was going to help them.

"Follow me," he said, before pushing off the bench and running towards his house.

Michael lived in Stevie's neighborhood, which was accessible from the alley where Stevie had hurled taunts at Tony, the Italian Ice man. They walked down a small maze of streets. Even though he was new in town, Michael, whether through some inner GPS or from walking the neighborhood so many times, crossed streets and made turns with authority and confidence. Michael's house was raised slightly on a small bluff at the end of a small, unpaved, dead end street. It was former farmland. Its isolation down a short dirt road, away from the rest of the neighborhood, added to its mystery. Stevie, accompanied by a friend or two, would often make the trip over to this strange house, daring each other to go up to the door and ring the bell before running away. Actually getting this close to it again made him a little nervous.

The house was coated with a dark stain on the outside. The picket fence that kept the world at a respectable distance and the shutters that flanked the front windows, had not been painted in recent history. There was no furniture on the vast porch that surrounded the entire front of the house, and the brown, weedy grass, which was sparse to begin with, needed attention. Simply put, the house looked uninviting, dark and foreboding.

Michael mounted the front steps two at a time and quietly bounded onto the porch. He pulled the screen door open, its hinges screaming in protest. It was only then that he noticed no one was behind him. As he turned, he saw that the others had stopped at the gate, which leaned against the gatepost, precariously hanging on by a rusty nail. It created a gap in the fence that visually threatened to swallow them whole. They looked at the spooky house, afraid to take one more step. Without voicing it, they were terrified that they would never be heard from again.

Michael, unaware of their angst, simply held up one finger and spoke to them as if they were moronic. "Come on, we have to go to my room before my mother finds out."

They looked at each other for what seemed to Michael to be an interminably long time until Brenda dropped her bike and opened the gate, breaking the spell. The two boys followed in a flash. The three of them approached the house together, and cautiously entered Michael's world.

Once inside the door, they tiptoed through the front hallway. The living room was to the left, the dining room to the right. Glancing in both directions, they discovered that Michael's house was...pleasant. The walls were painted a light, off-white color throughout, giving the entire interior a calm and comfortable appearance. The wood floors glistened, and there were some beautiful oriental rugs. There wasn't much furniture, but what there was looked expensive and was arranged neatly. Heavy curtains flanked the front windows, acting as a buttress for the billowing white sheers that rippled with the light breeze that flowed through the opened windows. The house looked as if it had been decorated by a professional, and, best of all, it smelled like cookies.

Michael's mother was out in the backyard so they all crept upstairs to Michael's room. If the downstairs of the house had been a surprise to them, Michael's bedroom left them stunned. It was bright and cheery, painted in pastel yellows and blues, giving it a seaside look. Pirate paraphernalia were on every shelf, on every piece of furniture, and in every corner of the room: models of pirate ships, pictures of pirates, and small plastic pirate figurines. Above Michael's neatly made bed, which was covered with a multi-colored bedspread sporting a ship's wheel, hung a poster of Johnny Depp as Captain Sparrow.

"You make your bed each day?" asked Stevie incredulously.

"My mom makes me do it before breakfast and before I do my other chores," said Michael off-handedly.

"You do chores every day?" persisted Stevie. "Even in the summertime?"

"Not everyone is as lazy as you, Stevie," said Brenda.

Stevie started to argue, but Bobby cut him off by getting right to the point.

"It's clear you know something about pirates, Michael. What do you know that will help us?"

Michael held up his finger and smiled at them all. "Everything," he said.

17

Michael didn't just know something about pirates. He wasn't just a fan of pirate movies. Nor was he merely a collector of pirate models and toys. Michael proved to be an expert about anything and everything related to pirates. Along one wall in his room stood a triple shelf crammed with books about pirates, both fictional and real. There were biographies about famous pirates, fascinating tales featuring fictional pirates, and book upon book of pirate history and lore. He told them he had watched every movie ever made about pirates. He loved the old Errol Flynn movies his mother bought him, especially *Captain Blood*, but confessed that the more recent *Pirates of the Caribbean* movies were his favorites. They were full of adventure and made him both laugh and cheer sometimes. He said he knew every word by heart to some of the movies because he watched them over and over on his TV.

Michael was about to tell them about some of his books when they all heard the stairs creak. They immediately got quiet and listened, their hair standing on end. There it was again, a bit louder this time. Michael had just put a finger to his lips when the door to his room creaked open, and a woman appeared in the doorway. She appeared to be deranged: her hair was disheveled, there was dirt smeared across her face, and she had a wild look in her eyes. She was holding a sharp object in her left hand and it was pointed in their direction. Stevie, who was sitting on the floor, involuntarily shuffled back against the wall.

"Oh, Michael," said his mother, pushing the hair out of her face, obviously relieved to find a group of children in her son's room rather than an intruder. "I heard voices and I was startled. I was out in the yard doing some gardening and didn't know you had guests. Why don't you introduce me?" She took off her gloves and slipped the gardening shears into her pocket.

It was then they realized they'd forgotten to tell Michael their names. Brenda volunteered her name and Stevie and Bobby followed. Bobby explained that he was from England on vacation and that they had been walking around Stevie's neighborhood when they saw Michael up the street in the front yard. They walked up to the house, and he invited them inside.

"I hope that was all right with you?" he asked her.

"Oh, of course, young man, I…I just didn't expect to see anyone. I'm Mrs. Kelleher, Michael's mother. Please, all of you, pardon my appearance, I must look dreadful. I'll go downstairs, freshen up, and bring you some homemade chocolate chip cookies and milk." She cast a questioning look at Michael who was holding his mouth to prevent himself from laughing at the white lie Bobby had told. His mom seemed to know something was going on, but she let it go for the moment.

As soon as she left, they all breathed a sigh of relief.

"Sorry, Michael. I didn't want to lie to your mom, but I thought it would be better than telling her you snuck out of the house. I didn't think she would have appreciated that."

"Thanks for not getting me into trouble," Michael, said, finger pointed towards the ceiling, continuously reminding himself to speak slowly.

Stevie was still glued to the back wall. "What just happened? Are we still alive?"

Brenda threw a pillow at him. They all laughed a nervous kind of laugh.

Bobby brought them back to reality. "Michael, can you really help us?" he repeated.

Michael was leafing through a pirate comic he had just picked up. Keeping his nose in the comic, he simply said, "Yes, I can, because there were pirates here once upon a time. I read about it in a book we bought before moving here. Would you like to see it?"

"Absolutely," they all said.

Michael led them to his bookshelf and plucked a large volume from the top shelf: **Buried Treasure: Where Is It Now?** by Professor Jonathan Ambrose.

Bobby read the inside jacket: "*This book, complete with drawings and illustrations, offers the reader a variety of intriguing hypotheses as to where some of the more famous and infamous pirates may have buried their ill-gotten treasures.*" As Bobby scanned the book for any reference to their town and the surrounding area, the door opened and the aroma of fresh homemade cookies wafted in.

Mrs. Kelleher carried a large tray with four glasses of milk and a plate of chocolate chip cookies, still gooey from the oven. Stevie was the first to reach for a couple. The others joined him, and their munching, slurping, and contented sighs filled the room for several minutes.

"Mrs. Kelleher, these are even better than the ones I get at home," said Stevie. "My mom uses the frozen dough."

"These are made from scratch. I'm glad you like them."

Mrs. Kelleher felt awkward, mostly due to not having to face this situation very often. Friends in her son's room were not a common occurrence, and she didn't know how to respond. Were they truly being friendly? Or were they pretending to be friendly, only to torment and tease her son later? That had happened before, and she would not let it happen again. These kids seemed nice, though, and she wasn't quite sure what to do. She had taught him about social graces and what to do in certain circumstances. She taught him what to accept and what not to accept in the behavior of others. She knew he'd paid attention and she thought it had sunk in. She was just going to have to trust in her son.

"Okay, kids, I'll take the glasses downstairs and let you be. Let me know if you need anything." She left and shut the door behind her.

"Nice mom you got there," said Stevie. "I could tell as soon as she first entered the room," he added with a smile.

Bobby picked up the book he had been scanning. "It says here that there are several Connecticut destinations for buried treasure and several pirates who plied these waters. It doesn't list any names for this area, unfortunately, but does confirm what Michael told us. There were pirates around here."

Brenda sat on the edge of the bed. Michael leaned against the foot of the bed as he sat on the floor. Stevie was leaning against the wall. They were all focused on Bobby as he spoke. Bobby's accent, as well as the compelling story he told, captivated his audience.

Bobby scanned the page. "*Those suspected of being in this area were known for their brutality...did not value life at all...extremely cruel and clever...sailed the Long Island Sound looking for a possible place to hide their vast wealth...favored Connecticut for its navigable rivers, like the Housatonic.*"

Bobby stopped there, thinking about what all this might mean. The others were just as enthralled, especially when hearing about the reference to the Housatonic River, which skirted Mountain Lake. The room was silent, except for their breathing.

He scanned the rest of the chapter and read the last sentence: "*Although there is no known physical proof that treasure is buried in northwest Connecticut, the author believes that it is so.*" He was deep in thought for a few moments and then looked at his mates.

"You know this book is all about theories, right? I mean you know it isn't filled with facts, right? That it's just supposition? That means it may or may not be true." Bobby tossed the book on the bed in frustration. "Maybe *I'm* wrong. Maybe I *did* dream the whole thing up. Maybe we're just reading into things. But if it is true, there's got to be proof, and we need to find it."

"What about Madame Tarot?" asked Brenda.

"Who's that?" asked Michael.

"A palm reader at the carnival. She fell into a trance when we visited her, and spoke like a pirate. I'll fill you in on the details later," Stevie whispered to Michael.

"Perhaps our imagination is going a bit wild here, too," said Bobby. "Maybe what Madame Tarot said wasn't as bad as we thought, and had absolutely nothing to do with anything. Maybe, maybe, maybe!"

"Yeah, maybe it was just the corndogs and ice cream you ate at the carnival," joked Stevie.

A dejected look crept over their faces replacing the hope and excitement that had been there just a few minutes ago. They had really thought they were on to something, but now they realized that a mystery involving the return of a pirate was a theory—possible, but a theory nonetheless. Self-doubt dampened their resolve.

They stood up and gave every sign of preparing to leave. Michael looked them over and wondered if they would ever be back.

"Michael," said Bobby, "we can't thank you enough for bringing us over and getting a chance to meet you." The others nodded in agreement.

"We should leave now, but I would like to come back soon and examine more of your books if that's all right."

Now, Michael was nodding in agreement, smiling too. They made their way down the stairs and towards the front door. Once outside, they waved goodbye to Michael, picked up their bikes, and walked them towards town once more.

"Well, that was a bust!" said Stevie.

"Not so," said Bobby. "Michael proved the mayor wrong—there were pirates in the area. That's something to go on."

It was a warm, summer day. They reached Baker Street just in time to hear a wailing siren and see the sheriff's police cruiser flying down the road towards the café. They raced to follow the smoke kicking out of the car's exhaust pipe. The cruiser stopped directly in front of the café.

Outside on the sidewalk were a few of the patrons, as well as Sharon, complete with pink uniform and popping gum, chewing a bit faster than usual. Each time she bent forward to peek in the large front window to see what was happening, the pencil in her hair hit the window, causing those inside to look up and see who was tapping. Bobby, Brenda, and Stevie came to an abrupt stop just outside the entrance, leaning their bikes against the wall.

As Bobby reached for the door handle, Sharon shouted.

"Hey, don't touch that! Sheriff Musgrave doesn't want anyone inside while he talks to the mayor. He said it's extremely important and made us all leave."

"What's so important?" asked Brenda.

"How should I know?" exclaimed Sharon. "He don't want to talk to me, now, does he?" She looked inside again, inadvertently tapping on the window.

The door opened and Moss and Jinx filed out. Moss was arguing that they shouldn't have to leave since they were part of the *inner circle,* but the sheriff ordered them out.

"Why are his shorts all in a bunch? The mayor will tell us everything anyways," Moss grumbled.

Jinx, with toothpick bobbing and weaving, leaned over to the kids and whispered, "Well *I* know what's goin' on here. I heard the sheriff tell the mayor just before we was thrown out."

He punctuated every syllable of his next statement in a snarl.

"*Someone's been murdered.*"

Part 6

The Game's Afoot

Inside the café, Sheriff Musgrove looked pale, sweaty, and nervous. His gun was in his holster, and this time there was an actual bullet in it, a very rare occurrence. He paced back and forth, his hat in one hand, and in the other a handkerchief to wipe his neck and forehead.

"Mayor, I'm telling you. Nothing like this has hit this town for as long as I can remember. This is big. Way big. Maybe too big. Maybe we ought to call somebody in. Maybe somebody like the state police or the FBI."

"Calm down, Hank. I know this is bad, but the FBI? The state police won't want this either," the mayor whined. "This is in our jurisdiction, not theirs. And there isn't any federal law broken here that I can see. Based on what you know so far, it appears it was just a random killing."

"Just?"

"Oh, you know what I mean. Start at the beginning again and tell me what you know so far."

"We got a call about thirty minutes ago from the office up at the cemetery. Some gentleman was visiting a relative's gravesite when he noticed a pile of clothes near one of the newly dug sites. He walked over to check it out and saw that the pile of clothes was actually someone lying face down on the pile of dirt. He panicked and ran all the way back to the office like his pants were on fire. Somebody at the office walked up to the site to verify that there was indeed a body. Once they stopped puking, they called us. They said it was their gravedigger and that it didn't look like an accident since his head had been bashed in. I immediately dispatched Deputy Carver to hustle on up there and seal everything off. I also called Detective Robinson. Then I hightailed it over here to get you. I figured you might want to be in on the initial decision on what we do about this."

"A smart move, Hank, and I appreciate it. Two heads are better than one and all that. Now, ...ah... it seems to me we need to visit the crime scene and check things out before that nosey Bill Glean of the Daily Mirror gets involved. What do you say?"

"You bet. No comments to anybody until we find out exactly what happened," said the sheriff.

With a plan firmly in place, the sheriff and mayor put on their official game faces. Looking suitably concerned, but definitely in control, they made their way to the front door.

"Here they come!" shouted Sharon, pencil busy tapping a rhythm.

Word had spread fast about the murder and half the town had arrived at the coffee shop. People were on edge, hoping for some sign that all was well. But the look on the faces of their two top officials soon dispelled any such hopes. The mayor put his head down, grabbed onto the sheriff's belt, and together they serpentined their way to the sheriff's car, resembling a funereal conga line. They dodged shouts from the curious, and formal questions from Bill Glean of the *Daily Mirror*. On their way, the mayor glanced over to his right and spotted Bobby. Their eyes locked for the briefest of moments. "How did you know?" the mayor's gaze asked. The moment passed quickly, though, and the mayor and sheriff were soon through the milling crowd. Both officials fell into the police car, which seemed to take off even before they hit their seats. The car kicked up a smoke screen that protected them from the nervous and frightened folks of Mountain Lake.

A momentary hush settled over the confused crowd as they collectively watched the retreating police car. Sheer pandemonium followed. Everyone seemed to be talking and rushing in different directions all at once. Bill Glean was shouting questions, primarily at Sharon, but to anyone really, hoping someone would have some kind of an answer to questions they didn't yet know to ask. Some people continued to peer into the café window, half expecting something to be going on in there, even though the place was now empty.

The kids stood still, stunned by the sudden development.

"First your father, now this. Brenda, we have to see Michael again and right now," Bobby whispered, and off he biked. The others stood with dazed looks on their faces, wondering why they had to revisit Michael so soon, and then tore off after him.

The sheriff's car was out of sight within five seconds. Sheriff Musgrove had never driven that fast in his whole life, not even when he took a course in evasive driving techniques at the State

Police Academy. Mountain Lake was no longer the quiet little town where nothing ever happened. It was now a town with a murder.

"For God's sake, Hank," said the mayor, "he's dead. It's not like he'll be upset if we're late, and there's no need to add two more to the obituary list. Slow down."

"Okay, Mayor," muttered the sheriff, slowing down only slightly. "Right now I've got a deputy up there who needs direction and an investigator on his way who is going to need some help. I don't have the kind of manpower they have on *Law and Order*, you know."

"You got a point there," agreed the mayor. "Your deputy couldn't find the seat of his pants with both hands, a map, and a compass, but as long as he roped off the area like he was told, Luke Robinson can go about doing his job as a detective, which, by the way, we paid handsomely to train him for. So, the only thing he will need you to do for him right now is to get him some coffee. Speaking of which, Hank, we're going to be up there for some time. Let's pull into the 7-Eleven and get some supplies, Okay?"

The sheriff expelled a deep breath. "That makes sense, I guess."

The sheriff pulled into the convenience store just on the edge of town. He jumped from the police car and held the front door open for the mayor. Picking up chips, pretzels, Twinkies, and Twizzlers, the two men swam up and down the aisles like sharks in search of an overdue dinner. The mayor loved Twizzlers. He called it his diet food. He reasoned that with Twizzlers, he chewed a great deal but didn't seem to swallow a whole lot of calories. Throwing it all in a big heap on the counter, they asked Harry, the owner, for four large coffees with cream and sugar on the side.

"What's going on, Mayor? Goin' campin'?" Harry asked, half laughing. He knew that going camping was definitely not on his two customers' list of favorite activities. He also knew something was up, though, and he didn't have a clue as to what it was. These guys never came in here to get such a large cache. He was determined to find out why they wanted it.

"Can't talk about it, Harry," clipped the mayor. "Official business."

The sheriff grunted in agreement and emphasized his point by scowling, looking grim, and nodding his head vigorously. "Wish we could tell you, but we can't."

Harry tried to feel them out with some food suggestions. He hoped that a particular choice might indicate something. "Need any hot dogs? Going to stay overnight where you goin'? Hot dogs will stay warm in the aluminum wrapper, you know."

"No, Harry, we don't need any hot dogs!" the mayor barked. "Nor do we need potato salad, green beans, or corn on the stinkin' cob! We just need what we got here, and the coffees if you please," he added as if he were talking to a complete idiot.

"Okay, okay," said Harry with his hands raised in surrender. "I'm just tryin' to help is all."

The sheriff reached over, grabbed the bag off the counter, and gave Harry one last serious look. Before he could take the bag away, the mayor held up his hand to stop him. Never taking his eyes off Harry, he grabbed a handful of Slim Jims and stuffed them in the bag. "Put it on my tab, Harry."

They were out the door before Harry had time to protest. The car sped away spinning its wheels and kicking up a cloud of dust in its wake.

Bobby, Brenda, and Stevie rode hard and were out of breath when they arrived at Michael's. Nevertheless, they jumped off their bikes and leaped up to the porch two steps at a time before punching the doorbell.

Michael's mother opened the door, somewhat befuddled by their reappearance.

"Can I help you?" she asked.

It was Bobby who caught his breath first. "We need to see Michael, please."

"He's upsta..." she started, but they were already racing up to his room.

She stood there slowly closing the door, wondering what was going on and, as always, worrying that whatever was going on might hurt her son. Obviously, something was amiss, and if it involved her son, she was going to find out what it was. She hurried back into the kitchen, removing her apron along the way.

Bobby pushed open the bedroom door and the three comrades tumbled into Michael's room. Michael was at his PlayStation, actively engaged in a game of *Pirates of the Caribbean: At World's End.* Bobby walked over and placed his hand on Michael's shoulder. He leaned in and spoke between breaths.

"Michael, things have gotten worse. Someone has been murdered and we're going to need all the help we can get. Will you help us?" Bobby gasped.

Brenda and Stevie weren't sure what kind of help he would be, but were willing to go along to find out what Bobby had in mind.

Without taking his eyes off the monitor, Michael lifted his index finger in the air and whispered a reply. "My mom is either already listening at the door, or she is creeping up the stairs and will be soon."

The other three immediately turned towards the door as if expecting to see through it.

"We better look busy then," Brenda whispered.

Stevie immediately jumped over to the bookcase and picked up a comic to read. Brenda plopped on the floor and began setting up pirate figures. Bobby just leaned in closer to Michael, whispering encouragement as Michael battled evil pirates on their ghost ship. Within seconds, they all heard a quick knock followed by the squeaky door as it opened.

Michael's mother appeared, once again carrying a tray full of fresh chocolate chip cookies.

"I brought you some more treats," said Mrs. Kelleher. "I heated them up just a bit to get them warm. Don't they smell great? I'll give them to you in just a moment," she said, pulling the tray away as Stevie reached out for a few, "but first, what's going on?" she pointedly asked.

All four stared at the ceiling as if the answer lay among the star decals Michael had posted up there. Even Mrs. Kelleher glanced upward and wondered what it was they were looking at. None of the kids made a sound while their minds searched frantically for a response. Mrs. Kelleher's question hung out there like a rotten fish; they could all smell it, but no one wanted to touch it. Michael stopped his game, looked between his newfound friends and his mother and hoped someone would derail her curiosity, if, for no other reason than to get his hands on some more cookies.

"I'm sorry if we came in a bit too fast, Mrs. Kelleher," said Bobby, coming to their rescue once again. "We were downtown and uncovered a mystery that we need Michael's help to solve."

The others in the group gave Bobby a long, surprised look. They wondered about the wisdom of telling Mrs. Kelleher that they wanted to involve her son in helping to solve a murder. It didn't seem like a good opening strategy and they feared Bobby was going to tell her too much, too soon.

"You see," he continued, "we were at the comics store doing research on some things Michael taught us about pirates on our first visit." Brenda and Stevie glanced at one another. Maybe he wasn't going to mention the murder after all.

"We discovered that there may have been some pirates here in the area once upon a time and came back to verify this with Michael. When we were here earlier, we noticed he had quite a collection of books on the subject and wanted to take advantage of his expertise." Bobby was being less than honest once again. At the very least, he was guilty of the sin of omission, given that key words like murder, corpse, violence, spirit, ghost, and treasure did not feature in his tale.

"Hmmm," Mrs. Kelleher wondered aloud as she studied Bobby intensely. "Well, okay then, I'll just leave these on the edge of the bed for you." She placed the cookie tray on Michael's bed and quietly left the room, not quite believing their story but once again willing to let it go for the moment.

When they heard her retreat down the staircase, they all stopped what they were doing while Bobby brought them closer together.

"We need a plan of action," he said.

They huddled at the foot of Michael's bed where they could bend over and whisper, sure not to be heard outside of the room. They were also strategically within arm's reach of the plate of cookies, which pleased Stevie as he grabbed a few.

"Someone's been murdered," continued Bobby, "and I'll wager if we find out who it is, it will tell us something about who is helping our pirate."

"Who was killed?" piped Michael.

"I don't know," answered Bobby. "We're going to need to split our resources and gather as much information as we can," said Bobby. "No sense running about with our knickers in a knot."

"Knickers in a what?" Stevie asked, befuddled by Bobby's quaint expressions.

"Never mind that now, Stevie," Brenda admonished. "What do you suggest, Bobby?"

"Brenda, I think you should locate Moss and Jinx. Find out if they heard who's been murdered. Since they're close to the sheriff, they may have important inside information. I'm going to the library to see if I can dig up any information that may be helpful by verifying what we've learned so far from Michael's book and if there's anything else I can discover. And you, Stevie…" he continued, but Stevie was way ahead of him.

"I know what I'll do. I'm small and can snoop around like a ferret. I'll track down some of our suspects and see if I notice anything suspicious. I'll start with Mr. McCormack. I know where he lives. I was there once last year and played a practical joke on him at Halloween. I took a pumpkin off his front porch and stuck it on a fence post. He never knew it was me."

"Great idea, but be careful. Don't take any foolish chances. And Michael, would you see what else you could find in your books regarding pirates in this area? Focus on Mountain Lake in particular."

"I'll be happy to," said Michael, finger in the air.

"We'll all do what we have to do and then meet back here around 4:30. Then we'll quickly share what we have, since most of us have to be home around 5:00. Sound good to everyone?"

"Yes," they chorused.

"All right, then, hands in the middle."

Bobby was the first to extend his hand out, waiting for the others to place theirs on top of his. Brenda, and then Stevie, quickly followed him. They all looked at Michael in anticipation. Michael looked back at them, willing, but not able to comply at first. He had never been in a group before. No one had ever asked him to join anything. As small a gesture as this was, it was a monumental decision to commit himself to something that might cause him anguish and disappointment. He hesitated briefly, but then jumped in with his right hand and a big smile.

Then everyone jumped into action. Michael removed his game from the PlayStation and turned to his personal library. Bobby headed for the door along with Brenda and Stevie. Once outside the house, Bobby leaned closer to speak softly.

"We must be careful," he said. "Particularly you, Stevie, since you have the dodgiest task. It won't be easy sneaking up on people, especially if one of them is dangerous, and I am sure that one of them is. There is a connection between the attack on Uncle John, the murder at the cemetery, and the pirate of my dream. We need to find out what the connection is before anyone else gets hurt."

"No problemo," said Stevie warming up to the task. "This kind of thing is right up my alley. I'm not only sneaky, but also quick. I can outrun any of those clowns if they notice me. And if they get too close, I also have a few round stones in my pocket that I carry for their ease in throwing. I think you saw what I did to those balloons at the Carnival," Stevie boasted.

They all nodded to each other and went their various ways.

Brenda took off towards town and the café. She was sure the dynamic duo would be there holding court. They would be bragging about their inside contacts and spouting information like busted sewer pipes. Her main concern would be sorting through the nonsense for a nugget of truth.

Stevie produced a coy smile and sped off in the direction of Cobble Road. He headed out to the McCormack farm as his first stop, sure that the misused tools McCormack had wanted to exchange at Brenda's father's store were a key to the mystery. This was just the kind of thing he enjoyed doing, being on the edge of danger and using his wily skills.

Armed with directions from Brenda, Bobby went to the library near the school. He wasn't ready to share with the others what he was feeling at the moment. He had an overwhelming feeling that more people would get hurt soon.

20

The ride to the cemetery didn't take long. The sheriff contemplated using his siren again, but decided against it. He didn't want to attract undue attention. The day was heating up in more ways than one. He was decidedly agitated and was sweating. Even though they had the air-conditioning on in the car, they rode with the windows open, as if the warm breeze could somehow blow away the uneasy feeling that cloaked them both. The Shady Rest Cemetery loomed over the next hill. A rounded, wrought iron sign, welded right onto a large and unwieldy gate, marked it's opening. The gate was flanked by tall evergreens that rose above the attached rusty fence as far as the end of the property line. The evergreens had grown higher than the fence long ago, emphasizing the impression that anyone who came to the cemetery was there to stay.

As Mayor Block and Sheriff Musgrave approached the entrance, it was clear that deputy Tim Carver had been busy. Unfortunately, not all of his accomplishments were to the sheriff's liking. The deputy had roped off much of the area with police caution tape, making it look like some macabre Christmas gift. His deputy had also shut and padlocked the metal gate at the entry. While it was a good idea to keep out a nosey public, it also made it impossible for the sheriff to get in. Carver had also dragged official police barriers onto the lone cemetery road that led up a hill to the gravesite, and locked them together with chains. He did so to prevent any traffic foolish enough to try and drive up the paved hill to get to the crime scene, if they somehow managed to get through the gate in the first place. Unfortunately, as a result, the only way past the horses and up the hill was through the muddy lawn flanking the road. An early morning rain had made the mud as mucky as quicksand. The crime scene was secure alright, but also unreachable. Deputy Carver clearly didn't think of the effect his work would have on the arrival of the mayor and sheriff.

"That dunderhead," complained the sheriff. "I'll try to call him on the walkie-talkie and get him down here to let us in."

He tried several times, but there was no answer.

"You don't suppose he's hurt, do you?" inquired the mayor, suddenly feeling apprehensive. "Maybe a victim himself?"

"He better have a good excuse for this," muttered the sheriff as he went to his trunk to retrieve the snips that would cut through the chain holding the padlock, "or he'll wish he was a victim!"

Meanwhile, Deputy Tim Carver was up at the gravesite feeling quite proud of himself, as he surveyed the final details of his work. After checking the corpse for a pulse and finding none, he had leaned back against the front fender of his car, when, out of the corner of his eye, he saw the mayor and sheriff crawling up the muddy side of the hill. They did not look happy.

"Dang it, Tim, what were you thinking making such an obstacle course?" panted the sheriff.

"Uh, gee chief, I thought I was following standard procedure for a crime like this. You know, to keep out people who want to see what a murder scene looks like."

The sheriff's face reddened until it resembled an overripe tomato. "First of all," he huffed, "there ain't no standard procedure for an event like this, 'cause we ain't never had an event like this. Second," he boomed, "there are no busybodies coming up here 'cause they don't know that anything happened up here yet. And third, you imbecilic horse's patoot, my new shoes are muddy and you nearly gave me a heart attack. And where's your walkie-talkie?"

"Sorry, chief," his deputy mumbled, "I sort of left it in my car 'cause I was in such a hurry to secure the crime scene."

"Well, Mr. CSI," the sheriff said calming down just a bit, "you can walk down the muddy hill and un-secure it by clearing those barriers. Then you can drive my car up here when you're done. Here, take my keys! And don't forget to take your walkie-talkie with you."

The mayor stood there all this time, bent over, hands on his knees, trying to catch his wheezy breath.

The sheriff placed his hands on his hips and looked around. He took his hat off and wiped his head with his handkerchief. The day was very warm. The air was still. The only sound was the mayor's breathing.

"Strange," the sheriff murmured, "how quiet it can be in a cemetery." He wanted to poke around a bit, but he was conscious of trampling all over the crime scene. He didn't want to do anything that would come back to bite him in the can later in court, so he kept a respectable distance and viewed things from afar. Over to his right lay a prone body, draped over a mound of dirt, arms and legs spread-eagled. There was an obvious wound to the back of the head. Blood coagulated amidst the tangle of greasy hair. A large pool of it had gathered around the corpse's head making it look like a crimson halo. He saw no signs of a struggle, but he would let his detective sort out the details.

The sheriff wiped his forehead again, and put his hat back on.

The mayor, who had caught his breath by now, leaned in and almost whispered. "Is it Zeke Hansen?"

"Looks like him from behind."

Zeke, the town's gravedigger, had worked for the Shady Rest Cemetery for the last ten years. He sometimes needed help from one or two of the town municipal workers, but there were so few funerals at any given time in Mountain Lake that he often worked alone, which was mostly how he liked it. He would take his time digging the grave of the newly departed and then fill it back up after the funeral. Once the pallbearers helped him set it up properly, he would lower the coffin into the grave with a winch. He was as strong as an ox, which left the sheriff wondering how anyone could have bested him. Maybe he knew the attacker? Maybe he was tricked somehow? At any rate, he hoped he would know more once the detective and coroner reports came in.

The mayor must have been thinking the same thing and disturbed the sheriff's musings. "How could anyone get the drop on a man that big? Surely he would have heard someone trying to sneak up on him, right?"

The sheriff grunted and was about to add something when he heard his car laboring up the hill with his deputy at the wheel. There were two cars, though, the other belonging to Luke Robinson, his part-time investigator. Both men pulled their cars up to the top of the hill and parked out of the way of the roped-off area. They got out of their cars and moved towards the sheriff and mayor. Luke carried a black backpack slung over his shoulder.

"Hey, Sheriff."

"Hey, Luke. You got your stuff?"

"Yup, right here in the bag. I'm going to put on the rubber gloves and booties and walk around for a bit, check over the site. I want to see if I notice anything that shouldn't be here. The rain this morning might have helped with footprints. Then again it might not have. It may have succeeded in washing away anything of value."

"Geez!" said the sheriff, shaking his head. "What about time of death?"

"We'll need the coroner for that. I called him before I left and he's on his way too. Well, guess I better be at it." Luke put on his booties and rubber gloves, walked over to the site and ducked under the caution tape, which was wrapped around several neighboring headstones. He bent over to examine the body and then sectioned off the surrounding turf into grids, much like an archaeologist would do.

The mayor and the sheriff walked over to the sheriff's car, which was still running with the air-conditioning on, and sat in the front seat awaiting news of any kind. His deputy stood there, looking a bit lost, so the sheriff shouted out his window.

"Tim, take your car and go down to the main entrance. Make sure that no one comes up without my authority just in case someone does get wind of this."

Glad to have something to do, as well as get away from his boss, deputy Carver ran to his car like he was being chased.

"Yes, Sir!" he shouted as he dove behind the steering wheel. He slammed his car into gear and raced downhill in seconds.

"He couldn't get away from you fast enough," muttered the mayor.

"Good to keep him on his toes."

The mayor grinned and looked over at the detective, whose head suddenly popped up.

"Sheriff!" he called.

"Yeah! What is it Luke?" the sheriff called as he pulled himself from the car and raced over to the yellow tape. "Whaddya got?"

The mayor tried to get there fast enough to hear the conversation.

"This is odd," Luke said, and held up a gold earring. It was shiny in spots, but mostly mottled from age and the elements. "I would swear this earring is an antique."

21

Brenda got to the Baker Street Café as quickly as she could. She was tired and sweaty from the heat of the day, but the recent events gave her an adrenalin charge that kept her moving forward. She parked her bike on the street and crept up to the front entrance. She was afraid to enter, because this place was now connected to the murder investigation and seemed scary and foreboding. It was silly, of course. The cafe had become ground zero for anyone seeking information about the murder, as this was the place where everyone had originally found out about it.

Peeking in the door didn't help much. It looked quiet inside, as if there were no customers. Made sense to her, because people would be spooked by such frightening news and might want to get as far away as possible, afraid that what happened would somehow rub off on them. As her eyes began to adjust, she could see bodies towards the back. It didn't take much imagination to figure out who some of them were. Opening the door carefully minimized the sound of the bell, but did not eliminate it entirely.

"Hey, come on in, we're open, whoever it is," shouted Sharon from the back. She lifted her beehive head to peer over some booths and saw Brenda. "Be right with you, honey," she called.

"That's all right, I'll come to you," Brenda announced, and she walked briskly to the back of the restaurant.

Moss and Jinx were in their usual spots. A full cup of steaming coffee sat in front of each of them. Sharon half stood and half sat against the edge of one seat back, coffee pot firmly in her grip, ready to pour at the slightest provocation. There were two booths filled with four other locals and a handful standing around, too nervous to sit. Everyone was paying close attention to the constant flow of misinformation dribbling onto the table from the mouth of Jinx.

The place had been packed with people shortly after the sheriff and mayor whisked out of town. All of them were seeking word—any word—about what was happening. The wiser members of the community, however, either knew they would get nowhere with these two, or had heard their drivel and left. Others pulled themselves away when they determined there was nothing new to be learned.

Moss' ego wouldn't allow him to think he wasn't a celebrity in town, but Jinx always harbored some self-doubt. And so he was using this opportunity to develop celebrity status for being "in the know." Not only did he declare himself a "personal friend" of the mayor and sheriff—he would do quotes with his fingers when he said this—he also bragged that the sheriff confided in him about this headline event, "*even before he told the mayor.*" He made this last announcement with great drama by dropping his voice an octave, tucking his chin, and popping his eyeballs when he said it.

Brenda resisted making a face or giving any indication that she was anything less than enthralled.

"Wow," she said dutifully, "I'll bet you know exactly what's going on around here. Nobody else seems to have a handle on things. Not even Mr. Glean. I'll bet he doesn't even know where the sheriff and mayor have gone." She was fishing, but Moss and Jinx were too wrapped up in themselves to notice.

"He doesn't. I can tell you that!" exclaimed Jinx. "In fact, he's so slow it took him a good deal of time to find out there even was a murder."

"But I know who it was that got killed and where it happened," he pronounced with great fanfare. "And," he whispered, "I also heard they found a major clue." He leaned back with a smirk, taking in his audience.

Moss looked like he wasn't surprised at all about anything that was being said, even though it was news to him. In fact, he just sat there nodding his head in agreement like a bobble-head doll on the seat of a moving ATV.

Brenda couldn't help herself. She tapped her foot and shook her head, getting more frustrated by the second. "So, who is it?" she blurted. Even Moss looked at Jinx in expectation.

At first, Jinx seemed stunned by the question. He was enjoying the idea of having a secret no one else seemed to know. Now he was disappointed to have to give it up.

"I have a friend," he started. "He works up at the cemetery. He called me a little while ago and told me that Zeke Hansen had his head bashed in. Said Deputy Carver told him that. He also said they found an old earring on the site." He drew this statement out for what seemed like ten full minutes, each word reluctant to fall from his lips.

Some people nodded their heads, some looked aghast, and others a bit skeptical. Whatever Jinx expected from this revelation, it wasn't a change of subject.

"Did you hear what happened to my dad last night?" Brenda asked innocently. "I wonder if these two events are connected in some way?" She tried to set Jinx up to see if the sheriff or his deputy had mentioned anything about her father's incident, or made any connection to the recent murder at all. If she thought she was going to get anything of substance on that issue, she was sorely mistaken.

"Don't be silly, little girl, there ain't no connection between those two things. Anybody can see that!" offered Moss, not wishing to be left out of the discussion entirely. "You see, in one instance—that being the one with your father—he was hit on the head and robbed. It was a simple assault with robbery as a motive. This here one today, well, that's a different matter altogether."

Not quite sure he nailed his point, he turned to look at Jinx. "Right, buddy?"

"Right you are, my friend. I've been a student of these type of things for a long time," Jinx said, warming to his audience, "and I can tell you with absolute certainty that these two things aren't even close to being related. I have seen every single episode of *Law and Order* and they have provided me with certain legal skills over the years. In fact, not only was I once considering a career as a private detective, the local police do at times ask me to consult on a case." He said the word consult as if it were two words: *con* and *sult.* He then sat back with his arms folded, a smug look drifting across his face.

Sharon, despite her natural inclination to avoid these two, found herself enthralled by the wild speculation bouncing off the walls in her normally cheery café. This was better than *Judge Judy* and *Jerry Springer* combined. She hung on their every word as if they were all part of a reality TV show.

However, even some of the more dimwitted in the audience found Jinx's comment about being a legal consultant hard to swallow and were beginning to lose patience with the puffed up version of events he served them.

"What other cases have you actually been 'consulted' on?" Oscar Lee, who sold seasonal fruits and vegetables at the Saturday open-air market at the church, asked slightly annoyed.

"Uh, you see, I uh..." Jinx stammered. He then continued with a more defensive attitude. "I don't recall which ones offhand. It's sort of a thing where I'm on call and the sheriff asks me my opinion and then I give it to him. We have an understanding, him and me. And he only calls me when it's a case that's difficult to solve and he needs a fresh pair of eyes to look at it."

"I guess he doesn't have to call very far since he's usually sitting right across the booth from you," Mr. Lee dryly observed.

Not knowing how to respond to that, or even realizing that he was being insulted, Jinx nodded in agreement and took a large glug of coffee, emptying the cup. As he held up his cup, shook it gently and called "Sharon," no one even noticed the sound of the bell as Brenda quietly slipped out.

As Bobby headed for the library, he played and replayed the events surrounding this mystery, from his nightmares in London until the present murder. He let his mind flow freely, trying to make connections and examine his thoughts without prejudice, as if he were studying them from outside his own body.

Who was this spirit who tormented his dreams? What was *his* intent? What was *he* after, and how did he, Bobby, fit into all this? Who had been murdered and why? There were far too many questions and far too few answers. Bobby's mood was in stark contrast to the warm and sunny day around him.

He coasted down Turner Road and passed the school on his left. He continued on with Brenda's directions, knowing that the library would soon appear on the same side of the road as the school. Only a few cars passed and fewer still came from the opposite direction. Butterflies fluttered among the wildflowers that dotted the countryside on either side of him. Their fragrance floated in the air as he bore down the road. It looked like any other beautiful day at this time of the year, but Bobby sensed an undercurrent of something sinister in the air. Even the bees' intense zigzagging seemed more agitated than usual. Few people seemed to be out and about after the news of the murder.

The library shot up from the horizon as he rounded the next hill. Its spire pointed to the sky like Michael's finger. The spire was a lightening rod, placed there decades ago by a fast-talking traveling salesman who convinced the town leaders at the time of the need for such a device on all their public buildings. Because of the spire, the large, traditional brick building looked like a church. Doors and windows trimmed in a bright white, it seemed new, although it had been around since 1955.

Bobby left his bike on the rack on the left of the building, approached the entrance and opened the wide front door. There on his left was the circulation desk and the town librarian, angrily gluing loose bindings to over-abused books she was sure were skimmed and not read properly. The place had a faint musty but agreeable smell. It was even comforting in a way, reminding him of the small library in the Cotswold's he used to visit with his mother, a memory that gave him a pang of homesickness.

"Hello, ma'am, are you open?" he asked.

"Of course, young man, and what a delightful accent. Are you from the UK?"

Pamela Smith, as her nameplate indicated, was short and squat, not much taller than Bobby. She was wearing a tight dark skirt that fell below her knees and kept reaching for the floor, as well as a loose white blouse made of something silky. Her hair was combed straight back, secured in a tight bun that resembled a small inner tube. Her glasses, attached to a sparkling braided cord on either side of her face, perched on the very edge of her nose. They hung there as if peering over for a quick look before leaping. The cord that kept them from falling shimmered in the light as she moved to glance at him. They accentuated her pronounced jowls.

"Yes, ma'am, I'm here on holiday visiting my cousin, Brenda Watson."

"Oh yes, I know Brenda. A delightful child." She clearly liked the word delightful. "She can be a bit rude, but then what child isn't these days?" she sighed, unaware of the irony of her statement. "How may I help you, young man?"

"If you please, I'm interested in finding out some specific information. I would like to know whether this area has been visited by pirates in the past, and if so, who they might be." He let that question hang in the air for a moment, expecting her to be taken aback by his direct request. Somewhere in the back of his mind he even thought she might guess what he was up to and try to drill him for more information that he was not willing to provide.

"That's an odd request. But it isn't the first I've ever had, and won't be the last." She paused, thinking for a minute. She raised one eyebrow, scrunched her nose, and picked up her sharpened # 2 pencil. She put the eraser between her teeth and chewed as she fired up the synapses in her brain, formulating an attack plan like a general going to war.

"Begin with a basic reference source, like the encyclopedia," she told him, now pointing the pencil directly at him. "Look up pirates, specifically those who traveled the Long Island Sound.

Then check out some local history books followed by historical newspaper references, which we have on microfiche. You go to the encyclopedia to get started, and I'll pull together the local histories and set up the microfiche." With that, she pushed off her stool, threw down her pencil, and pointed him in the direction of the reference section.

Bobby raced over. Knowing he had only a limited amount of time, he wanted to explore the other resources before he had to leave. He was almost sure he would come away with something worthwhile, but knew it would not be easy to find. This wasn't going to be like picking up solid gold chunks off the ground, plain in sight and ready for the taking. He was going to have to dig for what he needed. He drew some comfort in knowing that at least he had some help figuring out where he should dig.

He picked up the appropriate volume of the Encyclopedia Britannica and began reading the article on pirates. He found it to be too general, lacking specific information about the area in question. Frustrated, he decided on another tack. He was good with a computer and certainly knew how to navigate his way around Google. He darted over to the bank of computers for public use and shot a look over at the librarian, who was still hunched over pulling local histories off the shelf. He sat down and Googled *Pirates of Connecticut.* Not much helpful information came up. So he did an advanced search, including the phrase "buried treasure." Brilliant! This time he had some great hits. Below the first article on Captain Kidd was a general article on pirates in Connecticut. Clicking on that, he found a list of five pirates. He couldn't believe his good fortune, having more specific names to guide his further research.

"Oh my goodness, what are you doing?" exclaimed Ms. Smith. "I deliberately didn't send you to the computer because I wanted you to start your research the way it should be started: slowly and methodically."

"Sorry, ma'am, I don't mean to be rude, but I am in a bit of a hurry. I thought the computer might provide me with quick information."

Ms. Smith glared at him from over the top of her glasses and sniffed. "Hmmph. Young people today! Nobody has time to do things properly, no matter what country they're from, I guess. Everything has to be rushed. Your local histories are on this cart, and you can explore them or not, depending on how much of a *hurry* you are in," she added. She then hustled off to her desk and once again took up her position as chief repairer of shoddily treated knowledge.

There were eleven books on the tall, wobbly-wheeled mobile shelf. Some were on the history of Connecticut, some general books on pirates and outlaws, and a handful on the Danbury-Mountain Lake area specifically. Bobby sat at the table next to the parked shelf and dove into this latter collection. He immediately went to the index of each book, searching for any of the names he had pulled out of his Google article. He found three in the first one, two in the second, and four in the third book. Two of the names were common to all three books. He wrote the two on a piece of paper and decided to focus on those.

Bobby finished scanning the third book and gently placed it back on the mobile shelf. He stood, a bit wobbly himself, and felt more tired than when he first came in. He glanced at the clock on the wall behind Ms. Smith, and noticed it was 4:15 p.m. He ran to the front door, shouting his thanks as he dashed for his bike.

"Well…I suppose you're wel…" she started, turning around in her chair. "Kids today absolutely need manners beaten into them," she mumbled. Once again, the irony of her statement was lost on her.

As Bobby rode out of sight, he failed to notice that Conan had arrived at the library to return a local history tome tucked neatly under his arm.

23

Stevie was nothing if not cautious. He had paid a quick visit to his dad's tool chest before venturing out to the McCormack property, taking a flashlight, powdered graphite, and a utility knife. He was reckless at times, but when he knew there was real danger involved, he took special care to be prepared. He was short and wily and proud of it. Those qualities had served him well in the past and they weren't going to let him down now. They often allowed him to slip into and out of places most people wouldn't even fit. Today was going to be a piece of cake. He knew the terrain, having pulled a Halloween prank at the site once before. He knew that Mr. McCormack had a violent temper, but he wasn't too concerned. Knowledge like that was useful on a mission. Instead of scaring him, it gave him confidence. He knew what he was up against, and he also knew that when people have a short fuse they are loud and make mistakes. He was sure he would see or hear Mr. McCormack coming from a mile away. Assured, he rode on to his destination on Cobble Avenue.

The old fruit stand on the edge of the McCormack property was empty with no signs of life. He didn't expect to see anyone there today, but it was good to be sure. He pulled over to the side of the road and made as if he were checking the air in his bike's tires. As he bent down on one knee into the dust, he glanced up and took in the surrounding area. He didn't see any parked cars or recent footprints. That was good. Seeing what he expected was a sign that things were going in the right direction. He paused as he stood up, checking out the driveway that led to the house. The tire tracks appeared to be coming out onto the road, going towards town. He didn't see anything going in, and the driveway was big enough to fit two cars going in opposite directions. A car going out and none coming in meant nobody was home. Still, he wasn't going to take any chances. Not after hearing about the murder.

He straddled his bike and pedaled past the McCormack property towards the lake. He knew of a path off the main road, not too far from the lake entrance, that led onto the McCormack property. He had used it at Halloween last year and he would use it again today. He knew he had to find out what he could quickly and head back to Michael's, but he was going to remain cautious. If he didn't make it back in time, so what? He could call later and let Brenda know what he'd found out.

He was approaching the entrance to the lake when a truck with darkened windows passed him. It slowed as it came up behind him and then accelerated as it went by. The parking lot by the lake was just a quarter of a mile ahead. The path he sought turned off the main road just before the lot, its entrance marked by a telephone pole. The path in turn connected to a marked hiking trail that began in the parking lot just up the road and ended at the lake on the other end. Another older footpath branched off the main trail and onto the McCormack property as you progressed towards the lake. A NO TRESPASS sign at the head of that path warned people to stay away. That's exactly where Stevie was heading.

When he got to the telephone pole, Stevie looked both ways and saw no traffic. He was taking no chances; he wanted no one to see him. He then ran his bike onto the footpath and headed towards the main trail. Just before getting to the trail, he laid his bike down behind a tree and covered it with some loose brush.

Now on the main trail, he began to run towards the juncture he sought. It wasn't far, but he was in a hurry. The hiking trail was typical for this area, forested all around with ferns and smaller bush in between tall deciduous trees. It provided perfect cover. No one was on the trail today. After all, it was a workday, and late in the afternoon. Most hikers liked to get an early start to avoid the heat of the day. Better for him, anyway. The fewer people there were, the less explaining he would have to do if he saw anyone he knew. Or worse, if he saw anyone his parents knew. Here it was, finally, the juncture that led to the McCormack property. It was a small lane almost covered with underbrush. Most people didn't even see it. After one last look around, he darted down the path and was swallowed by the surrounding woods.

Once out of sight Stevie slowed to a more leisurely pace. Everyone knew old man McCormack and no one ventured onto his property, so Stevie didn't expect to run into anyone. He passed the NO TRESSPASS sign, and read the handwritten statement underneath: "Violators will be dealt with harshly." That said it all. The man was nuts, so caution was a necessity.

The footpath dead-ended right into the back of a farmed field at the edge of the McCormack property. The field was loaded with corn, another blessing because the stalks gave him cover. Stevie negotiated his way around the field, pausing every few steps to listen. All he could hear was the wind whistling through the corn stalks, rustling the husk's leaves. Every once in a while he thought he heard footsteps, but when he turned he didn't see anyone and told himself it was just the wind. He took a deep breath and tried to relax. He had been in tight spots before and managed to slip away. And besides, he had a pocket full of stones for extra protection, picked for their ease in throwing.

The front of the field opened up to the back of the McCormack barn. The last time Stevie had been here he only took a peek inside the barn, but this time he meant to explore it. He wasn't quite buying the idea that the murder and the attack on Mr. Watson were connected. But if McCormack was involved with stealing those tools from Brenda's dad, he'd probably hid them in his barn. Wouldn't it be great if he could pick up a tool or two and ride it right over to Brenda's? Truth be known, he was a bit jealous of Bobby, and such a find would greatly impress Brenda.

Stevie inched his way to the front corner of the barn, careful not to be exposed to the main driveway that circled in front. He saw no car and no rising dust, and he heard no engine.

Cautiously, he looked around the corner. The house seemed locked up; no open windows or doors, and the front door seemed shut tight. There were no lights on in the house.

Satisfied it was safe, he slowly backtracked to the side door of the barn. It was locked. He wasn't getting in that way. He moved again towards the other side of the barn, taking the same precautions as before. He inched his way up to the front corner and snuck another look at the house. This time, he had to duck under the one window that was on this side of the barn. Seeing no one again, he edged his way back to the window. He glanced in, noting how dark it was inside. He would have preferred slipping in an open door, but this would have to do. He lifted the window. It was stuck! The paint was severely chipping and it wouldn't budge. This had happened at his house last fall with the basement windows. He had watched his dad bang on the windows on both sides and then coat the tracks with powdered graphite. Stevie was glad he was prepared.

He checked around once more and then banged both sides of the window hard, just once. Then he paused to listen. If he heard a door open, he'd be gone. But he didn't hear anything. He pulled out the tube of graphite from his shirt pocket and sprayed it onto the window tracks. He reached under the top of the bottom window and pushed. He pushed as hard as he could and didn't seem to be getting anywhere. He pressed until his arms ached. Angry, he banged the window once again and shoved harder. He felt a gentle move at first. Then all of a sudden, it went up with a bang!

He paused again, listening. No sound but the woeful cries of a few noisy crows outside and a few clucks from the chickens inside. He knew it was now or never. He hoisted himself up over the open window and disappeared into the dark interior.

"Maybe it's an antique," mused the sheriff. "Or maybe it was dropped by someone visiting another grave site. I don't see how this could be of any value," he concluded as he examined the earring his detective had found.

"Could be, I guess," agreed Luke. "But right now, this piece of jewelry is the only solid piece of anything that even resembles a clue. And the victim had it clutched in his right hand."

"I guess you're right, Luke," he said with a sigh. "Just put it into an evidence bag and tag it for me. Nothing like this ever happens around here. Now we have an assault and a murder all within the same week. How do you account for that, Mayor?" he asked, turning towards the mayor.

"Can't," muttered the mayor, as he nervously chewed on his fourth Slim Jim.

"Gee, that's helpful," mumbled the sheriff. "I'm beginning to wonder if I'm in the middle of some Stephen King novel, where all the people go crazy or dead, and I'm the only normal one left.

Present company excluded, of course," he added, when the mayor shot him a look.

The sheriff got into the car, shut the door, and turned up the air-conditioning. The outdoor temperature was rising and he was hot. Mayor Block had been sitting there on the edge of his seat and staring intently at the body lying across the pile of dirt. Even with the air conditioning turned up, the mayor wasn't looking so good. In fact, he began to look downright pale. Perhaps it was the heat, or the Slim Jims he had dug into a little while ago. Or perhaps it was the fact that he had never really seen a dead body. The sheriff knew the mayor would sometimes attend a wake as a representative of the town, but he never actually went up to the body. As if dead bodies scared him and he didn't want to look. Right now, though, he noticed that the mayor's eyes were glued to the lifeless lump across the way. The sheriff later said it must have been all three factors: the growing heat, the greasy food, and the "viewing," as he called it. Because without preamble, the mayor leaned forward and puked a raging river. Vomit tumbled from his mouth in torrents, landing on the dash and the floor of the front seat passenger side of the sheriff's car.

At first they were both shocked. The mayor, looking a ghostly gray, glanced at the sheriff with bulging eyes and a yellowish liquid dribbling from his chin. His mouth moved up and down without closing as if he were silently praying for deliverance. The sheriff instinctively pulled back, scrunched his massive frame against the door, and let his mouth fall agape, not sure what to say, if anything. And then, more of the downpour. No human, thought the sheriff, could have eliminated that much in the way of internal fluids without completely disappearing. For the briefest of seconds, he entertained the notion that the mayor was a zombie and he had been right about that Stephen King novel after all. Soon his senses took hold and he did what any normal person would have done. He reached behind his back, grabbed the door handle, and scrambled out of that car as fast as he could.

The sheriff twisted and hit the ground with both hands before his legs could catch up with him. Once his left foot made contact, he sprinted like an Olympian out of the starting block, gagging a bit himself. As he ran around the back of the car, he reached for the hankie in his back pocket to wipe his face and head. He had left his hat on the front seat to fend for itself. Luke, who was focused on the murder scene, hadn't seen the mayor lose his lunch, but did hear the sheriff bolt from the car choking and cursing.

"What happened, Sheriff?" he called, a bit concerned. "Everything all right?"

"God, no, everything is not all right. His highness just puked in my car," he stammered, getting out the words in between gulps of fresh air.

Luke was stunned. "Oh boy," was the best he could do. Right now he was glad to be on his side of the yellow tape. "I'm a little busy right now," he said tentatively, "but is there any way I can help?"

"Yeah," said the sheriff. "Get on your walkie talkie and call my genius deputy up here. I've got just the job for him."

Deputy Carver got word his boss needed him pronto. Knowing that he was the first to arrive on the scene and secure it, even if the chief did have an issue with how he'd done it, he believed Sheriff Musgrove now needed his criminology expertise.

Perhaps that showoff Luke Robinson, Mr. La-Di-Da Detective, couldn't figure something out. Maybe the sheriff needed a real crime fighter up on the hill. Someone who knew how to look for clues. Someone like him. Well, he thought, *better not waste any more time down here.* He hitched up his belt, straightened his hat, got behind the wheel of his car and headed on up the hill with swagger.

When Carver got there, Luke was still combing the area. *The sheriff must be punishing Luke for his lack of ability to find anything useful,* he thought. The sheriff was leaning against the back fender of his car looking dejected. *I guess he's upset that his golden boy detective needed help. Ha! I'll show him,* thought Carver.

He put his car in park and slowly got out, looking like a real officer of the law, not some namby-pamby detective who had received nothing but some bogus training. He pulled himself up to his full height of 5'4", put his thumbs into his belt buckle and nodded towards his boss.

"You called me, Sheriff!" It was a statement, not a question.

"Yeah!" his boss answered. "The mayor puked all over the inside of my car. Take him home and drop him off. Then go to the Baker Street Café and pick up those useless mokes, Moss and Jinx. Tell them to get their rear ends back to their shop and clean out my car. I don't want any smell left, you understand? If there's any smell left, you'll clean it! Now throw me your keys and get out of here!"

"But...wha...I don't under..."

The chief turned his head sharply towards his deputy. "Something you don't understand?"

"Uh, no, Sir. No, Sir," Carver repeated.

The sheriff held out his hand. "Keys."

Deputy Tim Carver swallowed his pride, tossed his boss the keys, and gingerly lowered himself behind the wheel of the sheriff's car.

He drove out of there quickly with the driver side window wide open. His head was hanging out of the window and he was holding his nose with his left hand all the way back into town. The mayor, clearly exhausted, just sat in a puddle of his own vomit, leaning against the car door and looking comatose.

As they were leaving, a dark sedan pulled in. It was Tom Kimble, the county coroner. Tom was a friendly but humorless man. He waved to the deputy and didn't quite understand why he didn't wave back. He hadn't noticed that the deputy had his nose firmly pinched and cheeks puffed from trying to hold his breath. He did see another body in the car on the passenger side, however, and based on the complexion, he thought briefly that it might have been the corpse he was called to examine.

When Kimble arrived on the hill and got out of his car, the blast of warm air hit him like an open furnace, even though the heat didn't seem to affect him much. The coroner looked like he was sent by Central Casting to star in a movie about coroners. He was five foot nothing and wore shoe lifts to appear taller. He wore a long black coat, black pants, a white shirt, and black tie. He always looked as if he was dressed for a funeral. Given his choice of occupation, one may have thought the coroner would try to compensate with bright, cheery clothing, but he preferred an appearance that bespoke his task and the mood it evoked.

"Hank."

"Tom. Got one for you."

"Yeah, Luke filled me in. What do you need right now?"

"Time and probable cause of death. I won't hold you to it until you do an autopsy, but I'm working blind so far and need some information."

"You don't look so good. Something wrong?"

"Long story. Just get me that information as soon as you can, will ya, doc?"

"Sure, you hanging here?"

"No, I'm going back to the office. Call me as soon as you got something."

"Okay." The coroner then went over to converse with the detective.

The sheriff got into his deputy's car—with no guilt whatsoever—and started back to his office. He was not even halfway there when his radio crackled. He picked it up. "Yeah," he barked. It was Luke.

"Coroner did a quick take. Time of death was probably between midnight and 2 a.m. We found an empty whiskey bottle under the vic, so he was obviously drinking while working last night. Not unusual for him, apparently. Looks like he was attacked and hit over the head with one of his own shovels. Funny thing, though. There was money in his pocket, but his keys were stolen."

"Ten-four," said the sheriff and hung up his radio. "Now, why would anyone want the keys of a gravedigger?" he wondered aloud.

Stevie landed with a thud. He scrunched down on the ground and looked around, allowing his eyes to adjust to the darkness. The larger area was already somewhat visible, but the dark corners and stalls were impenetrable at the moment. Within minutes he was able to see fairly well. He listened intently. Besides the noise of some chickens, he didn't hear much of anything, confirming that he was quite alone. Nevertheless, he kept one hand on the windowsill until he was absolutely sure. One odd sound and he was going to slip back out the way he came in. When he was sure he was in no danger, he took out his flashlight, which he had also retrieved from his father's toolbox, and began to look around.

The flashlight cast a sharp, direct beam, giving light to only a small area. He took one step at a time, moving the shaft of light from side to side, all the while listening for anything out of the ordinary. Stevie wondered what to do about the open window. If he left it open, there was the danger of having someone outside notice it and start looking for an intruder. If he closed it and someone was in here, he would be trapped. He opted to take a risk and leave it open. If someone was outside and closed the window on him, he might still be able to run for the side door and get away. If someone was in here and the window was closed, there would be no escape. The thought made him shudder.

He moved towards the rear of the barn and looked for any type of trunk or box.

He reasoned that if a thief was likely to hide anything he had taken, that's where he might store it. Because his eyes were still adjusting, it was difficult to see clearly without the flashlight. There was a hayloft in the barn with an upper doorway to the outside, but that was closed. If opened, it would act like a skylight, allowing the sun to pour through the interior of the barn. Closed as it was, it caused the darkness to lick at the corners of his vision as soon as the flashlight swept past.

He continued his slow pace to the back of the barn. Closed fencing reached towards the ceiling and stopped about halfway up, separating the rear of the barn from the main section. Two pieces of fencing ran perpendicular to the sides of the barn with an opening of about six feet. There was no gate or door to the opening, only the gaping maw of a black hole. He stopped at the breach, flicked his flash to the left and moved it into the darkened corner of the belly of the beast. He noticed a tall wooden locker with a handle and no lock.

Suddenly he heard a rustling noise from the corner on his right. He immediately shut off the light and crouched. His heart was hammering like an oil derrick. Sweat poured off his forehead and ran down his back giving him goosebumps. He gripped his flashlight so tight he thought he would break it in half. His panic turned to fear and he couldn't think straight.

He gradually realized that he hadn't heard any footsteps. He glanced to his right. It was pitch dark. He stood up, using the fence post at the opening to lean on. He decided to shoot the light down the darkened corridor and react based on what he saw. If anyone was there, he would sprint for the window and dive through it. Methodically, he raised the flashlight and pointed it. He placed his finger on the on-off button and pushed.

Light filled the black hole. A long, dark mournful face stared directly back at him. It was huge and it was ugly. His split second reaction did not go as planned. He dropped the light, stumbled backwards and tripped on his own two feet. He scrambled crablike towards the window and nearly made it until he fell down… then he burst out laughing. It was more of a silent laughter, but one borne from frayed nerves and uncontrollable fear. When he regained his breath, he moved back to the fence opening, picked up his light and shone it once more to the right.

Mr. McCormack's cow stared directly back at him. Tethered to her stall, she was no danger to him. He shook his head at the absurdity of his reaction.

Just as he got comfortable again, he heard a noise he could easily identify. A car pulled up in front of the barn. He looked around for a place to hide. Off to his right, stairs led to the loft. He took them three at a time and dove into the loose hay above. He wiggled his way into the pile just as the barn door was unhitched and swung open. Peeking through the hay he saw Mr. McCormack enter the barn.

Mr. McCormack actually looked meaner than usual, if that were possible. He strode into the barn and walked directly to the back. He mumbled something incoherent to the cow as he untied her and led her outside. He then let out the chickens that knew enough to race out into the yard for the already scattered corn. He started to walk back out when he paused for a moment. He sniffed the air as if he detected a slight disturbance in the atmosphere. Then, as quickly as he came in, he left, gently shoving the barn doors behind him, leaving them partially opened.

Stevie knew it was time to go, but he wanted to check out that storage locker first. He waited another minute and heard the house door open and close. That was his signal to move. He slithered down the stairs. The ambient light cast from the slightly parted barn doors was enough to guide him and keep him from using his flashlight. He approached the cabinet by feeling his way along the fence until he finally reached it. He turned on the flash and reached for the handle. Standing there were two shovels, just like the tools stolen from Mr. Watson's store. He bent down to examine the sticker on the head of the tools and saw "Mountain Lake Hardware" prominently displayed. Looking closer, he noticed something like blood staining both the sticker and a section of the shovelhead.

It was time to go. He closed the door and shut off his flashlight. Too dangerous to take the tools now. He would tell the sheriff. He made his way back to the entry in the fence. He could see the window across the barn and made a beeline for it. One last quick glance at the open barn doors and through the window he went. He landed softly outside, picking himself up and dusting himself off. He stole another quick look at the house. Maybe, if things were quiet, he would even sneak up and peek inside.

He drew up to the corner of the barn and once again found himself inching his way around for a glimpse. He saw the chickens feeding around the front of the barn on corn that Mr. McCormack must have thrown about before he came inside. The cow was off eating grass on the far side of the barn. The car was parked directly in front of the house on the circle between the house and the barn. The front door was definitely closed and lights were on in the house.

Someone's hand slammed down hard on the back of his neck and gripped it like a steel vice. The other hand swooped around his face from the left side and held a white handkerchief over his mouth. It was wet and had an odd smell. He heard quiet laughter, felt the strength go out of his limbs, and then fell into complete and utter darkness.

PART 7

COMPLICATIONS

Bobby was in a rush to get back to Michael's house. Despite his success at the library, he had a strong sense of foreboding. He hoped Brenda was able to learn something useful. Michael, he was sure, was going to contribute in some large way. "And what of Stevie?" he wondered aloud. "I wonder how he is doing?" He knew that Stevie had the most difficult task, certainly the most dangerous, but he hoped that Stevie was being cautious. He also wondered how many of the suspects Stevie was going to encounter in the short amount of time he had this afternoon. Perhaps Stevie could continue trailing them tomorrow with his and Brenda's help.

He rode past the school and gave it a quick look. Cold and uninviting, it stood far back off the road. He felt a definite ripple of panic as he passed the building. It was a nervous kind of feeling—one that someone might get walking down a dark street on a moonless night. He shook it off as he flew past, focusing on the information he was bringing to their gathering.

"Time is of the essence," his mum would often say. Right now he missed her greatly. He realized how often she was right in what she said. Even though she trusted in him and had faith in his gift, what he was now thinking was so far-fetched even she would have difficulty accepting it. He knew he would have to have something more concrete, something more substantial, for anyone to ever believe his theory.

He pulled into Michael's street with aching legs and burning lungs. He was exhausted from the ride, but it didn't prevent him from plowing through the front gate and leaping onto the porch. He punched the doorbell. Mrs. Kelleher answered the door with a smile. "Michael's upstairs," she said, happy that her son was receiving so much attention. She knew how difficult it could be for Michael to make friends. It was one of the challenges of his condition. He didn't pick up on the social cues that came to other kids naturally. That had caused him great distress in their previous community. He worked very hard at trying to get it right, often role-playing a variety of social situations with her. She hoped it was beginning to pay off. Perhaps this new group could see beyond her son's challenges. Perhaps they could see the brilliance that she knew lay just underneath, like a rapidly flowing underground river. If they could just get past the surface, they would be in as much awe of Michael's talents and knowledge base as she was. With a glimmer of hope, she smiled briefly and returned to cooking dinner.

Bobby entered Michael's room. Brenda was already there. Michael was still on his computer and didn't even turn to say hello. Bobby smiled at her, but Brenda looked disappointed.

"Hey," she muttered.

"Were you able to find out anything?" he asked.

"Not much!" she revealed. "Jinx did say that he thought that it was Mr. Hansen who worked at the cemetery who was killed. He also said they found an old earring as a clue. But it was hard to tell if anything Dumb and Dumber said was accurate. And," she continued with emphasis, "those two geniuses think there is no connection between the murder and my father's attack."

"I know they're wrong about that," Bobby said. "There is something very dangerous and menacing at work here, Brenda. Something far worse than I imagined at first. Now it's become deadly."

Bobby looked at Michael.

"How's our new friend doing?"

"He's playing his game again. I don't know if he learned anything yet because he can't seem to break away from it."

"And what about Stevie? Have you heard from him?"

"No, nothing yet."

"I've managed to discover something of substance and I believe that Michael can help us with it."

That news perked Brenda up and she stood to see what he'd found. Bobby shared the scrap of paper upon which he had scribbled two names. He had written the names Black Bart, which they had already encountered, and Hiram Quincy, another strong possibility.

"Both of these men were vicious pirates and known to travel through here, according to some obscure local sources. They were both tall, bearded, and had a reputation for brutality. It's suspected that Black Bart killed over thirty men and Hiram Quincy just about the same."

Bobby walked over to Michael.

"Hello, Michael, how are you doing?" Michael didn't respond, but looked annoyed that he was being interrupted in his game. Bobby paused, unsure how to proceed. He knew Michael was different and therefore had to be approached differently. He looked to Brenda. "Wait here."

Bobby dashed from the room. Brenda could hear him clomping down the stairs. She wondered what he was up to. Just when she started to get impatient, she heard him racing back up to the room. A second later, he burst into the room and waited to catch his breath.

"What were you do…" Brenda began, but Bobby held up his hand and nodded in her direction as if to say he had everything under control. He walked up to Michael and gently placed a hand on his shoulder.

"Michael, can you hear me?" he asked.

"Of course he can hear you," Brenda said, "he's not deaf, you know."

Bobby mouthed the words, "I know" in her direction and continued.

"Michael, if you can hear me, please say 'yes'."

"Yes, I hear you," he said in a bored monotone, as he continued to defeat a collection of ghosts and pirates.

"Good," continued Bobby, "I'm going to leave these two names here on your desk. I would like you to research them. They are a key factor to this mystery and I'm counting on your help. Find out anything you can. Will you do it?" Bobby waited, but it appeared as if Michael was back in his own world and not coming out. He was about to ask the question again when Michael responded.

"Yes, I'll do it, just as soon as I'm done here."

"Thank you, Michael. We'll check with you tomorrow."

He glanced at Brenda and tilted his head towards the door. It was time for them to leave.

"What about Stevie," Brenda whispered.

"It's getting late," said Bobby. "We're going to have to call him later."

Once outside, they shared notes. Brenda told him once again how fruitless she thought her day had been, having run up against the wall of stupidity that was Moss and Jinx.

"It was a bit of a stretch to get anything useful from them anyway," Bobby said kindly, "but don't be discouraged, you did find out two things we hadn't known before. We now know who was murdered. And we know that an old earring was found. I would wager that earring belongs to our pirate."

"If you look at it that way, I guess my day wasn't a total waste."

Bobby then told her about his experience at the library. "Finding those names was a stroke of luck. My research confirmed some of what we know and gave us one more name to verify or eliminate. Now, at least I feel better knowing that we're on the right path."

"Terrific, but how is Michael going to help? He can't even tear himself away from the game he's playing. And where did you go before?" she asked, almost as an afterthought.

"I went to see Michael's mum. I told her I wanted to tell Michael something and couldn't seem to get his attention. She was thrilled to tell me more about his specific challenges and how I might help Michael listen to what I had to say. She had worked on this very skill with him herself. And it seemed to have worked," he added.

"Yes, you got his attention all right, but now what? What's he going to *do*?"

"His mum assured me that if he acknowledged me, he not only heard what I had to say, but he would act upon it."

"Bobby, I know you believe in what you're saying about this pirate-turned-ghost-theory. And you know I believe in *you.* It's just…well, it's just that I'm finding the whole thing difficult to accept. What if it's just some crazy guy running around doing these things? What if it is Mr. McCormack, or that wild tempered Tony, or our lunatic school custodian? Or maybe even somebody else we haven't even thought of?"

Bobby stopped his bike and looked tired. "You're right, Brenda," he told her, looking at the ground. "There are times when I doubt myself, too, but I don't now. I am now one hundred percent certain that the pirate that appeared to me and spoke to me is involved in the evil that is occurring in this town. I know how this fiend made me feel when I met *him* in my dreams. I could feel *his* anger and smell *his* fear. I know how cold, lonely, and helpless I felt confronting *him* at Madame Tarot's when *his* threats touched my mind. And I know how sick and frightened *he* makes me feel whenever I think of *him.*" He looked up at his cousin. "*He* is real, Brenda. And *he's* dangerous. Nobody else will believe me, so if we don't stop *him,* no one will. *He'll* kill again. I know *he* will."

Brenda nodded. "Okay," she said. "Let's get home. We'll have dinner, call Stevie to see what he found out, and meet up with him at the carnival tonight. Then we can continue our search tomorrow. If my parents say anything about the murder, though, we should probably say we don't know anything. We don't want to give them the idea we're mixed up with that in any way."

When they pulled into the driveway, things appeared calm. Brenda's home now stood as a sanctuary from the evils that lurked just outside the front door. They entered through the mudroom door, and were immediately overcome by the smell of roasted chicken basting in the oven.

"Hello, children," sang Auntie Arlene. "I trust you had a wonderful day in this beautiful weather."

"Yes, Auntie," said Bobby. "We biked around town, spent time at the library, and even made a new friend."

"How nice, dear," she responded absently as she whipped potatoes. "Now run along and wash up, you two, and we'll have dinner shortly."

They did as she asked and returned just in time for the arrival of Brenda's father. He shouted his usual refrain.

"I'm home, does anybody care?" This time, there was a heartfelt, "We all do!" when he came into the kitchen.

Dinner was a nice respite, with all of their fears forgotten for the moment. They enjoyed each other's company, talking and laughing throughout their meal. Besides discussing the carnival, Uncle John recited some jokes he'd heard earlier. Each one made them all laugh heartily. Brenda was so afraid of milk going up her nose because she was laughing so hard that she refused to drink anything. Auntie Arlene tried to tell a joke of her own, but when she got to the punch line she realized she had forgotten it. That brought more peals of laughter than the joke itself ever would have garnered.

They were enjoying themselves so much they barely noticed that the phone was ringing. Finally, Auntie Arlene jumped at the sound. "Oh my, the phone!" she exclaimed. She ran over and plucked it from its cradle. She stood there listening for a moment, her smile gradually fading. It was replaced with a look of concern.

"There's been a murder in town!" she gasped. "John, why didn't you tell me?"

"I didn't know, Arlene. I spent most of the day in my accountant's office out on the highway. I saw the sheriff when I returned to the shop, just before coming home, to talk about my attack, but he didn't mention anything about a murder. I told him that Tom McCormack was upset with me, and he seemed to think that was important. Who was murdered?" he asked.

Without answering him, Arlene posed the same question to the person at the other end of the line. Only moments later she turned to Brenda and Bobby.

"It's Mrs. Nichols, Stevie's mom. Do either of you know where Stevie is?" she asked.

A momentary look of panic crossed their faces. Brenda was the first to speak. "No, mom. We haven't seen him all afternoon," she said truthfully.

Brenda's mom resumed her phone conversation for another minute before gently returning it with a soft click. She slowly turned back to the group with a mixed look of compassion, sympathy, and fear.

"Stevie didn't come home for dinner tonight."

Earlier in the day, the sheriff had been perplexed, to say the least. He had never had a more difficult problem to solve in his many years as a police officer. His peaceful little town was getting turned upside down, and he didn't like it one bit.

After leaving the cemetery, he had gone back to his office. There, he sat in his chair, an old model that someone had picked up at a yard sale long ago. It had a black cushion at least six inches thick, creased like a well-used map, with a wooden back and arm rests. The back of the chair had wide wooden slats to hold up his sizeable frame and it tilted way back allowing him to grip his hands behind his head and stare at the ceiling. When he lowered his eyes, it gave him the appearance of looking down at people when he spoke to them. The really neat thing about his chair, he believed, was that in order to raise or lower it you had to turn it like you were screwing the top onto a bottle of fine wine. Despite his advanced age, he found this amusing and would sometimes spin around, going higher or lower whenever he was trying to think.

His office was a windowless cave, made of cinder block construction, painted an institutional gray like the metal desk and filing cabinet. The carpet was threadbare with bald patches to match his head. Whenever he was interrogating someone about one of the more sensational crimes in the community, like the rare example of graffiti on public property, or who might have taken the gnome in front of the flower shop in town, he would put on his hat, lean back in his chair, and stare down the suspect who sat in the chair on the other side of his desk until they folded like a cheap suit.

Most people found his office depressing, but not him. He enjoyed the solitude it provided. Here he had the time and privacy to think things out. He also enjoyed the aura of power it gave him. He was "The Sheriff," and this was "The Sheriff's Office." It didn't hurt that it scared the daylights out of any kid brought in for questioning. The guilty squirmed for no more than a few minutes before spilling the beans. Those who weren't guilty usually knew those who were and could be persuaded to share that information in record time.

Today he wasn't interrogating anyone, though. He was thinking, and thinking hard, only this time he decided not to spin. After seeing what had happened to the mayor today, spinning in circles was not in the cards.

He mulled over what he knew about the recent events. One day, John Watson takes a hit from behind and gets nothing but a couple of tools and cheap torches stolen. Money is left in the register. Nothing else is taken. Then they find out that someone takes batting practice on the back of Zeke Hansen's head for no apparent reason other than to steal his keys. His keys, for cripes sake! He had checked with the manager of the cemetery and his key chain held nothing except his car keys, his house key, and the key to the storage shed. He had asked his detective to check it out and report back.

The phone rang as if on cue.

"Yeah."

"Hey, Sheriff. Luke here."

"Luke, whatcha got?"

"Checked out that storage shed for you." There was a pause.

"And..." Sometimes he enjoyed teasing information out of his detective, but today he was in no mood.

"That's the funny thing, Sir. There's nothin' in that shed 'cept some tools, you know, the kind of stuff Zeke would use to dig graves and such." Another pause.

"And...?" the sheriff asked, getting irritated.

"Manager says the only things that seem to be missin' are the mini-backhoe and the winch he used to lower the coffins."

"A backhoe and a winch? Do you mean to tell me someone's been murdered for a mechanical shovel and a portable lift? What the heck is going on here?"

"Manager says the backhoe was the kind that's small enough to fit on the back of a pickup or inside a U-Haul rent-a-truck. A Toro model, weighing about 600 pounds."

"Great. Far too many people around here own a truck for that lead to take us anywhere, but call around to the U-Haul rental places and check on it," ordered the sheriff.

"Already did that. Nobody has rented anything recently. Last ones were for a few college kids comin' home from school in May. Nothin' since then."

"Okay, Luke," the sheriff sighed, "thanks. Nice work."

The sheriff hung up and sighed, rubbing his eyes with the heels of his two massive hands. He went back over the file regarding the assault on John Watson and decided to pay him another visit. He left the comfort of his office knowing the only way he was going to get anywhere on this was to shake things up. So far, he was coming up empty. Maybe by pushing people he would find out something useful.

He drove over to the hardware store in his freshly scrubbed car. It smelled like pine disinfectant, which didn't help much because it reminded him about what had happened that morning. He arrived just in time to catch John Watson as he was closing up shop for the day after returning from his accountant.

"Hey, John, do you mind if I go over a few things with you about that attack?"

"Sure, Hank, but I already told you everything I know. Can't see how this will help."

"I know, but I got nothin' so far, and if you can just bear with me, sometimes things that have been forgotten will surface. Tell me again what happened, and start from the beginning."

"Like I said, I was working on Joe Johnson's mower when I was suddenly hit in the back of the head. Didn't hear anyone come in and didn't see anything. When I came to, I called the police. No money was taken, just some shovels and some torches."

"And the doors were locked?"

"Yup. Locked them myself before I started the job."

"Any idea at all who might have done this?"

"No Sir! Although…" he added.

"Although what?" asked the sheriff driving that question through the narrowest of openings.

"Oh, you know Tom McCormack, Hank. He's an old drunk and full of hot air. He stopped in my shop the other day and we had a bit of a row. He said I cheated him by selling him faulty merchandise. He wanted a complete trade in, when the tools he brought in were broken from misuse. You know how rocky his property is in spots. Anyway, I offered him a discount, but he cursed me and stormed out of here all upset."

The sheriff took notes, excited that for the first time in this investigation he had a lead.

"Did anyone witness the argument?" he asked.

"No, no one heard the actual argument, but my daughter and her cousin were outside and saw his truck speeding away. They said he even ran the stop sign."

"Geez, John, why didn't you say something about this? Or file a complaint?"

"Because I don't think Tom is a threat to anyone. He can be a real pain sometimes, but I wouldn't call him dangerous."

"I would. Everybody knows he has a mean temper. I'm going over to see him right now."

The sheriff bid farewell with a tip of his hat and raced to his car. He called his deputy for backup and then the judge for a search warrant. Within an hour, he was at the entrance to the McCormack property. His deputy was already waiting at the edge of the driveway.

"We firing up the sirens, chief?" asked Deputy Tim.

"Of course not!" bellowed the sheriff. "We don't know anything yet. And we don't want to tip him off that we're coming. Just get in your car and follow me." He shook his head in disgust and got into his car.

They approached the entrance to the house and got out of their cars, stretched a moment, and looked around.

Tom McCormack came to the front door of his house and didn't look happy. "What do you two want?" he barked with more growling in his voice than a watchdog.

"Hello, Tom. Deputy Carver and I are here on official business. Heard you had a fight with John Watson."

"So."

"So, shortly afterwards, he gets hit in the head with a shovel and has some tools stolen."

"What's that got to do with me?"

"Maybe we'll find out. We got a search warrant for your property."

"Wait just a minute, Sheriff, I got rights. You can't just come in here and..."

"Oh, yes, we can, Tom, so just stay out of the way or risk being arrested."

Tom McCormack was no shrinking violet, but he looked a little pale at the threat of arrest and started to stutter.

"Tom," said the sheriff, "you just sit over there while I search your barn. Deputy Carver will keep an eye on you. Go on, sit on your porch there."

"You have no right..."

The sheriff waved the warrant in front of him. "Sit down."

Tom McCormack sat on the steps to his porch and dropped his head in his hands. The deputy looked at him sternly, thumbs hitched into his belt. The sheriff opened the barn doors wide and strode in like he owned the place. He turned over cans, and looked behind bags. He wasn't quite sure what he was looking for, but hoped to find something that would tie Tom McCormack to the attack on John Watson. At least then he would have one mystery solved.

Finding nothing in the front of the barn, he proceeded to the back. Carver nervously tried to keep an eye on his charge, as well as listen for his chief. The sheriff poked around a bit and cursed at the smell of the chickens. He choked down a gag and noticed a tall, wooden storage chest close to the coop. He walked over to it and opened the door. He stared at its contents and whistled softly. Kneeling down to do a quick inspection, he whistled again.

It took just ten seconds from that moment for him to arrive back at the entrance to the barn. He looked at his deputy as he held two shovels in his surgical glove-covered hand. One of the shovels had blood on it.

"Cuff him," he said.

More bad news greeted the sheriff when he returned to his office to lock up McCormack for the night. Word had just arrived of Stevie's disappearance. He turned to his deputy.

"Tim, I want you to lock up our prisoner, then take these shovels over to the state lab in Danbury. Tell them I need a positive ID no later than tomorrow. I'm going over to the Nichols residence to check on the disappearance report of their son."

"Right, chief." Deputy Carver grabbed Tom McCormack by the arm and led him to his cell, as the prisoner complained the entire time.

Sheriff Musgrove drove over to the Nichols' residence to speak with Stevie's parents. While he was concerned about the boy's disappearance in light of all that's happened, he wasn't alarmed after speaking with Mr. and Mrs. Nichols. In fact, after Mr. Nichols told him that he and Stevie had an argument, and Stevie stormed off, he was sure that at least this mystery would be resolved within a day.

Given that a murder had taken place, and the fact that Stevie was missing, Bobby, Brenda and her parents had forgotten all plans of returning to the carnival that night. After dinner, Bobby and Brenda went upstairs to Brenda's room. They sat side by side on the edge of her bed, each struggling with the idea of what to do next.

"I shouldn't have let him go," said Bobby.

"You wouldn't have been able to stop him," said Brenda. "Once Stevie decides he's going to do something, no one can stop him. What do you think happened?" she asked, turning to Bobby.

"I don't know, but I've got a bad feeling about it."

"Maybe we should go to the authorities. Stevie may be hurt, or worse," Brenda worried.

"You're right," said Bobby. "So much has happened, I don't think we can do this alone. We need help. We should go down and speak to your dad."

Fearful of the kind of reaction they received from the mayor on their first attempt to secure adult help, they grudgingly made their way downstairs to speak to Brenda's dad. He and Auntie Arlene were alone in the kitchen, speaking softly about what might have happened to Stevie. They looked up when Bobby and Brenda approached.

"What's up, guys?" asked Uncle John.

"It's about Stevie," Brenda started. She decided to tell her parents what they were up to, but would leave any mention of Bobby's theory out of it.

"I'm afraid we were playing detective about your attack. Stevie decided to go out to the McCormack farm to check things out."

"What?" Uncle John exploded. "He did what?" Without waiting for an answer, he ran to the phone and was patched through to Sheriff Musgrove. Before John got to relate what Brenda told him, the sheriff assured him that he was on top of this, that he had a pretty good idea where Stevie was, and that Uncle John should keep his two young ones in the house and in bed for the night.

When he got off the phone, he was still perplexed, but turned to Bobby and Brenda. "The sheriff seems to think he knows where Stevie is, but he, and the two of us, want the both of you to stay home tonight and stay up in your rooms."

"Is he OK?" asked Bobby.

"Where is he?" Brenda blurted out.

"I don't know," said her father. "The sheriff didn't share that information with me. But I'm sure he's on top of it. It's police business, and none of yours."

"But…" Brenda started, but her father would have none of it.

"No buts. You two go upstairs."

Reluctantly, they agreed.

"Where do you think he went?" asked Brenda once they had closed the doors to her room. "And why would the sheriff know where he is but not tell us?"

"I don't know," said Bobby. "But I don't feel any better now than I did before. If he isn't home tomorrow morning, we're going to have to look for him."

They sat in worry a bit longer before trying to get some sleep, but it didn't come easy. The wind was strong. The tree branches pawed at the side of the house scratching the windowpanes, a constant reminder of their growing fear. Brenda lay awake with her arms under her head as she stared intently at the ceiling. Tears welled in her eyes. Stevie was her best friend. She had a hunch the sheriff didn't have a clue as to where Stevie was, and she feared he was as dead as the gravedigger at the cemetery. Stevie was loyal to a fault and did whatever he could to please her. He was eternally grateful to Brenda for saving his life, and she just couldn't rest while he may be in danger. She *wouldn't* rest if he was in danger. She was going to do whatever it took to help him, even if it meant putting her own life at risk.

Bobby was just as restless. He lay in bed with his arms folded and his brow knotted. Looking out the window in his room, he searched for answers that weren't there. A lone tear fled the corner of his eye as he thought about Stevie. He wasn't so sure that the sheriff really knew where Stevie was, either. Instead he had a strong sense of the malevolent force at work, and the thought of what that beast might do to Stevie scared him. He was determined he would not let his fear paralyze him. He would see this through to the end. Too many people he cared for were getting hurt. He would double his efforts at finding a solution, even if it meant putting his own life at risk.

After a fitful night, Bobby and Brenda fell into a light slumber before dawn. They then awoke with more fatigue than if they hadn't slept at all, and were listless at breakfast. Auntie Arlene was almost mute, a rarity for her. Uncle John ate quietly, but then, after clearing his throat, spoke to them before going off to work.

"Okay, you two. Listen up. I called Stevie's house this morning. They confirmed what the sheriff told me last night and believe Stevie will come home later this morning. But I'd like to know from you two. Do you have any idea where Stevie is? Did he run away from home for some reason? If he did, whatever happened can be worked out if we know that he is safe."

Brenda offered the same partial truth she had given the night before. "Dad, really, we haven't seen him since early yesterday. Okay?"

Brenda's father sat there for a moment staring at the both of them. "All right, honey, I believe you. But if he does get in touch with you, please convince him he needs to call his parents. Fair enough?'

"Sure, Dad."

"And you two be extra careful today. I want you to stay together until all of this is resolved. Don't go anywhere except to town and back. No exploring or hiking through the woods for a while. Understand?"

Brenda rolled her eyes a bit, accompanied by a heavy sigh.

"Brenda Jean..."

"Okay, okay, I promise we'll be careful."

Uncle John stood up from the table and bent over to kiss his daughter, winked at Bobby, and left for work.

Bobby leaned in to his cousin. "We need to go."

"Thanks for breakfast, mom, we're going outside now."

Her mother grunted her approval, added her own comments about being careful, and proceeded to clean up the dishes. Bobby and Brenda were frantic as they raced for their bikes.

"We have to find the sheriff and find out where he thinks Stevie is. If we think he's not right, we need to somehow convince him to see things our way."

"What, you want to tell him about the spirit of the pirate? He'll laugh us out of town!"

"If we have to," Bobby would gladly be ridiculed by the sheriff or anyone else if it meant that they'd find Stevie. "Where do you suppose the sheriff might be right about now?"

Brenda smirked. "Where else?" she posed.

They went straight to the Baker Street Café and locked their bikes before going inside. Sure enough, the Regulars were all seated in their usual cubby. Everyone was present: Moss, Jinx, and Sheriff Musgrove. Even Mayor Block was there, now fully recovered from losing his guts at the cemetery. Moss and Jinx occupied one side, with the mayor and sheriff crowding each other out on the other. They both had such girth the sheriff was actually perched on the edge of the seat. Each person had a full cup of java, and Sharon had wisely set a fresh pot down in the middle of the table. The mood was somber, as the discussion centered on recent events and what to do about them.

The bell over the door announced Brenda and Bobby's arrival. They walked to the back of the café as if going to Saturday morning detention. What seemed like such a good, even uplifting, idea before now seemed stupid and downright foolish. Who was going to believe them? They didn't before, and they wouldn't now. They panicked, as they got closer. Both sensed that they were making a mistake, but then both thought about Stevie.

"Sheriff Musgrove?" began Brenda. "We have to talk to you. It's about Stevie Nichols, my best friend. We may have some information that could be helpful concerning his disappearance."

The polite smile on the sheriff's face faded with each word she spoke until he was left with nothing but a look of stern reproach.

"What do you know about the boy's disappearance, young lady?" he asked.

"We...that is my cousin, Stevie and I, we were looking into the connection between the recent murder and my dad's assault. Stevie was tailing one of our suspects yesterday and..."

"You what? " the sheriff exploded. "Did I hear you say you were tailing suspects?"

"Not us, exactly, but Stevie was. That's what I'm trying to explain. You see..." Brenda's lip quivered and then she broke down and cried, all the tension she felt in the passed twenty-four hours coming out in a torrent of tears.

Moss and Jinx were transfixed, unable to pick up their mug or take a sip. Mayor Block began to look like he had up at the cemetery. The sheriff unconsciously sensed this and moved further into the aisle.

"Why don't you start from the beginning, young lady, and tell me exactly what you know," demanded the sheriff.

The tears kept coming, however, and were hard to turn off. Sharon came to the rescue. Wrapping her arms around Brenda, she helped her over to the counter, and produced a glass of water to help calm her down. The sheriff started to protest, but then turned his attention towards Bobby. His eyes bore into him like a laser.

"Okay, young man, let's start with you. What do you know about all this? And tell me everything."

Bobby took a deep breath. He knew full disclosure was the way to go, for this was a last ditch effort in trying to get official help. He began with the day he woke up in his new home in London and how he knew from his dreams that something was wrong. He told the sheriff about the dream on the plane where he first met the pirate, his ghostly encounter while craw fishing, and the ominous warning he received through Madame Tarot. He continued with the conclusions he had drawn regarding the evil spectral force at work, how he must be soliciting someone's help in town, and how they all believed that recent events were connected. He finished with a brief description on how they had been conducting their investigation and Stevie's role in tailing some of their suspects. He told the sheriff that Stevie had planned to go to Mr. McCormack's house.

When he was finished, Bobby glanced at his audience and tried to gauge their reaction. Moss and Jinx had the same dull look they always had, although it did seem a bit duller. The mayor, leaning across the table so he could see around the sheriff, had his mouth open in shock. A bit of drool pooled on the table in front of him. By this time Brenda was feeling better and back at Bobby's side. The sheriff looked at them both with a mixture of anger and frustration.

"Listen to me, the both of you. I don't know if you're trying to be funny or if you are really serious, but I've never heard anything so ridiculous in all my life. Ghosts? Pirates? Connections between random crimes? You are letting your imaginations run absolutely wild. Your friend, young lady, probably ran away from home for the night. He had an argument with his dad the day he went missing, something about missing tools, which I'm sure you did not know about. His dad says that Stevie's done it several times before when they've had an argument, and usually camps out in a friend's backyard before coming home for lunch the next day. Shucks, I did that myself when I was his age. But, just to cover all the bases I have my deputy out looking for him, and I will speak to Mr. McCormack to see if he knows anything about it. I will also speak to your father about you all running around 'tailing' people, which is dangerous as it is. I expect the two of you to go straight home and stay out of trouble. Do you both understand?"

"Yes, Sir," responded Bobby.

The sheriff looked at Brenda, who gave him a brief nod.

"And I'm going to stop by your father's store and fill him in on what you just told me. You two scoot on home, and I mean now!"

As soon as Bobby and Brenda emerged into the late morning sun, Bobby declared, "That's it. I'll never ask another adult for assistance in this. They just won't understand. And now we can't go home, or we'll be grounded by your dad. Stevie is missing and it's up to us to find him. We must go to Michael's first."

"You go on to Michael's," Brenda said, "I'm going to try and retrace Stevie's steps. Maybe I can turn up something that will help us."

"I'm not so sure that's wise, Brenda. It may be too dangerous. We shouldn't split up. Let's go to Michael's first and..."

"Look, Bobby," Brenda interrupted. "We don't have much time. We have to split up. But don't worry, whatever happened to Stevie, he didn't see it coming. I'm forewarned, so I'll be doubly careful. Besides, I know Stevie better than anyone, so I stand a good chance of finding a clue as to where he might be."

"Okay," said Bobby. But we'll meet back here at no later than 5:00. Then we'll decide what to do."

Brenda went in the direction of the McCormack property, and Bobby biked towards Michael's house. Both had a sick feeling they were rushing headlong into trouble.

Bobby arrived at Michael's house, now anxious to hear what he may have found out. Michael's mother came to the door with a smile. She was clearly pleased to see Bobby. "Michael's not here right now," she said. "But could we just sit on the porch for a moment?"

Bobby was in a hurry to see Michael, but he fought back his frustration and said, "Yes, ma'am."

Bobby noticed that there was new furniture set on the front porch, that had not been there the first time they visited. Besides being comfortable, the white wicker frame and thick, colorful cushions of the chairs took away the mysterious and foreboding look of the house. It still needed a paint job, but the furniture softened the look considerably. Bobby sat down on one of two chairs flanking a small table.

"It is Bobby, isn't it?"

"Yes, ma'am."

"Bobby, I need to talk to you about Michael. I know that you know that Michael is...different than other kids. That is, he responds differently to situations where most people have a shared, common response."

"Yes, ma'am, you mentioned this yesterday."

"The thing is, Michael makes quick attachments and he has grown quite fond of you and your friends. He sometimes has a difficult time showing that, and may even appear to ignore you at times, but I assure you his affection is genuine."

Bobby sat squirming slightly, wondering where Michael was and whether or not he was going to find out anything today that would be helpful. The wriggling was not lost on Mrs. Kelleher.

"The thing is this," she repeated, but getting to the point, "Michael was hurt where we used to live. Not physically, but hurt nonetheless. You see he has something called Asperger Syndrome, and he struggles with how to relate to people. They say it's a form of autism. Do you follow? "

Bobby shook his head yes.

"On a dare, some kids in our old hometown befriended him. When they were done with their little game, they abandoned him, but that wasn't the worst of it. They then started teasing and taunting him. Michael tried to take their betrayal in stride. 'Easy come, easy go,' he would say. But he was truly upset by their abuse. So much, we thought it better to move. Can you understand what I'm trying to say, Bobby?"

"I think so, Mrs. Kelleher. I'm not really sure what autism is, but the three of us knew Michael was different from the beginning." He didn't bother to relate Stevie's unfriendly comments. "And I will say that we ignored him because of it. We didn't want to be mean. We just didn't understand. But since we've come to know him, I do think that we might all become good friends."

Bobby didn't know if he said too much or not enough. But then he noticed the tears forming in Mrs. Kelleher's eyes.

"Thank you, Bobby," she whispered. "What you said means the world to me. I'll just say one more thing and then let you go. If you ever tire of Michael, please just be honest with him. He responds to a direct approach much better."

She took out a tissue and blew her nose. "And now, I've taken up enough of your day. Thank you again, and please know that you and your friends are welcome here at any time."

"Mrs. Kelleher, do you know where Michael is?" asked Bobby, trying to mask his growing desperation.

"Oh, of course. He went to the library. He insisted on going alone. He said he was doing a research project, but he wouldn't tell me what it was about. He has a lot of interests and I'm trying to ..."

Before she could finish her sentence, Bobby had thanked her and run off. As he grabbed his bike, he looked at Mrs. Kelleher one last time. "Michael really is a great kid." He didn't see her wipe her eyes again as he sped to the library.

Brenda pedaled as fast as she could towards the McCormack property. Stevie was in trouble, she knew that for sure. She decided that she didn't believe the sheriff's story about Stevie's whereabouts. Stevie would have contacted them, even if he did have a fight with his dad.

She refocused and tried to think like Stevie would think. He was nothing if not cunning. He would be devious about his approach to the McCormack property. He would enter from an angle, sneaking up to it like a secret agent. So, she wondered, where could he do that?

She pondered that as she pulled up to the McCormack driveway. Definitely not this way; if he went straight down the drive, he could be seen a mile away from the house or the road. The only way that a clandestine entry appeared feasible was to the north, towards the lake. If he were going to be sneaky about it, that's the way he would have gone. She hurried towards the lake. Just before the parking lot, she noticed the small path Stevie had told her about when he pulled that pumpkin prank last Halloween.

She walked her bike over and tried to see where it led. She walked in a bit to get a better view. As she walked, she kept looking to her left and right as well as behind her. She had the eerie feeling she was being watched, but tried to dismiss that thought as quickly as it came. "How could someone be watching me?" she murmured. "No one even knows I'm here." Nervous as she was, thoughts of Stevie in trouble spurred her forward. She could see the main trail and raced on ahead, her heart beating rapidly.

She arrived at the juncture of the two paths and paused. *This new one comes from the parking lot,* she thought. It occurred to her that from here Stevie would have gone on foot, so he probably stashed his bike. She looked around for a place where he might have hidden it and noticed a flash of light. The sunlight bounced off the rim of what looked like a tire. She rushed over, moved some loose brush, and, yes, there it was: Stevie's bike!

Bobby got to the library in record time. He pushed through the entrance and searched for Michael. The library was crowded today, with youngsters taking advantage of the special summer programs. The librarian, Ms. Smith, was perched at her desk like a hawk-eyed sentinel, making sure no one escaped with an unstamped book.

She saw Bobby and her back stiffened. On his last visit she had identified him as another short-cutter on the road to research.

Bobby looked at the computers but didn't see Michael. After a moment's panic, he noticed that Michael was just beyond the computer bank, sitting at a long table all by himself. Michael's head was buried in an old book, one that still bore a lot of dust and had a musty smell that didn't seem to bother him. It took Bobby three more steps before Michael finally caught sight of his new friend.

Bobby's "Hi, Michael" was quickly followed by a loud "SHHH!" delivered by the librarian. Michael didn't lift his head out of the book, but acknowledged Bobby with a raise of his hand.

As Bobby took a seat next to Michael, Michael got up without a word and went to place the timeworn book back on the shelf. Bobby understood that Michael had his own internal clock and nothing could move him beyond it. So he waited.

Finally, Michael returned and sat next to Bobby. "I have something to tell you," he began. But they were met with another loud "SHHH!" from the circulation desk. Michael got up and headed outside. Bobby, confused at first, followed. On his way, Bobby grabbed three very heavy reference books off the shelf and dropped them into the return slot. Ms. SHHH! would have a little work to do putting those away.

Once outside, Michael stood there in the warm sunlight with his arms folded and a wide grin.

"I have your pirate," he said with his finger pointed towards the sky.

"You what?"

"I have your pirate. I researched the two names you gave me. The Housatonic River is in one of my books at home. It mentioned the diary of a sailor. I found more information about the diary in a book at the library, called *Black Bart's Treasure.* The diary had a story about a night where everyone aboard the ship had to stay below decks or be killed on orders of the captain. It says the ship was docked down the river from a mountain that looks like an old man. That's our mountain. The captain of the ship was Bartholomew Jones, also known as Black Bart. He was a vicious pirate who killed lots of people. He hijacked lots of ships and lived around the Long Island Sound. I think he buried his treasure by our mountain," Michael concluded.

"I know you're right, Michael, I can feel it! Brilliant work!"

"Why are we looking for someone who is dead?" asked Michael.

"Michael, I know it's hard to believe, but this pirate lives. At least as a spirit. He's been haunting my dreams and searching for his treasure. I know he's somehow responsible for an attack on Brenda's father and a murder up at the cemetery. He's working with someone here in town and we're trying to find out with whom. No adult believes us or will help us. Do you believe me?" Bobby asked after a brief pause.

"Yes," Michael said simply.

"Why would you believe me when no adult will?" asked Bobby, somewhat incredulous.

"Because I don't think you would lie to me," said Michael. "I can't always tell when people are lying, but I know you're not."

Bobby couldn't believe his ears. Here was someone who was supposed to have trouble relating to people, but was willing to put his faith in Bobby's fantastic story. He promised himself not to let that trust be misplaced.

"I'm afraid there's more bad news, Michael. Stevie is missing."

Brenda ran along the path towards the lake. She kept looking left towards the McCormack property for an entry point as she ran. Moving on a bit further, she saw a small footpath breaking through the underbrush. After a few feet she saw the "NO TRESPASS" sign with the not so welcoming comment underneath.

Brenda ran as fast as she could to the barn in the distance. She was panting when she got there. She noticed an open window on the side of the barn and guessed that was where Stevie must have entered. She walked around to the front, noticed no one was home and the barn doors were wide open. She went inside to look around.

It was dark in the barn—the kind of darkness that demands walking and speaking softly. "That's a foolish thought," she murmured. But she also knew that sometimes it was foolish to disturb the dark. Conquering her fear, she cleared her throat. "Stevie?" she called out. "Stevie?" she continued, more boldly this time.

All was quiet, but then she heard a noise near the rear of the barn. Tip-toeing to the back, she picked up a stick along the way and held it like a baseball bat. As she peeked around the fencing in the back of the barn, she saw chickens meandering outside their cages on one side and a cow on the other. She breathed a sigh of relief, but was disappointed to find no trace of her best friend.

She walked back outside and looked at the house. *Was he in there?* she wondered. *And if so, did McCormack catch him? And if he was caught, where would he be now? Did McCormack hold him prisoner somewhere?* After a moment's consideration, she decided on the basement as the most logical choice. She tried the front door first, which was locked. She then went to the door at the rear of the house. It was locked also. No windows were ajar either. Examining the basement windows, she saw that they were big enough to sneak through, but also locked. She looked around and picked up a good-sized rock. She broke the glass, reached in, and unlocked a basement window. Pushing it open, she slipped in feet first and stepped onto a thin table pressed against the wall.

She waited a moment. Her eyes needed time to adjust to the dim light. The air was stale, musty, and smelled like wet charcoal. When she could finally see, she jumped off the table and picked up a flashlight that lay there, searching the large room. She flicked the light into the dark corners looking for something—anything—that would indicate Stevie had been there. She found nothing. Disappointed, she climbed up the creaky stairs that led to the first floor and tried the handle. Locked. She pounded on the door screaming for her friend. She was so desperate, she didn't care if anyone else heard her too. Nothing but stillness and sore fists for her efforts.

She wanted to cry, but stopped herself. This was no time to lose it. She wiped her nose and decided she would go onto the front porch and break another window to get inside and search the upstairs. She walked over to the table and climbed on. She reached the window and began to pull herself up. As she scurried out onto the grass, two strong hands grabbed her wrists and pulled her upright.

She stared into the face of a nightmare. "You!" she screamed.

One of those hands covered her face with an odd smelling cloth. In seconds she saw nothing but night.

Part 8

Day of Reckoning

30

Bobby spent most of the afternoon confirming the information Michael had given him and thinking about a plan of attack. Fear gripped his heart and squeezed it like a vise. "How are we going to do this?" he wondered aloud. A feeling of self-doubt crept in, threatening to rob him of his will.

As he struggled with a plan, thoughts of Stevie crept into his consciousness. He had no sense of Stevie being killed, no feeling or vision in that regard. But he did imagine his new friend tied up, alone, and worried that no one knew where he was. The thought of that filled him with anger. He hurried back to the café, as he had much to tell Brenda when she got back.

Armed with information that he hoped would guide them all towards their final destination, they needed to strategize for the eventual rendezvous with their nemesis. Bobby parked his bike in front of the café and waited outside for Brenda. It was already late afternoon and there was no sight of her. He waited for an hour, until it was 5:00, a nervous feeling creeping up from his stomach. *Maybe she went home already*, he thought. Bobby stayed for another five minutes and took off in the direction of Brenda's.

Bobby parked his bike in the garage and noticed Uncle John's car was there. He came in through the mudroom and greeted his Auntie Arlene, who was preparing dinner.

"Hello, Auntie, hope you had a good day."

"Hello, Bobby dear, and yes, all things considered, it was okay," she said, the worry about Stevie written all over her face.

Bobby looked around and didn't see Brenda either helping her mom or sitting at the table. "Is Brenda home yet, Auntie?"

"Isn't she with you?" she asked, alarmed.

"No," said Bobby. "I needed to go to the library for something, and Brenda decided to stay uptown for a while. I haven't seen her since late this morning."

"Oh my," she said softly. "Then where...John!" Auntie Arlene shouted while drying her hands on a small towel. "John!"

Uncle John walked briskly into the room, troubled by the tone in his wife's voice. "What is it? What's the matter?"

"Oh, John," she sputtered, "it's Brenda. Bobby said she was going to stay up town this afternoon, but she hasn't made it home yet. Did she stop in your shop?"

"No, I haven't seen her at all today."

"Oh, dear!" Fear for her missing daughter was rising slowly.

"Now wait just a minute," he said with his hand up like a stop sign. He turned to Bobby, who had thought that Brenda would certainly have been home before her dad.

"Bobby, when did you last see her?"

"This morning, outside the Baker Street Café. I was going over to Michael's house and then the library, but she wanted to stay up town for a bit before coming home," he said, now worried that their plan had gone awry.

"Oh, dear God," his auntie implored, while wringing her hands.

"Bobby," his uncle continued, "do you have any idea where she might be?"

"No, sir, I really thought she would be home by now," Bobby said. Although he had grown to like and respect his Uncle John, he remained adamant about not telling another adult about his suspicions and their plans. Still, he now knew that Brenda was in peril. If he told his uncle the full story, perhaps he would listen. But what if he didn't? What if he thought his story was ridiculous rubbish, just like the sheriff and mayor? His uncle would probably be angry with Bobby and keep him at the house, forbidding him to go out and search for his cousin. *No,* he thought, *I know what I need to do.*

"I'm going over to the sheriff's office," said Uncle John.

"I'm coming with you!" Auntie Arlene said, ready to leave that very instant.

"No. I'm going out to search for Brenda with Hank or I'll be looking for her by myself if he's not in." Uncle John held her shoulders. "I know this is hard, but we don't know anything yet, and you have to be here in case she shows up or calls. I'll be home as soon as I can." He then kissed her on the forehead and left in a rush.

Once he was gone, Bobby put his arm around his auntie and tried to console her. He sat her down at the table and told her everything would be all right.

"I'll just go upstairs for the rest of the night, if that's all right with you," he told her. His auntie sat there and stared into nothingness before burying her face in her hands.

Bobby went to his room. He had decided that he and Michael were on their own now. Something told him that time was running out, and he had to act immediately. So he went into Brenda's room and grabbed a backpack. He stuffed it with a flashlight and a Swiss army knife. He looked around for anything else that might be useful and grabbed a few more things on her desk, including a small mirror, and threw it all into the backpack. As he turned to leave, he paused at the doorway. He looked back at her room, nostalgic for her voice, worried for her safety. He hurried back into his room, jammed a jacket into the backpack, and climbed out the open window.

There was an old maple tree next to the house just outside Bobby's window. It had a thick, long, branch that reached just below the windowsill. It was easy for him to step onto it while holding the limb just above it. A series of lower branches led him to the backyard. Sneaking his bike out of the garage, he was on his way in minutes.

Thinking about his only daughter, John Watson was now in a state of controlled panic. Brenda was his only child and he was not going to rest until he found her. He pulled into the station with a roar and his car slid to a stop on the loose gravel. He turned off the engine, jumped out of his car, and jogged up to the door of the sheriff's office. He jerked open the door and yelled for Sheriff Musgrove.

"Hank! Hank, are you here?"

Marge Connors, the police dispatcher, who would normally be home at this hour, was on the job and very busy. Stevie hadn't made it home by lunch, as the sheriff had predicted, so there was now an all-out search for the boy in place. Some volunteers from the town, assisted by part-time police specials were canvassing the neighborhoods and handing out flyers. Marge was the one to coordinate their efforts, and she sat at her desk pouring over a map of the town. Before she even had an opportunity to respond to John, there was a shout from the rear of the building.

"Margie, who's there?" the sheriff boomed.

"Hank it's me, John Watson. My daughter's gone missing!" The comment made Margie's eyes go wide.

"What's that you say? Your daughter?" Hank queried as he hustled up to the front office.

"That's right. She never showed up for dinner, which isn't like her. I need you to look for her and I'm coming with you."

"Hold on, John, we can't just go off willy-nilly. And right now we're conducting a search for that Nichols boy." The sheriff looked at the floor and scratched his five o'clock shadow, looking embarrassed. "He didn't show up like I expected, but I still think he ran away from home for a day or two."

"Well, now my daughter hasn't shown up, Hank, and I don't think she ran away."

"Maybe she's with the Nichols boy, John. They are good friends, right? But, let's start at the beginning. Do you have any idea where she might be?"

"No," he said a bit taken aback, "I don't. She stayed in town this afternoon, but she's always home by five o'clock, Hank. She is never late. Never. Not without telling us. She's missing, Hank, like her friend Stevie, and I can't sit home and do nothing. I just can't. "

"All right, all right, I understand. Let's think this through. Who was the last one to see her?"

"My wife's nephew, Bobby."

"Where was that and when?" said the sheriff, trying his best to sound important, official, and in control as the chaos mounted.

"Late morning in front of the Baker Street Café. He said he went to the library while she stayed in town. That's all I know."

"Did you say this morning… in front of the café?"

"Yeah."

"Hmmm," mused the sheriff. "I tried to get over to see you today, John, but I had to interrogate my prisoner over the disappearance of that Nichols boy. Then I just ran out of time and forgot to."

"See me? About what?" he demanded.

"Your kid and her cousin came into the café this morning to see me. They said they had some information on their missing friend, Stevie Nichols. I heard them out, John, I swear. The mayor was there as well. I mean, their story was so utterly ridiculous, no one would believe it."

"What did they tell you?" he asked, his voice high and shrill.

"They gave me some wild story about a lost treasure, spirits appearing to your nephew and threatening him, and how the murder up at the cemetery was related to your attack, as well as to the disappearance of that Nichols boy. They even said they were trailing suspects, if you can believe that. I told them they were letting their imaginations get the better of them, that they were going to get into trouble, and they should go on home and let us do the police work. Or something like that. Look, John, I gave them what I thought was sound advice—the same advice I'm sure you would have given," he finished, sounding defensive. "I was going to stop in to tell you about it, but I got distracted and just plain ran out of time."

John Watson didn't know what to think, as he clenched his fists and tightened his jaw. Why hadn't Brenda mentioned any of this to him? It was a fantastic story and not at all believable, but did he have to point out the obvious to the sheriff?

"Even if their imaginations were running a bit wild," he shouted, "don't you think a rash of incidents like this is a bit too coincidental?"

"Maybe so," the sheriff reluctantly agreed, "but I didn't want them to get hurt by following people like Tom McCormack."

"Isn't he in jail now?" John asked, furrowing his brow.

"No, I couldn't keep him, actually. I had to let him go this afternoon. He claims he never saw the Nichols boy and wouldn't know him if he tripped over him. I had nothing else to hold him on, so I sent him home. Also, the reports came back on that shovel with the blood on it, and it turned out to be what he said it was: chicken blood. He butchered one of his chickens with it last week. I thought for sure we had him dead to rights on your assault, but I guess I was wrong," he said, rubbing the back of his neck.

Brenda's father became very excited all of a sudden, the words tumbling over each other to get out.

"Hank, don't you see? You let him go this afternoon. My daughter's been missing since this afternoon. Another coincidence? I don't think so. I'm going out there to check for my daughter. Now."

"I can't let you do that, John. Letting you go out there all upset and angry wouldn't be right. And you could make matters worse."

"I don't care about right, Hank. I'm going out there, with or without you."

The sheriff paused, thinking about how to handle this. "Oh all right, I'll drive and you can come with me on two conditions," he finally said. "You let me do the talking and you don't go crazy when you're out there. If you do, John, I swear I'll put you in handcuffs and make you sit in the back of the car. Understand?"

"Fine, let's go."

Sheriff Musgrove radioed his deputy, who was home on a quick break eating pizza in front of the television and catching up on what Vanna was wearing on *Wheel of Fortune.*

"Yeah chief?" said Tim Carver.

"Another kid's gone missing, Tim. John Watson's girl, Brenda. She's been gone since this afternoon. John is here in my office. He and I are taking a ride out to Tom McCormack's. I want you to meet us there, pronto. Capisce?"

"Yes, Sir, I'm on my way. Ten four." He gobbled the remaining slice of pizza, took one last look at his digital ladylove, and ran to his car while buckling his holster.

They all met at the entry to the property and proceeded up the long drive to the McCormack house. Deputy Carver didn't dare ask the sheriff to turn on the sirens. Before they even got out of their cars, Tom McCormack was at the front door.

"What now?" he shouted.

"Simmer down, Tom, we're here on official business."

"Oh really, and here I thought you came by to have a beer and discuss politics." He looked at the deputy standing there with his feet spread, his thumbs in his holster belt, and his hat drawn down over his brow. "And what are you posing for, the cover of *Rambo* magazine?"

"I said, simmer down," the chief said firmly. "We've got another missing person, John Watson's little girl, and I plan to ask you a few questions about it."

"Oh you do, do you? I'm sorry the girl's missing, but I ain't had nothin' to do with it, or any of the other crazy stuff you're accusin' me of. Sure I got a temper, and no, I don't like kids, but I never hurt one, and I never would. If any of 'em showed up here I'd just chase 'em off, with maybe a boot in their keister for good measure. And I ain't seen anyone else since you turned me loose after a false arrest. If you really want to earn your salary, why don't you find out who it was that vandalized my property since you arrested me? My basement window's been busted and someone was down there."

The sheriff and his deputy checked out the broken window. Then the sheriff and John Watson went inside and looked around the basement while his deputy checked the outside grounds. The footprints in the basement dust looked like a child's print about the size of Brenda's foot. The sheriff and Brenda's father shared a worried look. Suddenly, they heard a cry from Deputy Carver. They ran out and found him not too far from the window. He was holding something up with a pair of tweezers he always carried in his shirt pocket.

"Chief, I found this hanky in the bushes over there." He pointed towards a grass pathway leading away from the house. "Smell it, chief."

The sheriff took a quick sniff. "Chloroform," he whispered. Turning to his deputy he added, "Bag it, Tim."

The sheriff turned and pointed at Tom McCormack. "We're going now, Tom, but don't you go anywhere. You're still a suspect."

McCormack just snorted as he banged the door shut.

"Let's go, John," the sheriff said. "We'll talk in the car."

John Watson gave the sheriff a disbelieving look. He raced after him and jerked open the car door.

"Why are we leaving?" he shouted, once inside the car. "My daughter was here, Hank! Those were her footprints and there's a chloroform soaked rag out there! Tom McCormack must have something to do with it! What more evidence do you need?"

"I don't think so, John. Think about it for a minute. McCormack's the one who drew our attention to the basement break-in, remember? If he hadn't said anything, we might have asked him a few questions and left. We wouldn't even know of the break-in. And that rag was dropped in the bushes away from the house, towards the path to the lake area. Tim and I saw some footprints leading in that direction. Whoever it was, they went over to the lake."

"Then let's go over there and look!"

"We will, John, but I'm afraid it's getting too dark to do a thorough search. There's no moon even and the lake area is huge. We're going to need help, and it takes time to organize a search of this magnitude. I'm calling in the State Police. I'll have them issue an immediate Amber Alert for both your daughter and the Nichols boy. The State Police will be out here with a boat and helicopter at first light so we can check the lake and surrounding area. It will take them a few hours to get their equipment here. Until then, you and I and Deputy Carver will search all night in some of the more accessible areas. Then you and I and Mr. Nichols will go out on the boat with the Staties at dawn"

31

It was getting dark. Without a light on his bike it was hard for Bobby to ride on a moonless night. There were streetlights to go by, but they were not as bright as a good headlight. If any cars approached, he would see their lights in plenty of time and pull off the road to avoid getting hit.

He arrived at Michael's without a firm plan. To knock on the door was to invite unwelcome scrutiny from Michael's mother, so he walked around to the back of the house. He could see Mrs. Kelleher in the kitchen. He walked to the side window of Michael's bedroom and noticed that the light was on. In the hopes of getting Michael's attention, he picked up some pebbles to throw up to the window. He grabbed a small round one and leaned back to throw. Just as Bobby was ready to release it, Michael surprised him by raising his window. He then dropped what appeared to be a rolled up, all-weather fire escape ladder. Bobby walked over as Michael reached the bottom step.

"Hi, Michael."

"Oh, I didn't see you," said Michael. Bobby had startled him. "Why are you in my yard?" Michael asked.

"You didn't see me? I thought you noticed that I was out here and you were coming out to join me."

"No, I'm going out because I discovered something important. I have to sneak out because my mother won't allow me to go out at night alone. She thinks I've gone to bed early. Why are *you* here?" asked Michael.

"Because now Brenda is missing, also. And I think I know where to find her. We need to try and find her now! There's no telling what this fiend could do to her. "

"I'll get my bike," said Michael.

"Wait a minute, Michael! What did you find out, and where were you going?"

"I was upset when you told me Stevie was missing. So I thought about it and I think I know where he might be. I was going to rescue him."

"What? You know where he is? How? Where?"

"When I first moved here, my mom took me to the school to see if I liked it enough to start there in the fall. The principal introduced me to the custodian, who was in the office. His name is Carl. I didn't like him, though. He acted like the kids who teased me at my other school. You had told me that he was one of your suspects, so I looked for information about him on my computer. I found out that Carl's middle name is the same as the first name of the pirate you wanted me to research. So I was thinking that is a coincidence except I don't believe in coincidences. Next, I found out where he lives and I called him up to ask him about it. He got very angry with me. He said that something bad could happen to me, like what happened to other people in town, if I don't mind my own business. That made me think Carl might be the person you are looking for. And if he is, then maybe he took Stevie and hid him someplace, like his office at school. That's where I was going, to check it out."

As soon as Michael had told him about this, Bobby bent over with a visionary headache. In his mind, he saw a picture of Stevie hanging somewhere, groaning in pain, and heard deep and disturbing laughter.

"Are you okay?" asked Michael.

Bobby stood slowly, shaking his head. "I'm fine, Michael," he said. "I need to think for a second." Bobby felt intuitively that Michael was right. He knew, though, that this was a gamble and he didn't have time to waste. He also knew that if they found Stevie, the three of them could then go after Brenda, increasing their chances for success. He decided to trust Michael as well as his instincts.

"You showed faith in me, Michael, so I'll show faith in you. If we don't find Stevie, maybe we'll at least find a clue to his whereabouts. So let's go!"

They quietly retrieved Michael's bike and rode to the school, avoiding any scattered traffic on the way. Within ten minutes, they were pulling into the long drive that fronted the school entrance.

Bobby thought about Carl being the one suspected of helping Bart. It made sense that it was a relative. A relative would be someone Bart could connect with more easily. Especially someone with a weak character, like Carl. Remembering Carl's look and behavior when they were playing ball at the school made it even easier to accept.

The school looked frightening in the dark. It was as if the brick walls had soaked up the vileness of its custodian during the day, only to leak it into the air at night. To Bobby, it hummed with evil. Buildings, Bobby believed, took on the essence of their inhabitants. Without the laughter and happiness that children bring during the school year, this building had no one but Carl to fill its days, and that wasn't a good thing.

They passed the front entrance and saw nothing but blackness. Although emergency and security lights were on at all times, they appeared dim, almost reluctant to share their lumens. They rounded the side of the school and headed towards the rear entry where the custodial office was located.

There were two ways to get to it. One was through a steel door in the boiler room that opened directly onto the asphalt playground. That would be impossible to open without a key. The other was through the main rear entry doors that led directly into the hallway. If they could get into the building there, they could reach the custodial office door. With a bit of hope, they tried the steel door first. No luck, it was locked tight. There was no window in the door and no way to open it from the outside. The main entry doors to the school were also shut and locked. The window glass in those doors was shatter resistant. That would not be an easy entry for them either. They were stumped.

"Come with me," Michael said, with his finger in the air, reminding himself to speak slowly and clearly.

"Where are we going?" Bobby asked.

"When the guidance counselor gave me a tour of the building, she told me about the interior courtyard. I asked her what would happen if someone got caught in there. She thought it was an odd question but said that if you're on the roof and fall into it, the doors to the school are not locked. That way, if you get into trouble, there is always a way out. They don't want anyone trapped in the courtyard even though they don't belong there."

"How does that help us?" Bobby inquired.

"You don't have to fall into the courtyard," Michael said matter-of-factly. "You can climb onto the dumpster by the cafeteria to get onto the roof. From there you can walk over to the courtyard. Then, we can hang from the roof, jump into the courtyard, and open the door to the school."

"Why would you even think to ask the counselor such a question?" Bobby asked him.

"When I saw the courtyard, I imagined being trapped in there," Michael said. "I wouldn't like that and so I needed to know how I'd get out."

Bobby was amazed at his friend's resourcefulness. How strange it was that Michael continued to be helpful in trying to aid the only one of their group who had tormented him.

They stashed their bikes, stood on a milk crate outside the school cafeteria, and stepped onto the dumpster. From there it was an easy climb onto the roof of the school. They ran across the flat roof, careful not to make much noise. When they got to the courtyard, they simply hung from the edge of the roof and dropped onto the loose gravel that covered the ground. They paused to look around and then raced for the door. It opened without fail.

32

Brenda started to come around. She felt drugged and was still in a dream state. Her eyes fluttered open and immediately began to tear. She wasn't quite sure at first what had happened or where she was. She felt pain in her shoulders, and quickly realized that her arms were twisted backwards with her hands tied behind her. Her knees were bent and her tied feet were connected to her hands behind her back. Lying on her side, she took in her surroundings. Flaming torches stuck into crevices along the wall in the corner of a large, domed shaped space. There were deep shadows all about her, dancing to the flickering light. There seemed to be a four-foot wide opening to the outside on one end. She could see a few stars in the night sky. The other end had a wider opening, but it was much darker, leading to the interior of the mountain. A damp smell and a strong undercurrent of body odor mixed with the burning fuel that lit the torches. She thought she was alone at first, but then heard rustling in a far corner. She glanced over, and knew immediately that she was in deep trouble.

A man that resembled a large bear was bent over at the waist, rummaging through a chest filled with clothing. "Where's my earring?" he muttered. When he didn't seem to find what he was looking for, he stood up to his full height of over six feet tall. He had long, black, stringy hair that looked unwashed. He wore a long coat that fell below his waist, almost to his knees, with wide, tapered sleeves that billowed at the wrists. Instinctively, he whirled around and looked in Brenda's direction. She found herself staring into the face of pure evil. His smile showed a row of sharpened, yellow teeth. His deep black eyes held no mirth. His shadowed face couldn't hide the downturned mouth that formed into a sneer.

With a jolt, she remembered what had happened and who was now standing before her. Her heart beat rapidly and her hurried breathing could be heard through the cloth tied around her mouth. She panicked and started hyperventilating. She knew she had to calm down and get control of herself, or she was going to pass out. She closed her eyes for a moment and forced herself to breathe more slowly. It took a few minutes but she finally relaxed.

"I thought we almost lost you again, miss," her captor laughed.

She was certain she was looking into Carl's face, but the accent wasn't his. It was him, the mean custodian, but then again it wasn't.

"You young ones are nosey and that will get you all killed. I warned the one from England. He wouldn't listen and now it will get him killed as well. I'll look forward to that one, I will. I'll take great pleasure in taking care of him," he said with wicked glee. "I'll save you for when I catch him and bring him here. I'll make him watch while I dispatch you, and then I'll take my time with him. He's meddlesome and dangerous. He has a power I've not seen before. I didn't want him to come here and use his power to interfere with my quest in any way, but he wouldn't listen. I'll rid the world of him soon, and then depart with my treasure."

Brenda began to choke on her gag. Her captor reached into his belt and withdrew a sharp knife, perhaps twelve inches in length. He grinned as he saw Brenda's eyes widen with fear. Taunting her, he stroked the tip of the knife, as if making sure it was sharp enough. He stood at her side, his dark, scuffed boots not two inches from her prone body. He reached down with the knife and she panicked again. He placed one hand on the side of her head and pressed. He slipped the knife under the gag tied around her mouth and sliced through it in seconds.

"Not yet, miss, oh no, not yet. Your time will come. Just be patient. I'll have time for you and your friend later. Oh, yes I will. But I'm busy right now, retrieving my goods."

"Who are you?" she managed to ask, her voice shaky and tentative.

"Who am I?" he repeated. "Why, I am the feared one, lass," he hissed. "I am the one who makes them shake in their boots when they see my colors flying. I am the one who was here long before you, and now that I have this new body to inhabit—the last of my line—I will be the one who will be here long after you."

Brenda had no idea what he was talking about. He seemed crazy, and so she didn't dare interrupt his strange tirade.

"I have roamed the spirit world far too long. I have come for my treasure and I will have it by sunrise. There is nothing to stop me now, certainly not that fool in the cemetery, who was friend to my heir, Carl."

"So you killed ...?" Brenda was horrified.

"Yes," he smiled proudly. "I am now a part of Carl, you see. My spirit inhabits his pathetic body that I now dominate, but a part of him still fights me. Soon I will be strong enough to subdue whatever remains of his pathetic soul. I whispered to him in the night many times in months past. He thought he heard voices at first but then I revealed myself to him in a dream. I told him we would accomplish great things together if he would only let my spirit enter him. There were riches beyond his imagination just waiting for him. He need only accept me into his life and they were his.

He feared me, though. Oh, he was evil—almost as evil as I—but he also had a fear that kept me at bay for a while. The fool shared my secrets with his friend who dug graves at the cemetery and that upset me greatly. He was lazy, you see, and he sought help from his friend. He thought the two of them could overpower me and take my treasure. But I checked my anger and spoke again of sharing so much wealth with him. I told him that there was enough for all of us to be partners. In the end, he was more greedy than afraid, which was his downfall. He convinced himself he could control me and so he let me enter his soul.

But he was wrong.

Once I entered his body I forced him to go to the cemetery. With me in control, we killed the other one. We then took his machines and brought them here to dig up my bounty. Carl had stolen tools and torches from your father at first, but this digger we now have is far better. And after I use him to operate it, I will destroy his soul entirely. Then the only other ones for me to get rid of, my young miss, are you and the boy. *After that,* I will disappear into this new world with the body and mind of this spineless descendant I inhabit, but with my own soul to guide me. That's who I am!"

He turned and then stormed out of the cavern through a slim opening that led him away from her and farther into the mountain. She heard the dissipating sound of his footsteps echoing off the walls of her stone prison and watched the fading light of the lone torch he carried.

Brenda started to weep silently, her whole body shaking as she did. How did this happen? How could she have been so careless? She had been so sure it was Mr. McCormack who was the source of all this mayhem, and she was so concerned about Stevie that she had failed to take precautions. Oh, Stevie! What had happened to Stevie? And where was Bobby? What about her parents? The thought of her mom and dad brought fresh tears to her eyes and she cried with abandon.

She wasn't sure how long it took, but eventually she stopped. The tears dried on her cheeks and she tried to focus. She would not let this beast take her away from her parents. She would not let him win.

And if, by chance, she did lose, she was determined to go down fighting.

Bobby and Michael entered the school with trepidation. When the door squeaked on its hinges, they winced, and peered down the darkened hallway. It was filled with stacked classroom furniture, pitch-dark monoliths standing mute in the darkened surroundings. Some piles gave the illusion of being tall, unmoving wraiths silently watching the boys as they entered their wicked realm. Bobby wondered if they had made the right decision coming this way, since they had left themselves no way to back out. If something went wrong, the only way out now was forward through the halls and whatever lay ahead.

Bobby had scoped out their route while they were on the rooftop, and he knew they were on the far side of the school. They needed to traverse the length of this hallway and bank right before finding their way to the custodial office wing. They slow danced their way around the furniture, unable to get an adequate view of the entire length of the hall due to the obstructions. Bobby thought of using his flashlight but decided against it, since the hall was visible from the front of the building. He was fearful that anyone passing, or perhaps the sheriff on patrol, would see his light and come to investigate. So they marched on in darkness, careful not to trip on anything.

They reached the end of the hall and needed to turn right towards the other side of the building. There, more stacked furniture impeded their progress. All was dim and deadly silent as they bent and twisted their way to the custodial office. Neither boy wanted to break the stillness, both fearful it might unleash something evil.

At last, they reached the wing of the school where the custodial office could be found. Since this hall was not visible from the front of the building, Bobby confidently took out his flashlight and turned it on.

"You can take yours out, too, Michael," he whispered.

In the new light the mysterious hallway shadows were revealed for what they were: old and overused desks and chairs that had served countless numbers of children over the years. Feeling braver, they moved a bit faster down the hall and zigzagged their way around the summer debris. They could finally see the back door that led to the blacktop behind the school. That would be their way out when the time came, since it was locked from the outside, but not from the inside. Right now, however, they sought the office door of the custodian. Led by Michael, they crept a bit further on and there it was: a thick wooden door with a small shatterproof window, barely large enough to peek through. The plastic sign screwed into the door said "Custodian."

Bobby tried the door handle. Locked! He had hoped fate would be on their side and this particular door would be unlocked. But he was wrong and his frustration was building. He looked into the window and shined his light. He saw a dark room with a metal desk and chair, fronting a wall with a corkboard hanging just above the top of the desk. On the far wall were open shelves with a variety of tools laid out. Next to those stood a lone school locker. They had no idea what was in it, but they looked at each other and both feared the worst. Other than that, the room looked empty. Now what would they do? They had played the only card they had and came up empty.

Could they break in? This door was made of thick wood and seemed impenetrable. The glass window was too small to make a difference, and it was shatterproof anyway. As his irritation grew, Bobby started to move some of the loose items in the hall. He reached for a fire extinguisher.

"What are you doing?" asked Michael.

"I'm looking for something we can use to hit the door handle. If I can snap it off, the door might open and we can get in," he said, his eyes darting around like a hungry owl.

But Michael just turned and moved down the hall.

"Where are you going?" asked Bobby.

"I remember seeing this other door in the hall when I was here, and I asked about it. I'm very curious about things I don't understand. The guidance counselor told me it was the door to the boiler room. I had noticed all the classroom doors had locks in the handles, but this one didn't and I was curious and asked. She said it didn't have a lock because of a possible emergency. In case there was a fire or something and they needed to get into the boiler room quickly. The boiler room is attached to the custodial office. Maybe there is a door in the boiler room that leads to the office."

Michael went in the direction of the boiler room, and Bobby followed. The door opened with a swish. A quick look to their right confirmed what they sought. There *was* a door to the custodial office in here. They ran over to it and turned the handle. Locked! They each pounded it with both fists. Dejected, they leaned against the office door and sagged to the ground, as the boiler room door to the hallway slowly hissed shut on its air-compressed hinge.

Stevie was half asleep, secured tightly to the metal rings behind him. He had tried screaming for help, for hours in vain. He was exhausted and felt convinced that no one was going to come to his rescue. The school principal was on vacation and would not be back for at least two weeks. That's what his captor had told him and he had laughed when he had said it. Stevie couldn't believe that he had been caught back at the McCormack property. When he finally awoke from being drugged, he was tied up to the back end of the school boiler, his jailor taunting him. At first, he thought it was Carl who'd caught him. He certainly looked like Carl, but this person was far more sinister than Carl. This Carl-like person had told him that an old and vicious spirit had invaded the custodian's body and created a new and improved Carl. Stevie had no trouble believing this was a new Carl, but he didn't think improved was the right word. His kidnapper had tied him to the school boiler and adjusted the dials so it would blow up by morning. "There won't be a trace of you left," the Carl-thing said. As his captor left, cackling wickedly, Stevie had begun to scream until he passed out from fatigue. He hung there in a stupor for what seemed like hours, but was suddenly roused by the sound of pounding. *Am I dreaming?* he wondered. When he heard the soft click of the boiler room door close, he knew he was not alone.

"Help!" he called out in a raspy voice. "Is anyone there?"

Bobby and Michael were shocked. Did they both just hear that? That sounded like Stevie!

"Stevie?" called Bobby.

"I'm here!" he shouted with more vigor. "Over here, behind the boiler! Help me!"

Both boys raced over to the far side of the boiler. There, tied with rope and hanging from two metal handles welded onto the boiler was Stevie.

"What took you so long?" he squeaked in a hoarse voice.

Bobby retrieved his Swiss Army knife from his backpack and began cutting him loose. As he did, he explained how Michael had figured out where Stevie was, and how Michael had been on his way to rescue him when Bobby arrived at his home. Stevie was dumbfounded. He couldn't believe that Michael was the one who had saved him from certain death. Michael, who he had thought of as "limited." Michael, who he had teased and called retard, thinking of him as somehow on a lower social scale than the rest of them. At that moment, Stevie felt deeply ashamed of himself.

"Thank you, Michael," was all he could manage verbally, but he swore that somehow he would make amends. He would make things right.

"What happened to you, Stevie?" Michael asked, as Stevie slumped to the ground.

"I got caught," he whispered. "I never get caught, but this guy nailed me. It's embarrassing. I never had a chance."

"Never mind that now, anyway," Bobby said. "We've got to go get Brenda."

"Why?" Stevie jumped up from the ground. "What's happened to Brenda?"

"She's missing, too, and I fear she's in danger. And if we hope to save her, we're going to need your help. Are you strong enough?"

"Try and keep me away," Stevie said as he hurried for the door.

The three boys left the boiler room and raced through the door at the end of the hall. Stevie quickly turned and placed a stone in the doorway to keep the door from completely closing. Directed by Michael, they went back to retrieve their bikes. Michael told Stevie to ride double with him because he was pretty strong and could pedal them both. Stevie hopped on without hesitation. As they approached the door to the school they had just exited, Stevie asked Michael to wait a moment. He dismounted and ran back inside.

"What are you doing?" Bobby called after him.

"Pulling the fire alarm. That creep who kidnapped me set the boiler to explode in the morning. As much as I'm tempted to let her blow, it's probably best to have the fire department come and investigate and make sure it doesn't. I would have done it before, but I first wanted to make sure we had a fast way to escape."

Stevie pulled the fire alarm in the boiler room, setting off an ear-piercing distress signal that would soon register at the fire station. He then ran back outside and hopped onto Michael's bike. With fire truck sirens in the distance, the three boys were pedaling furiously down back streets, moving rapidly away from the school towards an undetermined destiny.

34

Brenda noticed that it was still dark in her cave, but a great deal of time had passed since her captor had left her alone. She could hear a machine, intermittently whining and slamming into the earth, making the ground vibrate. *He must be digging treasure,* she thought. She tried working the knots that tied her hands, but without success. No matter what she did, she couldn't loosen them. It hurt when she tried, but she knew it was her only chance. She could feel blood dripping down her wrists from the constant rubbing. Brenda thought of her mother in the kitchen, cooking up something special. She could almost smell the food. Then she thought of her dad coming home. She thought of him saying, 'Does anybody care?' Tears formed, but this time she wouldn't cry. She refused to give in.

She stopped for a moment, listening. It was what she couldn't hear at that moment that disturbed her most. She could no longer hear the machine he used and wondered if he had found what he was looking for. She didn't have to wonder long. Within a few minutes, she saw the glimmering light from the torch he carried, bouncing along the walls of the tunnel outside the cavern. Soon, she heard his boots scuffle along the hard floor. As he entered the cave, her fear returned, making her feel cold all over. His face was haggard. Lines of worry now crisscrossed his repulsive features. He looked at her with disgust, as if she were something that needed to be wiped off his boot.

She had decided to try and keep him talking. But now, with him right there in the room, Brenda was terrified to utter a single word, especially since he looked so angry. She floundered in indecision, afraid she was going to lose the moment. Finally, she swallowed her fear and formulated a question.

"Did you find what you were looking for?" she stammered.

He turned his head and stared right through her. His eyes were black as the night, his dark hair even greasier, hanging loose from exertion. He bared his teeth like a rabid carnivore, drooling with saliva, and spoke with words that chilled her, his voice low and menacing.

"Aye, miss, I found it. It's none too lucky for you, though. It brings you closer to your painful end."

Brenda suppressed her fear and continued her questions, hoping to distract him.

"Why don't you have it with you then?"

"It's none of your concern!" he bellowed. He looked at her with disdain, but then continued, as if he were talking to himself.

"A minor delay. I need to remove my treasure from the rotting chest. It will take a bit of time, but no worries, my dear. It merely gives you more time to picture what is going to happen to you."

He took out his knife again and pointed it at her. "Perhaps I should start now!" he threatened. "Perhaps I should cut you into pieces and let the rats have a feast, eh? What do you think of that?" He laughed a full, throaty laugh that echoed off the walls of their small room, and, she was sure, out to the lake.

"Did you hear that?" asked Stevie. "What the heck is that, a coyote?"

"No," said Bobby, "it's *him!*"

They had traveled a good distance through the night to get to the lake, directed by Bobby's intuition and Michael's research. It took them longer than it would have in broad daylight. The roads were dark, especially the farther they got from town. There weren't many cars at this time of night, but their progress was slowed each time they stopped to hide when cars passed. Finally, they had arrived at the parking area for the lake. It would be a while before the sun rose, but the sky didn't appear as dark as it had been. They headed for the main trail to the lake, which skirted the McCormack property. That led them to the southern end of the lake and from there directly to the mountain.

Traveling on a hiking trail at night by bike is nothing short of treacherous. Tree roots were everywhere. They would reach out from the base of every tree, tripping them up as they went by. They all knew without saying, however, that their own danger could not compare to the one Brenda was now facing. The strange howling they just heard gave them a burst of energy, and they bumped and twisted their way to the foot of the lake.

The pirate turned away from Brenda and picked up a variety of cloth sacks. Like a demon possessed, he strode from the room and carried his sacks to the site of the treasure. He had thought feverishly about his treasure and its rediscovery for centuries. And now, by using the body of his last heir, it would soon be his again.

Carl had known there was treasure to be found. Others in town had thought it just a story, a fairy tale, something they told to their children on listless summer nights. But Carl knew. His job at the school gave him access to the computer lab whenever he wanted. Over the years he had tracked down whatever scraps of information he could find. But it was his discovery of a reference in a comic book on local history that had led him on his frequent trips to the lake. He then uncovered other references online that spoke of the original point of entry to the mountain that his ancestor must have used, but that was no longer available to him. Damming the river years ago had flooded the entrance to the cave once used by Bart.

Carl found a newer entrance, though. It was one that was very difficult to find, at first. It did not appear on anyone's maps or charts. It lay behind some brush growing out of the mountainside. He had discovered it on one of his many scouting expeditions to the area. Once he squeezed through the narrow opening and crawled on his belly for a long time, the entry opened up into a large fissure. And that had eventually led him to the original trail.

Carl had found the trail, but he would never have found the treasure burial site. He had no idea which twists and turns along the trail would lead him to the exact spot. Carl alone would have been lost inside the mountain for years. Bart was only too willing to help Carl, but he had a price. He wanted to occupy his heir's body. Once Carl allowed that to happen, he knew he was engaged in a futile battle to save his miserable life.

At Bart's prodding, it was Carl who had assembled the cemetery's winch at the outside entrance to the cave. It, in turn, was used to lift the digging machine up to where it was needed. That pulley would also lower the treasure when the time came. Bart had to admit, Carl had been useful. The time was nigh, however, for Bart to lay Carl's soul to rest and take over his body completely. He knew he was almost strong enough and it would happen very soon. Unfortunately, so did Carl.

By nightfall of the next day this body will be completely mine, thought Bart. He would then have the body that would provide him a chance at another life, and the treasure to make a new life worthwhile. He started to chuckle as he was feeling quite pleased with himself. Then he broke into a full-throated laugh. His unearthly laughter caused the sides of his earthly body to ache, as the frightening noise reverberated on the walls around him.

At the new sound of that hideous howling, the boys dropped their bikes and ran the rest of the way around the lake and towards the mountain.

"We'll never find a way inside to save her!" lamented Stevie.

"On the contrary," remarked Bobby, breathing heavily. "We know several important things. One comes from an obscure local history at the library that confirmed something for me. This lake was dammed, submerging the entry our adversary had used originally. Therefore, if we think they're in there, there must be another way inside. Two, we know Brenda was brought here recently, so I'll wager there are footprints about that will help point the way. Black Bart isn't expecting anyone to show up here, let alone us, so he won't be too cautious. And three, if we just heard that foul creature, they can't be too far off. We must be getting closer. Quick, we've got to hurry."

They continued to run faster than their strength allowed. They ran on the trail going around the lake, which, when it reached the mountain, veered off sharply to the left. After fifty feet, it connected with other hiking trails in the surrounding forest. They stopped at this juncture, gasping for air.

"Now what do we do?" asked Stevie, nearly breathless.

Michael raised a finger. "I think we should follow the mountain until we find the entry."

"Don't be a re..." Stevie started to say, immediately regretting it. "I'm sorry, Michael, old habits and all. No excuse though. Let me try again. The trail goes off to the left here, so shouldn't we just follow it?"

Michael put his finger up again. "The trail goes that way, but he took her in there," he said, nodding towards the mountain, "so we need to find the way inside by following the base of the mountain." Michael looked at Bobby for confirmation and got a nod.

"I agree with Michael," said Bobby. "The mountain is our key. We've got to follow its base and keep a sharp look for any clues." Stevie sighed and shook his head, but agreed.

Now off trail, they walked through the brambles and pushed aside branches that held them back, as if to prevent them from going farther. They were getting scratched and disoriented. With each difficult step, their minds kept telling them that time was not on their side.

Stevie moved around a large thorny bush and stopped in his tracks. He tried to call the others, but he was so fatigued, what came out of his mouth sounded like a whimper. It didn't matter, though. It got their attention. Bobby and Michael rushed over and saw what had excited Stevie. It was a slight, barely noticeable footpath that led towards the mountain, made of a loamy soil.

And on it, recent footprints.

Brenda's father was frantic. He hadn't slept, and couldn't even if he wanted. The sheriff dropped him off in the middle of the night so he could update his wife and prepare for the continued search with the state police. As he got ready, he noticed Bobby's door was closed and tried not to disturb him, thinking he could use all the sleep he could get.

His wife wanted to join the search, but he insisted that she stay home to take care of Bobby, and provide a warm welcome for them when they returned. He knew she wouldn't be able to stand the tension if she had to wait on the shore of the lake, or worse, at the state police checkpoint with the press and other gawkers. He also didn't want her present if the news was bad. If that were the case, he would rather tell her himself in private.

John met the sheriff at 5:00 a.m. and they picked up Stevie's father enroute. The sheriff headed for the lake parking area to join the state police. He was told there would be a helicopter in the air soon and they would be doing a thorough, coordinated search for the missing children. He, Mr. Watson, Mr. Nichols, and a state police officer would be on a boat looking for signs in and around the lake while the helicopter searched from above.

The sheriff had sent his deputy up to the lake earlier to work with the state police to set up a perimeter. They needed to keep the curious at bay. Sawhorses were strategically placed to detour traffic around the other side of town, and no one was allowed to pass without official permission. State police cars, with rooftop lights flashing, let everyone know this was official police business. The officers stood by their cars with their Smokey Bear hats on tight. No one dared challenge them.

The sheriff came upon the southern checkpoint and, after a brief scan of credentials by the officer in charge, he and his contingent were waved on through. A small crowd of onlookers had already gathered. It amazed the sheriff how little time it took for them to assemble, like turkey vultures at a road kill party. He knew there were quite a few people who monitored the police band radio and bad news spread like cholera. Not only was Bill Glean of the *Daily Mirror* there, but also representatives from other media organizations who were crowding around trying to scare up a story. There were a couple of TV vans from the networks getting set up. They drove through the mini-circus and then had a clear shot to the lake.

There were two parking areas. One led to the hiking trails that ran like veins through the surrounding countryside. The other was farther north about three miles, where they headed. That lot led to a man-made beach and boat dock. Some state police cars were already there when they pulled in. They quickly moved towards the dock where the boat was waiting.

There was one man on board the boat. He was short and stocky, built like a fireplug and just as hard. He spoke in a gravelly voice.

"Hello, Hank. Gentlemen," he said, nodding at Brenda and Stevie's dads. "I'm Lieutenant Wayne Wetzel." All three men shook hands.

"Lieutenant," said Mr. Nichols, "just how is this going to work?"

"We will be in constant contact with our helicopter and coordinating our search around predetermined grids. We'll finish searching one area before we move on to the next. I promise you, if your children are here, we'll find them."

The two fathers nodded, concern etched onto their faces.

"Just for the record," he continued, "I'm not a fan of you gentlemen being on board in case we find.... But, the sheriff is a friend of mine, and I guess if it were my child, I'd be right where you are."

"Okay, then," the lieutenant barked, not wishing to waste any more time, "life jackets, if you please."

They slipped on their life vests and managed to find a somewhat comfortable seat before the engine coughed into life. Within minutes, they pulled away from the dock and headed for the north end of the lake. Lieutenant Wetzel explained to them that after exploring the northern area, which could take a good hour, they would make their way south until the perimeter of the lake was completely investigated. If the helicopter saw something, they could be directed from up above.

"Don't worry, guys," said the sheriff in a tender moment. "We'll find them."

"I just hope we're not too late," Brenda's father muttered, saying what everyone else was thinking.

"There's only one set of footprints!" noted Stevie.

"Yes, but they appear very deep set. I'll bet he carried her here on his shoulders and then on into the mountain while she was still unconscious," said Bobby.

The boys were energized. Like hound dogs on a fresh scent, they moved bent over, following the footprints with their flashlights. Eyes probing the ground, they almost hadn't realized it when they arrived at the base of the mountain. The sun was starting to rise, but it was at a low angle and not high enough yet to give them the light they needed. What little light they had cast deep shadows. They still needed flashlights. The footpath, which took a definite turn to the left, hugged the base of the mountain.

"Quick!" said Stevie and started to run down the path.

"Wait a moment," said Bobby, holding his arm out to stop him. "There are no footprints down that way."

"Maybe he brushed them up after himself so no one would follow. Come on, it's the only way!" said Stevie.

"Wait!" Bobby said again. "He wouldn't be able to do that if he was carrying Brenda."

Michael stood off to the side looking around. He walked up to Stevie and tapped him on the shoulder.

"What?" said Stevie, exhausted and cranky.

Michael held up his finger.

"Okay, Michael, what is it? I see that your finger is up, what do you want to say?"

Michael just kept pushing his finger up.

"Michael, we don't have time to play twenty questions, spit it out already!"

Michael reached over and put his other hand under Stevie's chin, tilting it upwards. Michael hadn't wanted to say something, he was pointing at something. Stevie and Bobby both gazed up the side of the mountain and saw that Michael was pointing at a large bush growing out of a shadowed area that looked like a thin, dark opening. They wasted no time scurrying up the incline to reach the vegetation. Once there, it became clear that just behind the shrub was a crevice—a long, thin opening that led to the blackened interior of the mountain.

"I think we found it," whispered Bobby. Before leading them inside, Bobby took out his mirror and placed it in his shirt pocket and pocketed his Swiss army knife. He held onto his flashlight and dropped his backpack to the ground.

"Let's go," he said, took a deep breath and led them into the inky darkness.

It was taking hours to unearth his loot, far longer than Bart wanted, and it was making him viciously angry. He kept filling sacks with rubies, emeralds, and gold, and hauling them back to his cave. He would wait until he had accumulated them all before he would use the winch to lower them to the spit of land that jutted out into the lake at the foot of the mountain. He had hidden a raft there—or rather Carl had. He had used the raft to carry the digging machine to the pulley. Later, he would use Carl's truck, which he had hidden down a dirt-covered fire road, to escape with his treasure. Carl's soul would be dead but he would have all of Carl's knowledge and memories intact to guide him through this world. Now, due to the delay in retrieving his treasure, Bart would have to wait until the dead of night to avoid any scrutiny in his escape. No matter. He would occupy his time during the day to rid the world of the girl and that other one with the power.

The boy might prove the more difficult of the two, but the lad didn't suspect Carl of anything. He was confident that when he was fully in control of Carl's body, he would be able to sneak up on the boy near his home. Then he would bring the boy back to the cave and dispose of them both where no one would hear their screams. After that, he would make his escape. A delay of one day, but not one he would mind once he took care of those meddlesome children.

For now, he had to concentrate on his treasure. There was still too much to pack and haul. He would have to work faster, he told himself. It was heavy work, but he could rest for a lifetime once his spirit fully melded with the body of his descendant. He had to devote his energies to that as well, for Carl was stronger than he thought and he was still resisting him. That struggle took much of Bart's energy making the retrieval of his loot go slower than expected.

Were he a weaker man, he would have lost the fight and been doomed to roam the spirit world forever, but he was slowly winning. He knew it and more importantly Carl knew it. He could feel Carl's spirit getting weaker by the moment. He knew that if he could hang on until the next sunset, he would dominate Carl completely. Then the future would look quite different.

Brenda was working desperately to break free of her bonds, but was frustrated at every attempt. She caught her breath and tried a different approach. She began to rock back and forth. It was excruciatingly painful as her arms and legs were locked into position by her ties. Her goal was to make her way over to the pulley.

Perhaps then she could rub her hand restraints on the pulley to try and loosen or cut them. If this didn't work, she might be able to scream for help from the opening. Maybe someone would hear her desperate cries.

She was making good progress. One more jerk in the right direction and she would start to roll. There! She did it, but oh, did that hurt. Her limbs were stiff and the ground was hard and uneven. Rolling under the best of circumstances would have been difficult. This was turning out to be near impossible. There was even a slight incline towards the opening, forcing her to have to roll up hill. She tried again and the pain shot through her body from head to toe. She focused all her energy and mental acuity on this one task. She pushed, squirmed, and strained until…yes, she did it again.

Two more rolls and she would be at the base of the pulley. Then she would at least have something substantial to rub the ropes on. Right now, it was her only hope.

She pushed herself beyond the bounds of pain and endurance. Her arms ached so badly they were numb. Her mind refused to register the hurt. It was too busy trying to get her where she needed to go.

"Once more," she told herself. "Come on, Brenda, you can do it!" She was speaking to herself out loud, acting as her own cheerleader, and pushing herself forward.

There! She did it. "Now, just once more," she told herself while panting. "And this time it really is once more." She took a final deep breath and wedged her feet against a bump in the stone floor to give herself some leverage. Realizing she was very close to success, her adrenalin kicked in. She exhaled and pushed hard against her meager toehold. Just as she was about to fall into her roll, she saw *him*. *He* was standing there near the opposite entrance, bags of treasure in each hand. She was so busy trying to get to her destination that she hadn't seen or heard *him* arrive. Her heart sank and she collapsed with fatigue.

"Well then, lass, that could not have been easy for you to do. A noble effort, but I will tell you that if you attempt it again, I will help you to the pulley myself…and throw you out the opening!"

He reached down and grabbed the rope that connected her tied hands and feet and dragged her back to the side of the cave. Bart then pulled out his knife and thrust it under her chin, drawing blood. "Try that again and I will end your suffering like I ended your small friend!" *he* said, still angry.

Brenda jerked her head in his direction.

"Oh, yes, miss," he said, enjoying the look of fear on her face. "I already took care of one of your group. He thought he was clever, he did, scampering about the same farm where I caught you."

"Oh no, Stevie," Brenda whispered. "What have you done, you filthy beast," she screamed.

"I dragged his scrawny body to the school, chained him to a boiler, and soon he will be blown to bits," he said calmly. He leaned in close, his hot, foul breath wafting over her, and said, "and you will join him soon." He turned and left.

Nearly fainting from the pain, and the realization that Stevie was soon to die, she no longer had the strength or the will to try again. She had failed, and was ready to accept her fate.

Lieutenant Wetzel powered the boat around the shoreline in the northern sector of the lake one more time. He explained to his passengers to look for bent grass, areas where a boat may have anchored, strips of clothing, or any floating artifacts. Any sign that there had been people in the area. They all looked hard, but didn't find a thing.

The two fathers were hoping beyond hope that one of them would see something—anything—that would lead them to their children. Every breeze that moved the tall grasses, every turtle sunbathing on the rocks, and every discolored leaf that floated on the lake became a potential clue in their desperate eyes. They knew they had a lot of lake to cover and they were getting discouraged with each passing minute.

"I'm going to call the copter," barked Lt. Wetzel.

"*Chopper 1,* this is *Marine 1,* do you copy?"

"Go ahead, *Marine 1,* I copy, over."

"I've pretty well exhausted this area with no success and am now moving south. Head for the shoreline on that end of the lake, over."

"I roger that and I will follow suit. I've seen nothing in this sector to warrant a second look, over."

"Over and out."

Both the boat and the helicopter made wide turns. They continued their efforts along the edge of the lake and forest beyond as they headed in a southerly direction. Anxiety ran deep among them all. Although they would not say so out loud, all of the passengers sensed intuitively that they were moving headlong into a dire end to their search, and their children would be lost forever.

36

Bobby suddenly had an overpowering image of Brenda being in imminent danger and grabbed the sides of his head. "Hold on, Brenda," he whispered softly. "We're coming."

The corridor they found themselves in was dark and dank. "It's pitch in here and we're going to need our flashlights," Bobby yelled to Stevie and Michael, who were just behind him. The corridor was about three feet wide and six feet high, just enough room for one person to get through and push or drag another along with him. The thought of that beast dragging Brenda through here made him sick. The light of their flashlights was soon swallowed by the heavy darkness. Only a few feet in front of them were illuminated at a time. A short distance in, it became stifling hot.

"How do you know we're on the right track?" asked Stevie. "We can't even see in here."

"Because this is where the footprints lead us, for one," answered Bobby. "And… I can almost feel Brenda's presence in here, like a disappearing dream just before you wake up."

Bobby continued to move forward, afraid that with each step, he might be leading his friends to their sudden death. His light was getting dim and he shook the flashlight. He was upset with himself for not changing the batteries before he left, but he hadn't thought about it at the time. Now, he was fearful of walking into an unseen crevasse in the darkness and plunging to his end before reaching his cousin. He knew this was the way, though. He could feel it with every step.

They soon lost track of time as they picked their way along in the dark, overly careful about where they stepped.

"The ceiling is lowering," observed Bobby. It won't be long before we're going to have to crawl."

Stevie's puffed up bravado was taking a hit. "I'm not sure I can do this," he whined. "I don't like being cramped. I nearly freaked out when I was stuck in that boiler room and never thought I would see the sun again. That same feeling is coming back, and I don't like it. "

"Don't worry," said Michael. "You can do it. You did it before, and this time it's for our friend, Brenda."

Stevie turned towards Michael. He was confronted with a smile and a lingering finger pointing up. That put a grin on Stevie's face as well. They continued on in silence for a while. The hot, still air made it difficult to breathe, and in the silence that surrounded them they could hear each other panting.

Step by laborious step they plodded forward until the lowering ceiling made them get on their knees and crawl. They finally reached a point where crawling wasn't even an option. If they were going to go further, they were going to have to get on their stomachs and inch their way along.

"I'm confident this is the way." Bobby crawled on his stomach like a soldier on the battlefield. Stevie decided he wasn't going to complain anymore. He had made up his mind that he would be safe as long as Bobby was in front of him, Michael was behind him, and that he was doing this for Brenda. He worked on controlling his breathing and focusing on the bottom of Bobby's sneakers, which wiggled just in front of him. The air remained hot and stagnant and it made their movements difficult. The area they inched through was wider in some spots and tighter in others, but they continued crawling in tandem.

They rested occasionally, and were feeling the effects of the low ceiling. Their elbows ached from pulling themselves forward on their stomachs. Their legs hurt from dragging them along on the hard and bumpy surface. Their necks were sore from keeping their heads low to protect them from the rock just inches from the top of their skulls.

The silence was deafening, only adding to their disorientation. They were frightened, in pain, and worried about losing all control so deep in the mountain. Suddenly, the deathly quiet was pierced by Michael who began to sing:

"Yo ho, yo ho, a pirate's life for me.
We pillage and plunder, we rifle and loot.
Drink up me 'earties, yo ho.
We kidnap and ravage and don't give a hoot.
Drink up me 'earties, yo ho."

Stevie couldn't help it. The tension he'd experienced to this point exploded in uncontrollable laughter. His body shook from head to toe, as tears raced down his cheeks. Bobby also could not hold it in. He joined Stevie in a frenzied fit of laughing, the tension finally finding an outlet that echoed off the dull rock around them.

"What?" Michael wasn't sure why everyone was laughing.

"Thanks, Michael, I think we needed that," said Bobby.

"I know lots of pirate songs from all the movies and books I read," Michael responded, realizing that his new friends laughing with him, not at him, and that made him very happy.

They all moved forward and Michael began again. "I learned a new one today. It goes like this:

Along this trail came Boot and Crag
Who carried a load and daren't drag."

Michael's recitation caused Bobby to stop like a bird flying into a window. That made Stevie crawl right into the bottom of Bobby's foot with his face.

"Hey, what'd you stop for?" Stevie shouted.

"Michael," Bobby said. "Where did you learn that?"

"At the library in an old book, but I can't remember the rest."

Bobby turned slightly to face his mates, shone his flashlight under his own chin to light up his face so they could see him.

"Rich we'll be, says Mr. Boot," continued Bobby, "When first we bury the Captain's loot." He was breathing hard, but this time it wasn't the heat that made breathing difficult

"It's what *he* recited in my head at Madame Tarot's. It's what you and Brenda couldn't hear, Stevie, remember?" Stevie remembered how skeptical he'd been at the time, but a lot had happened since and his skepticism had all but disappeared.

"But Michael, where did you read that?" asked Bobby.

"I read it in an old book that had a piece of a diary in it. A sailor on Black Bart's ship wrote it."

Bobby continued onward, having no doubts they were going in the right direction. He did, however, wonder if he'd ever be able to stand up again. After another half hour of edging forward, Bobby paused. "The air has changed," he announced. "I feel a slight breeze."

The good news spurred Stevie on, and he even began to think of getting out of this mess. Before long they were crawling on hands and knees again. Soon after, they were able to stand upright. The air had indeed changed. A breeze was coming straight at them.

"There must be an opening ahead," said Bobby.

After a ten-minute walk through an ever-widening cavern with a ceiling that now reached at least thirty feet, they came upon an intersection. To the right lay a thin opening to the outside of the mountain, a three-foot tall, straight up and down slit about three inches wide. They raced over to it drinking in the shaft of sunlight peering through the crack. They pressed against the fissure and took deep, delicious breaths of fresh air.

"I don't care how," said Stevie, "but I will find another way out of here. I will not go that way again," he added with finality.

"Be careful what you wish for," Bobby said.

"*Marine 1,* this is *Chopper 1,* do you copy, over."

"*Chopper 1,* this is *Marine 1,* I copy, over."

"Lieutenant, I've ID'd a set of bikes in the bush, over."

"What's their location? Over."

"South end of the lake head, just off the main trail, over."

"Uh, direct a couple of troopers on ATVs over there to pick 'em up and ID 'em ASAP, over."

"Roger that, over and out."

The lieutenant turned to his passengers. "That sounds like it could be something. We'll check it out and know shortly," he said, speeding in that direction.

The trio dragged back the other way, since the fissure was a dead end, reluctant to leave the only bit of light they'd seen in some time. They were on a wide trail running through the interior of the mountain, which detoured into and out of various cave rooms. They moved forward with their flashlights on, but progress was slow. They explored each cavern, looking for any signs that Brenda may have been there. After each one, they made their way back to the trail and continued onward. It got darker the further they went. There were several crossroads that indicated a left or right turn. Following some inner intuitive compass, Bobby stayed left. The others had bought into his leadership long ago and followed without question.

They came upon a large, open area. Bobby said, "Stop. Turn off your lights."

"Wait a second," said Stevie, "I'm not exactly fond of the dark and…"

"Just do it," said Bobby.

They turned their lights off simultaneously, and as soon as they did, it was as if someone had turned on a thousand nightlights.

The room basked in the glow of nature's illumination: phosphorescent algae cast a dim shine to the surrounding walls and ceiling, as if they were standing inside some giant planetarium painted with glow-in-the-dark images of distant galaxies. They paused in their difficult task and allowed themselves to marvel at the magic that surrounded them. Despite their overwhelming fear and anxiety, they were momentarily awed with one of nature's incredible wonders.

"Amazing," said Bobby, his voice muted.

"Awesome," agreed Stevie.

Michael gaped, with his finger in the air, but unable to utter his thoughts.

"Shhh," cautioned Bobby, "I hear something." Listening intently, they detected a low hum that sounded like a muffled conversation. They took slow, deliberate steps towards the source of the noise, careful not to overturn any loose stones. They didn't dare speak and hardly breathed. They soon became aware that in a short distance ahead they would no longer be alone. The smell of burning fuel, mixed with something else, assaulted their nostrils.

It was something vile.

Something rotting.

Something dead.

They edged around a corner wall. Snippets of firelight danced on the smooth flat walls ahead. They crept forward, crab walking up to a set of large boulders piled atop one another. Peering over the top, they stared and immediately froze with fear.

He was there. The demon of Bobby's dreams was within view. *He* was hunched over, stuffing bags with items that winked in the erratic light. Although *he* was alone, *he* was clearly talking to *himself*. One of the two voices appeared to be begging.

"Leave me. I won't harm you and I won't tell anyone, I swear. I don't need much. If you could leave me just a bit of your treasure that would be nice, but please, just leave me be like I was," said the one voice, trembling with dread.

The other voice sent chills up their spine as it spoke with a patient malevolence. "Oh, I couldn't leave you, Carl. You're my blood. You've made all this possible, don't you see? We're together now. We're a team, you and I, and by nightfall we shall be one." Knowing he was now clearly the dominant one in this relationship, Bart then laughed viciously, grabbed his bags of treasure, and abruptly left.

The boys had watched the eerie scene without moving an inch.

"Who the heck is that nutcase talking to?" Stevie whispered.

"It's as I feared," said Bobby. "Given this is Carl's body, but not his spirit, I guess Carl and Bart are having a conversation."

"So *he's* kind of talking to himself?"

"I believe so, yes," Bobby concluded. "But look, *he's* going back to his lair," Bobby whispered, "and wherever *he's* going is probably where we'll find Brenda. Come on!" The boys leaped over the rock formation and ran up to the hole. It was deep, with a ladder leaning against the side of the pit. At the bottom lay a decayed chest, spilling over with a few more gold coins, cups, and jewelry, all sitting on a pile of old bones.

"The treasure!" gasped Stevie.

"Looks like he got most of it out. He must be storing it somewhere," Bobby observed.

"Look, there are heads," said Michael, pointing at a collection of craniums a foot away from the treasure chest.

"Three of them," counted Bobby. "I'll be two of them are Boot and Crag," he added, not without respect.

The smell of dampness, rotting wood, and death hugged them all like a musty old blanket. Standing off to the side of the pit was a pile of recently dug dirt and behind that, casting a long shadow, lay a yellow mini-backhoe, like some brightly colored dinosaur in suspended animation.

"We've got to go before it's too late!" Bobby said finally. He took off after the pirate, now followed by his mates who took one more peek into the hole. They were astounded by the glow of the remaining treasure. Even that paltry amount was worth a fortune. They turned as one to follow Bobby. Quietly, not wanting to alert their antagonist, they moved up a winding incline that was partially covered with dirt. There were tire tracks here, indicating the way the backhoe was probably brought in.

Although the channel was dark, they dared not turn on their flashlights. Instead, they relied on their senses of touch and smell, feeling their way along the wall. Now and then they would catch a whiff of the rapidly departing fiend as they sniffed and scurried their way forward like three blind mice. The incline suddenly rose sharply. They knew they were nearing the end of their journey by the faint light ahead that crept into the tunnel.

A few more reluctant steps and they were standing at the opening of a large cavern. Light flooded into the corridor from a combination of the torches within the cave and the growing natural light peeking in from the opening on the opposite side. Bobby held his arm out to prevent the others from moving further. He turned in their direction and spoke softly. "*He's* in there. I can hear *him* moving about. I'm sure Brenda is in there as well. I'm going to risk a peek. Be still, will you?" Bobby inched his way to the opening, got onto his knees, and stole a quick and furtive glance around the bend.

When Bobby tiptoed back to his mates, he looked crestfallen. His shoulders were slumped and his face, sallow and glum.

"What is it? What did you see? Is she in there? Is she all right? Bobby!" whispered Stevie, in a rush.

"Yes, she's in there. But she doesn't look good. She's all hunched up on the floor and she's trussed up like a sheep. I don't know what to do. I brought a knife, but now I realize it won't be of much use against *his* brute strength."

Bobby was so forlorn that he hadn't noticed the look that transformed Stevie's face. A strange, numbing sensation overtook him. Brenda had saved his life once. Without thinking of herself at all, not for a moment, she jumped into an icy, cold river and rescued him. He had pledged then that he would always be there for her and the time had come to make good on his pledge. He walked the few remaining steps towards the opening and peered in to see for himself how bad things were.

There she lay, prone, defeated, and empty of hope. When he saw Brenda all tied up, on the cold, hard floor, feelings of tenderness for her and boiling rage against the monster struggled for a way out.

Without another thought, Stevie willingly stepped into a very bad dream.

"*Marine 1,* this is *Chopper 1,* do you copy, over."

"*Chopper 1,* this is *Marine 1,* I copy, over."

"Sir, those bikes. The local deputy ID'd them for us since they are registered here in town. One belongs to a Michael Kelleher. Please hold for the second ID."

The lieutenant looked in the direction of his passengers. Not knowing who Michael was, John Watson and Mr. Nichols, gently shook their heads no, but the sheriff looked perplexed. "Michael Kelleher? That's the new boy in town. He's not very sociable and keeps to his home mostly. What the heck is his bike doing out here in the woods? Don't tell me we got another missin' kid here!"

"Sir, we've got an ID on the other bike's registration. It's a boy's bike registered to the Watson family."

Suddenly all eyes on the boat lit up like a Christmas tree. Lieutenant Wetzel looked at John Watson with renewed hope. Nearly speechless, John stuttered out a response. "That would be the bike my wife's nephew is riding. I don't understand. He should be back at our house, in bed. What is the bike doing way out here?"

The lieutenant wasted no time.

"*Chopper 1,* this *is Marine 1.* I want you to radio central command. I want all personnel to focus on this sector. Please give them coordinates. I also want the local deputy to bring the parents of all the missing children to central command. We're proceeding down the lake on the side where that trail continues. I will notify you of anything we find. Over and out."

"*Marine 1,* this is *Chopper 1,* I copy, over and out."

Stevie ran into the room screaming, charging head first towards their enemy. Bobby and Michael were too stunned to react. After a moment's hesitation, they followed suit, but by the time they entered the room, they ran just two long steps and stopped. Standing near the outside opening to the cave was their adversary. *He* looked deranged, even a bit startled. *He* had Stevie in *his* grasp and things did not look good.

What had started as an act of sheer bravery and desperate courage had turned into sheer disaster. Upon Stevie's entry into the cave, Bart turned on his heels, clearly taken by surprise. But due to his superior size and strength, he quickly regained the upper hand. *He* encircled Stevie with both arms and lifted him off the ground, unsure of what to do with him. Stevie was kicking and screaming. Shocked that Stevie had somehow survived being blown to bits along with the school, Bart decided to toss him out to the lake below. He half-dragged him over to the cave opening, grabbed the back of Stevie's shirt with *his* left hand and as *he* pulled back to throw Stevie out to a certain death, in came the other two, shouting and screaming.

"What have we here?" the startled pirate said, reaffirming his hold on Stevie.

Bobby moved over to Brenda, who had awoken from her fatigue-induced trance when Stevie had burst into the room. He bent over and asked her, "Are you okay?"

"Yes …no …I mean, okay, I guess."

Bobby got out his Swiss Army knife and opened it in a second. He cut the ropes from her wrists and was working on the legs when Bart faced him and spoke again.

"Cut her bonds, it makes no difference, you fools! You've saved me the trouble of having to hunt you down! You cannot escape me, here!"

Bobby finished cutting the restraints off Brenda's legs and helped her to stand. She stumbled at first, not able to put her full weight on her feet, and leaned on her cousin for support.

"I told you I didn't like Carl," she said feebly.

All this time, Michael had been drifting to the left. He made his way around to that side of the cave by feeling with his hands along the wall behind him. He never once took his eyes off Bart. Stevie continued to squirm, as if possessed. He furiously kicked the shins of his captor, who didn't seem to feel it at all.

Bart suddenly turned to Michael with an angry glare. "You think you can sneak up on me? I'll rip your head off and feed it to the fish! It's time for you all to die!"

"Let him go!" shouted Michael, with his finger pointed at the cave's ceiling.

Bobby had an inspiration. He grabbed the mirror in his shirt pocket. After stepping away from Brenda, he tilted the mirror to catch the shaft of morning sunlight sneaking into the room and directed it into the evil pirate's eyes. Momentarily blinded, Bart reacted instinctively and loosened *his* grip on Stevie while trying to look away from the penetrating light. Stevie kicked *him* hard once more and broke free from his captor. Bart regained *his* senses and looked at Bobby with pure malicious anger. *He* was taking a step towards Bobby, when Michael suddenly attacked *him* from the left.

Michael raced at *him* with the wild abandon previously shown by Stevie, wielding a flaming torch he had torn from its moor. He hit Bart hard, smacking *him* on the head and igniting *his* bushy, stringy mane. Bart teetered dangerously to the edge of the opening and reached out in desperation. *He* grabbed Michael by the shirt as *he* stumbled backwards. Bobby and Brenda gasped, as they were about to witness their new friend being pulled to a horrible death.

It would only be a matter of seconds to their imminent plunge to the lake below.

When Stevie was released from Bart's grasp, he had run to the opening from which they all had entered the cave and turned quickly around. He pulled out a smooth, round stone, carefully selected for its ease of throwing, as he had said so often. Michael and Bart, embraced in a dance of death, were quickly stumbling towards their fearful demise when Stevie calmly took aim, reared back his arm and pitched a perfect strike with deadly speed and accuracy. He pelted Bart right between the eyes. There was a loud crack, which echoed through the cavern like a gunshot. Bart let go of Michael and reached for *his* forehead with both hands. Blood gushed into *his* eyes and the force of the throw made *him* stagger backwards where *he* tripped through the gap.

Then, as *he* pin-wheeled his way out of the opening with *his* bloody hands flailing and *his* head fully aflame, Stevie quietly said, "Go back to the hell you came from."

As the boat rounded the southwestern corner of Mountain Lake, those on board heard a hideous screech coming from the face of the mountain. They glanced upwards and witnessed a fireball shooting out of the smooth surface of the mountain, plunging to the small spit of lakeshore below. The fiery mass fell so far they heard the dull thud when it landed.

"What in God's name was that?" muttered the sheriff.

"We'll soon find out," responded Lieutenant Wetzel who gunned the boat's engine.

Their boat radioed the incident to the helicopter pilot, who flew in for a closer look at that shadowed spot on the mountain face. Shining a spotlight on the partially shaded area, the copter pilot was able to radio the sighting of four youngsters, standing arm in arm, waving to him.

"Radio that location to central and get the rappelling team up there right away," directed Lieutenant Wetzel.

At the central command center in the north parking lot, Mrs. Kelleher, Mrs. Nichols, and Auntie Arlene all waited anxiously for any word about their children. The confirmation of the sighting of four children brought a gasp of hope to all of the awaiting parents.

A crack state police SWAT team trained in rappelling leaped off the mountaintop towards the identified spot on the mountain's sheer face to rescue the children. What they found when they arrived astounded them.

Before they got there, Bobby had led a discussion among his group about what they were going to say. He didn't want to lie, but told his mates that sometimes the truth is what most people want to believe. None of the adults were going to want to believe a story about an ancient pirate's spirit inhabiting the body of a diabolical descendant.

Even if it was the truth.

So he proposed, and the others agreed, that they would blame Carl. After all, it was Carl's body they'd find and identify in an autopsy report. It was not entirely untrue to say that Carl was insane and viewed them as a threat to his plan to uncover his ancestor's treasure. This version of the story would be much easier for the adults to accept, especially if the three of them admitted to allowing their imaginations to get the better of them. They all knew the real truth, however, and they vowed to speak of it only amongst themselves in the future.

All four children, injured and exhausted, were rescued by the rappelling team and placed in waiting state police SUVs. The SUVs, with lights flashing and sirens wailing, much to the delight of Bobby, Brenda, Stevie, and Michael, brought them out of the bush and back to central command.

Deputy Carver rather enjoyed hearing the sirens as well.

When they got out of the police vehicles, their parents could stand still no longer. They raced over to the cars, grabbed their children, and hugged them tightly.

EPILOGUE

Eventually the police retrieved the treasure in its entirety. Most of it was claimed by the state, but the state legislature awarded a million dollar reward to the four children. Their parents spent a good deal of time in the immediate aftermath helping them avoid the inevitable national publicity that ensued. They did, however, give an exclusive interview to Bill Glean of the *Daily Mirror,* whose article was quoted on all the national news outlets.

Stevie and Michael became fast friends, each providing the other with skills the one possessed and the other lacked. Stevie became quite a student with a variety of new interests, able to do computer research as well as anyone. Michael became a relief pitcher for the school baseball team with Stevie as his trainer, guide, and protector in school. Bonds of loyalty are often forged by adversity, and these two had quite a shared experience that brought them closer together.

Brenda, who possessed great inner strength to begin with, recovered nicely from her wounds, both physical and emotional. She was happy to have become close with her cousin, thanking him, as well as Stevie and Michael, for rescuing her from the clutches of that vile monster. She was also happy to report to them that according to the local paper, the school had hired a new custodian. He was identified in the paper as a kind and considerate man named Sidney, who came from Colombia. He was already hard at work painting foursquare boxes on the school blacktop for the upcoming school year and was quoted in the paper as saying, "The school grounds should *always* have kids playing, even in the summer. It makes school a happy place."

When thinking about his visit, Bobby realized he had a new memory to last him a lifetime, knowing in his heart that his father would have been pleased. He understood, perhaps for the first time, that he needed to embrace the gift he was given and not fear it. He promised himself to try and understand it better, to pay more attention to it in the future, and to nurture its growth.

Uncle John told Bobby's mother everything that happened from start to finish, as he knew it. Deeply shaken by the events that took place, she immediately purchased a ticket on the next available flight to America. She wanted to thank her relatives in person for the good care they provided before bringing her son home.

A week later, back at Newark airport, as Bobby and his mother were preparing to return to London, Bobby turned to his cousin Brenda and gave her a hug.

"Next time," he said, "you'll have to come to England."

The End

About the Author

Jim Kelly has been a middle school teacher, a vice-principal, a principal, a Co-Director of the New Jersey State History Fair, a consultant for the New Jersey Foundation for Educational Administration, a current Board member of the Global Learning Project, a non-profit, and Past-President of the Morris County Association of Elementary and Middle School Administrators. He has been the recipient of numerous education awards such as the *New Jersey Governor's Teacher Award,* two *Geraldine Dodge Foundation Grants,* and by acclamation of his school staff, received the *New Jersey Principal's and Supervisor's Association Principal of the Year Award for Visionary Leadership in 2007.* Jim also authored two professional books: **Student–Centered Teaching for Increased Participation** and **In Search of Leadership**.

The Lost Treasure is Jim's first novel. His love of mysteries, adventures, and everything about Sherlock Holmes, helped in the creation of eleven-year-old Bobby Holmes and his cousin Brenda Watson. Jim is currently at work on a dark comedy for adults entitled **Tommy Ails: Good For What Ails You**.

Jim was born in New Jersey, the second oldest in a family of ten, and except for brief stints in Pennsylvania and Hawaii, he lived there most of his life.

Jim lives in Mountain Lakes, New Jersey and Sarasota, Florida, with his wife Bronwen. They have three children, Peter, Alex, and Brianna.

Visit my Facebook page: J.M. Kelly

CPSIA information can be obtained
at www.ICGtesting.com
Printed in the USA
BVOW06s1330031117
499478BV00007B/34/P

9 781484 084946